Lock Down Publications
and Ca$h Presents

Crime Boss 2:
Progeny of Tyrone Davis

by PLAYA RAY

1

Playa Ray

First Edition September 2023

Printed in the United States of America

Lock Down Publications
P.O. Box 944
Stockbridge, GA 30281
www.lockdownpublications.com

Like our page on Facebook: Lock Down Publications
www.facebook.com/lockdownpublications.ldp

Stay Connected with Us!

Text LOCKDOWN to 22828 to stay up-to-date with
new releases, sneak peaks, contests and more…
Or CLICK HERE to sign up.
Like our page on Facebook:
Lock Down Publications: Facebook
Join Lock Down Publications/The New Era Reading
Group
Visit our website:

www.lockdownpublications.com

Follow us on Instagram:
Lock Down Publications: Instagram
Email Us: We want to hear from you!

Acknowledgments

I want to dedicate this book to my dear friend, Ms. Jane Pennella, of Portland, Oregon. Thanks for being you!

R.I.P to my father, Michael Morris McCoy. I can't be mad at God. At least you don't have to suffer anymore. Love you always!

Another R.I.P Usle 'Cisco' Flemister Jr.You may not have been the best person in the world, but to your daughter, you were the best father in the world, You will forever be remembered!

"You can turn a blind all you want, but remember: a blind eye can see."
-Rachel 'Ray' Freeman
South Philly

Prologue

November 2022

"This should be a piece of cake, guys."

Marvin's statement pulled Anthony from his reverie, causing him to glance out at the building of the First National Bank, through the windshield of the SUV that was driven by his colleague. From where they were parked, they had a clear panorama of the entrance, and the four-cashier counter, despite the light drizzle of rain that utterly contradicted the weather forecaster's prediction of clear skies.

Before being pulled from his abstract musing, Anthony was thinking about his four-year-old son, Alex, to whom he'd just returned home from doing thirty-seven months in prison for residential burglary. Anthony knows that he hasn't been much of a father since Alex's birth, but he blames it on the economy, and his inability to land a decent job. Ex-convicted felons were treated as if they were still wards of the state. And, his lack of a high school diploma didn't make matters any better. Growing up in a house with a single mother, and no siblings, may have played a small part in his life's misfortune, but Anthony refuses to blame it on the fact that he was raised without a father, who, as his mother puts it, didn't want anything to do with him. Though, he promised himself to never neglect his baby, at this moment, he was feeling as if he'd already let his son down. That's why he was hoping that this heist was a success. With the money, he could move Janelle and Alex far away from the dilapidated contraption that they called home. Plus, being that he'd proposed to Janelle while incarcerated, and still haven't gotten her an engagement ring, he would make that one of his top priorities.

"As I've said," Marvin spoke again, causing Anthony to look over at him, "We can't afford no more than a three minute window. The manager is the only present employee with access to the vault, through Sen-Tech. Anthony, you already know what to do. What's your count, Bo?"

"Thirteen," Bo answered from the backseat, his deep baritone voice resounding off the truck's interior. "That's including the manager, cashiers, and security guard."

"Good count," Marvin responded, then locked his blue eyes onto the dark hue of Anthony's. "The love of money is the root to all evil, but greed will always be a man's downfall. I would love to have every piece of currency inside that vault, but that's remotely impossible. Grab as much as you can. Once I make the call, retreat. It's for our own good."

Anthony could only nod his consent as he wondered if Marvin had any kind of ulterior motives. It was hard to discern but, being that they'd met while incarcerated, and really didn't know much about each other, Anthony made a mental note to keep a close eye on him. He'd been knowing Bo since middle school and, at the inception of high school, they'd become Batman and Robin in residential burglaries. Therefore, his sentiments with Bo were neutral.

"Make that fourteen," Bo announced, as two customers entered the bank in the course of one exiting.

Marvin checked his watch. "Not one squad car since we've been here. Let's just hope that's a good thing. You guys ready?"

"Definitely," Bo rejoined.

Anthony heard the question but couldn't answer because he was pondering what Marvin had said about the love of money being the route to all evil, and greed being a man's downfall. The statement had actually sent chills up his spine. Now, he felt as if he had butterflies in his stomach, which could very well be a premonition.

"Let's make it happen," Anthony finally answered, as he rechecked his Rosewood .44 automatic with his gloved hands.

Marvin pulled the SUV out of its parking spot, and slowly drove around to the entrance of the bank. Once the truck had come to a halt, they all quickly donned ski masks, and dismounted, clad in black jumpsuits, boots, and large overcoats that concealed their Lockheart bulletproof vests. Anthony carried his .44, but Marvin and Bo both carried Bonner Brothers P.50 fully automatics. As they neared the entrance, a Caucasian female in her mid-twenties, exited. Seeing them, she stopped, apprehension in her eyes.

"Get back inside!" Anthony demanded, aware of the consequences of allowing her to leave at this moment.

Tears instantly cascaded down the woman's face, as she took in the trio of armed men, who were getting precariously close. Then, as if she were a sprinter in the U.S. Olympics, and a starter pistol had gone off to initiate the race, she bolted to her left with a speed that was possibly fear-driven adrenaline. Instinctively, Anthony stopped, and raised his gun, securing the infrared beam at the center of her back. She had only gotten close to ten yards out, before the gun discharged, and a bullet perforated her coat, hitting its intended target. Before her body could hit the ground, Marvin pulled the entrance door open, and entered, followed by Anthony and Bo.

"Everybody down!" Marvin bellowed.

Customers dove to the floor, as shots rang out from the right of them. That's when they realized that the bank's security officer was firing upon them, as if he'd already had his gun out, expecting them. Perhaps, he'd heard the initial gunshot, and was acting off of his cop's instincts.

The crew returned fire as slugs impacted Anthony's, and Marvin's vests, but the shootout ended as quickly as it started, with the cop losing grip of his gun as he crumpled to the floor.

"Go, go, go!" Marvin yelled out to his accomplices.

Anthony spun, broke into a run, and dove over the counter to the other side, where the four cashiers, and manager, lay face down on the only carpeted area of the bank. They already knew that the four women were all cashiers, so Anthony grabbed the Caucasian male by the collar of his blazer.

"Get your ass up!"

"Okay, okay!" The manager said, getting to his feet.

"Just so you'll know I'm not here to play with you," Anthony said, then shot the manager in his right knee.

The manager yelled out in pain, as he flopped onto one of the desk chairs, holding his wounded leg that could very well be permanently damaged.

"You can nurse that later." Anthony grabbed the manager by his lapel and pulled him to his feet. "You already know what I want. Let's make it happen. And, if you try anything stupid, Santa Claus can scratch you off his list."

Anthony shoved the limping manager over to the huge, steel vault. The only breach in the vault's sleek surface was the Sen-Tech palm reader, in which authorized personnel gained entrance by placing their right hand upon. The manager stopped at the vault, and looked back at Anthony as if he was lost.

"I hope you're not as dumb as you look," Anthony said, shoving the barrel of his gun into the guy's side. "Are you really willing to die for someone else's money? Do you think your family could live with the fact that you died for nothing?"

Apparently, the manager had ruminated on this, because he drew a breath and placed his right hand flat on the reader. First, there was a beeping sound. Then, Anthony could see a neon green line slowly glide up and down the screen beneath the manager's palm. Feeling that things were in progress, Anthony took this time to look out at his accomplices. Marvin was near the entrance, keeping an eye out for the authorities, and Bo was relieving the customers of their valuables, before cleaning out the registers.

Another beeping sound brought Anthony's attention back to the vault. At this time, the manager was sweating profusely, which gave Anthony the feeling that something was amiss.

"What's taking so long?" He inquired.

"I don't know," the manager replied. "It would usually be open by now. I was told it has some kind of electrocardiograph like sensor that would stall if it sensed that the user is nervous. I guess I'm a bit nervous."

"Well, you need to get un-nervous!" Anthony told him, now remembering a case on the news, where a bank manager endeavored to access the vault while in a nervous state, and the system automatically notified authorities.

"One minute!" Marvin promulgated, as Bo ransacked the registers.

"Shit!" Anthony mumbled, retracting the barrel of his gun from the manager's side. "Take a deep breath, and count to ten. Slowly."

The manager nodded, drew a breath, then began counting. Anthony looked around when his eyes landed on the water cooler, an idea formed in his mind. Leaving a hostage unattended was something that a seasoned criminal would never do, but Anthony was desperate, which had him anticipating something he'd seen on the Science channel when he was a child.

"Thirty seconds!" announced Marvin.

That was enough to compel Anthony into action. He turned and reached the water cooler in a few brisk strides. After filling one of the paper cups with the ice-cold water, he approached, and tossed the liquid into the manager's face.

The manager gasped. A millisecond later, there was another beeping sound, which was followed by a faint metallic click. The huge door pushed a few inches out, bringing a broad smile to Anthony's face.

"Merry Fucking Christmas!" He said to the manager, before smashing the handle of his gun into his skull, rendering him unconscious.

Not wasting another second, Anthony entered the vault, pulling the door back up without locking it. The steel shelves that lined the three walls were piled with stacks of bills. The sight of all of it had Anthony in awe because he'd never seen this much money outside of television and magazines. At this moment, all he could think about was the life that he and his family would live when this is over.

"Time!" Marvin's voice reached the vault, in almost a whisper.

"Wrap it up! Let's go!"

As if he hadn't heard Marvin's call, Anthony pulled out a can of Dresdol, and sprayed the contents over a vast number of bills on one of the shelves. He didn't have to wait, because the hidden electronic devices that release the dye packs were already buzzing, indicating that the illegally bought spray was doing its job of dismantling them. Once the can was empty, Anthony tossed it to the floor, and pulled two Gym Pro bags from his coat's pocket, just as Bo pulled the vault's door open.

"Yo, we gotta go," Bo announced with a worried look on his face. "Marvin said."

"Fuck Marvin," Anthony cut in, tossing one of the compressed gym bags over to his friend. "Come in here and fill that up! The quicker we move, the quicker we can get up out of here. Pull from this shelf."

Anthony tucked his gun, unfolded the bag, and began stuffing the neutralized bills inside. After another second of lingering, Bo joined him. Moments later, with the large bags of money over their shoulders, and guns in hand, they emerged from the vault, moving briskly toward the exit, where Marvin was still positioned.

"You really do a great job of sticking to the plan," Marvin spoke with acidity, regarding Anthony as they approached.

"And, you really do a great job of nagging," Anthony recriminated, brushing past Marvin, and exiting the bank with Bo at his heels.

The sound of sirens could be heard in a distance. Climbing into the truck, Anthony placed the bag at his feet, and inserted a fresh cartridge into his gun. Once Bo and Marvin were settled in, Marvin put the SUV into gear, and pulled out at a casual pace. Getting to the exit, they spotted two Atlanta Police cruisers coming in fast from the right of them. Not one to crack under pressure, Marvin nonchalantly initiated his right turn signal, and pulled out into the light traffic, momentarily cruising past the two squad cars, but keeping them in his sights via the rearview mirror as they rushed into the bank's parking lot.

"Somebody moved the body," Bo finally spoke.

"What body?" Anthony and Marvin asked in unison.

"The white girl you shot outside the bank," Bo answered. "She wasn't there when we came out."

Anthony shot Marvin an accusing look.

"I didn't move the damn body!" Marvin took umbrage.

"Weren't you watching the door?" Asked Anthony.

"Of course, I was watching the door."

"Well, you did a great job of that," Anthony accused, still sore about what Marvin had said about him doing a great job of sticking to the plan. "She got away and called the cops on us."

"Bullshit!" Marvin contradicted, a hint of doubt in his voice.

"There's no way in hell sh –"

"Ambulance," Anthony cut him off, nodding at the oncoming emergency medical vehicle that was preceded by another squad car. "They only show up after being notified that somebody needs medical attention. You do the math, Einstein."

Marvin didn't reply. In fact, no one spoke for the duration of the ride. When they'd made it to the wooded area where they'd stashed the other stolen vehicle, they quickly dismounted, knowing that, within five minutes, the footage of the robbery, and the black Ford Atlantic will be plastered all over every television in Georgia, interrupting every co-existing program. Plus, helicopters would be immediately dispatched.

Using the remote, Anthony started the gray 2020 Mercury Electra, to allow the motor to warm up, in spite of the below thirty-degree weather. Then, he tossed the gym bag he was holding onto the front passenger's seat.

"Trunk," Marvin said, standing at the rear of the Mercury. Anthony activated the trunk, then turned to Bo, who was approaching with the other bag. "Put it in the front," he told his friend.

Bo's visage took on a look of uncertainty, but he did as he was instructed. Once he'd deposited the bag amongst the others, he turned, and found himself staring down the barrel of Anthony's gun. His body tensed as he stood there, looking into Anthnoy's face as if he was trying to determine whether his friend was toying with him or not.

"It's been real," Anthony asserted, before squeezing the trigger.

The slug impacted Bo's forehead, sending mucus and brain matter exploding from the back, as his 5'11, 240 pound frame, fell backwards to the soiled earth. Anthony quickly turned to Marvin, who was standing in apparent shock, holding the gasoline can he'd pulled from the trunk of the car.

14

"Come on, Anthony," Marvin spoke, slowly shaking his head from side to side. "I can't believe you're doing this. I let you in on this robbery to help you take care of your family, and this is how you repay me?"

Saying nothing, Anthony moved closer, standing about eight feet away from Marvin, gun still aimed at his head.

"Look," Marvin went on, "There should be enough money in those bags for the both of us. Just give me half of one of those bags, and I'll go on about my life."

"Are you serious?" Anthony asked, in an incredulous tone. "I just killed my best friend. If I was gonna split the money with anybody, it would've been with my friend, don't you think?"

"This is not right, Anthony."

"Life is not right, Marvin."

"But, it doesn't have to be like this," Marvin countered. "You're letting your love for money surmount your better judgment. Don't forget what I said about greed, Anthony."

"Oh, I won't."

Anthony tightened his index finger's grip on the trigger. Before he could pull back on it, he heard a loud cracking sound behind him, as if someone had stepped on a twig. He did a quick glance over his right shoulder but saw nothing out of the ordinary. Then, another sound drew his attention back in Marvin's direction. That's when he saw the gas can flying toward him, it's content spewing as it spun uncontrollably. All Anthony had time to do was throw his arm up in defense. The can crashed into his forearm, but his impromptu shield did nothing to keep the fuel out of his eyes.

Anthony, with his eyes burning, and temporarily blinded, screamed out in agony as he fired a succession of rounds in Marvin's direction, panning the gun toward the truck, which is where he'd seen Marvin dashing, presumably for cover, before losing his sight. After the sixth round, Anthony kept his gun aimed as he listened for any signs of movement. At this moment, it seemed as if the drizzle of rain had picked up, in which he could clearly hear pattering off the fallen leaves. Then, there was the occasional cackle from a bird. Other than that, there were no....

Crack!

Anthony did a half-left flank and let off three more shots. At this point, he realized that Marvin may have retrieved his P.50 from the SUV that they were going to set a fire with the guns, masks, and gloves inside of. This is also when Anthony knew that Marvin could shoot him down at any time now. He continued listening for any signs of his nemesis as he mentally, and physically, braced himself for the inevitable.

But, despite the burning sensation in his eyes, Anthony was not giving up. He was confident that he could still take Marvin out if he could just catch the right sign, and make his shots count. Then, came a snapping sound from behind him. Anthony quickly turned in that direction, only to have the gun knocked from his grasp.

"Greed will always be a man's downfall," is the last thing Anthony heard, before some kind of solid object crashed into his skull, taking him to a place of pure bliss.

Chapter 1

Seven months later

"Objection, Your Honor!"

Ebony Davis shot another aggravated look over at attorney Rebecca Scarlatti, who was, for the umpteenth time, on her feet at the defense table, making another one of her petty expostulations. But no matter how paltry her objections seemed, she was doing a fantastic job at making Ebony look bad in front of the news reporters, and everyone who was tuned into the world news all over the world to keep up with the live trial of a multi-millionaire businessman, accused of murdering his wife of twenty-eight years.

"Under what grounds?" Judge Carl Jackson asked, clearly rankled by the attorney's antics.

"Prosecutor's questions are repetitive, and extraneous," Rebecca answered, her voice prominently displaying her Italian accent.

"Your Honor," Ebony spoke up, knowing that she had to defend her argument, "My line of questioning is germane."

"How so?" He asked.

"Your Honor, there are no medical professionals on this jury panel," Ebony pointed out. "What I'm trying to do is paint an easy, perceptive picture in their minds, through this pathologist. My job is to prove my case through illustrations, and substantial evidence, which is what I intend to do."

"Objection overruled," the judge rendered his verdict. "Wrap it up, Ms. Davis!"

"Yes, sir," Ebony said from behind the lectern redirecting her attention back to the state's witness, as

Rebecca retook her seat beside her client. "You may answer the question, Mr. Day."

The medical examiner cleared his throat before speaking. "I reported no carbon granules deposited in the bronchial passages, or lungs, and no carbon monoxide in the blood, or other tissues."

"But, the victim was found inside of a fire damaged house," Ebony pressed. "Could your report be wrong? I mean, couldn't it be off just a little?"

"Not at all," Mr. Day responded, confidently. "There were two separate tests conducted. I did the first, and another pathologist conducted the second one with no knowledge of my initial findings. Afterwards, we combined analyses, which were synoptic."

"So, you're testifying under oath that your report is conclusive?"

"I am."

Ebony regarded the judge. "No further questions, Your Honor. However, I would like to retain this witness for further examination."

"Any objections from the defense?" The judge asked.

"No, Your Honor," Rebecca answered to Ebony's surprise.

"Cross?"

"Yes, Your Honor."

Ebony returned to her table as Rebecca approached the lectern, graciously, with her long, jet-black hair, pulled back into a bun. She, as well as the whole world, knew that the outcome of this trial was highly anticipative, because she has an impeccable winning streak when it comes to cases of this magnitude. No matter how much evidence was stacked up against her clients, Rebecca "The Genie" Scarlatti had a way of discrediting every piece of it, which made her a threat to any prosecutor's winning streak. But Assistant District Attorney Ebony Davis didn't have a winning streak to speak of, being that she loses more cases than she could dream of winning.

"Mr. Day," Rebecca spoke, "I am Attorney Rebecca Scarlatti, counsel for the accused, Mr. Howard Brown. Now, as I understand, you were the appointed pathologist, am I correct?"

Mr. Day nodded. "Yes."

"You did the autopsy in this case?"

"Yes."

"Did you record all of your findings?"

"I did."

"I mean, it would be important to do so, right?"

"Yes."

Rebecca nodded as she glanced around the courtroom, using the momentary silence for effect. But this was a tactic that Ebony was all too familiar with. This is what prosecutors, and defense attorneys do when they're about to deliver crushing blows that could pretty much turn a trial in their favor. And, knowing Rebecca Scarlatti's reputation, Ebony knew that whatever the doyen attorney was about to do, could incontestably be detrimental to a win that she was in dire need of.

Rebecca directed her attention back to the witness stand.

"Mr. Day, you admitted to the prosecutor that there were two similar tests done on the victim in this case, am I right?"

"Yes."

"Are you familiar with state's exhibit nine?"

"I am," Mr. Day answered, shifting uncomfortably in his seat.

"Could you tell the court what state's exhibit nine is?"

"It's a replica of my analysis in this case."

"And, all of your findings are in there?"

"Yes."

19

"All procedures?"

"Yes."

"Everything's recorded?"

"Yes."

Rebecca raised an eyebrow. "Are you sure?"

"I'm positive." Mr. Day seemed to take umbrage.

"Mr. Day," Rebecca continued, as if she hadn't noticed his inflection. "I've had a chance to peruse your report, and I saw no indications of any subsequent testing being done by any other pathologist, as you've attested to today. Being that you've admitted that all procedures are recorded, I figured this second alleged testing would, somehow, be amended to your report with respect to my client, and the court alike. I mean, you said it yourself that such recordings of all findings would be important, right?"

"Yes, I did."

"Well, could you explain to the court why this particular procedure wasn't important enough to disclose to the court?"

Ebony exchanged glances with her assistant, Assistant District Attorney Samantha Gordon. For they did not need a psychic to tell them where this was going. Looking back at the stand, Ebony could tell that Mr. Day was as baffled as they were. His face had actually turned a few shades redder.

"I, ah," he stammered. "I wouldn't say that it wasn't important."

"But, it wasn't recorded," Rebecca pointed out. "Did this second testing actually take place, Mr. Day?"

Ebony was on her feet. "Objection, Your Honor!"

"No further questions," Rebecca spoke, before the judge could. Then, she retreated to her table.

The judge regarded Ebony. "Re-cross?"

"No, Your Honor."

"Alright. This witness will be retained at the state's behest," the judge stated for the record. "At this time, we're going to conclude until nine a.m., tomorrow morning. Court adjourned."

"I'll handle the evidence," Samantha offered, as she and Ebony gathered their things at the state's table.

Ebony stopped to look at her.

"I haven't forgotten what today is," Samantha said, a knowing look in her green eyes. "You already have to deal with the throng of reporters outside the courthouse. Let me, at least, relieve you of one headache."

Ebony mustered a plausible smile. "Thanks! You're the best."

Samantha smiled back. "I know."

Ebony grabbed her briefcase, exited the court, and caught the elevator up to her office, where she'd only stayed long enough to retrieve her pocketbook. Taking the elevator to the ground floor, she marched defiantly toward the exit, mentally preparing herself for the cannonade of questions that awaited her just beyond the large, mahogany double doors.

But, when Ebony exited the building, she saw that Rebeca Scarlatti had already stolen the show as she, accompanied by her client, stood atop the stairs like a prospective president. And Ebony noticed as she stood in the background, the mob of reporters were not as unruly as they usually were. It was as if Scarlatti had casted a spell over them because they were actually raising their hands and awaiting her acknowledgement before posing their questions.

"What were your reasons for attacking the validity of the pathologist's assertion of a second testing?" Ebony heard a female reporter ask.

"Article ten of the United States constitution entitles my client to a fair trial," Rebecca cited. "My job is to make sure that his rights are secured."

"If Mr. Brown is innocent," another reporter asked, after being acknowledged. "Why did he refuse the polygraph?"

"If you were accused of a crime that you did not commit," Rebecca responded, "Would you rely on an unreliable machine to prove your innocence?"

The reporter didn't respond.

"Next question?"

Ebony didn't wait around to hear the next question. She circled the crowd and made for the parking garage. Though she didn't feel up to dealing with the reporters, a part of her felt left out, being that this was her first high-profile case since becoming an assistant district attorney, over two years ago.

"Ms. Davis?"

Stopping, Ebony turned to see Linkton County Deputy Aaron Taylor, approaching. Aaron was married, but he seemed to make it his imperative to occasionally escort her to her car and engage her in mundane conversations. He had never blatantly hinted, but Ebony knew that he had a crush on her. It's not like she didn't find him attractive with his smooth, caramel skin, straight teeth, and light-brown eyes, because she definitely did. It was just that she was mainly focused on building her reputation as a prosecutor. Plus, she had Jason, and Samantha, to satisfy whatever needs she felt needed to be satisfied.

"I thought you called in sick today," Ebony said as he caught up, and they proceeded on.

"No," he answered, relieving her of her briefcase. "They had me in Judge Manning's courtroom. One of her deputies was out serving a warrant. I guess I missed out on your performance. How'd you do?"

Ebony sighed. "I guess I did my best."

"I'm sure you did." Aaron paused before going on. "You're not worried about Scarlatti, are you?"

"The Genie?" Ebony asked, sarcasm in her voice. "They don't call her that for nothing."

"That may be true," Aaron replied as they neared Ebony's 2021 Cadillac Seville Retro. "But I think she'll need a little more than magic to get Howard Brown out of this one. You're a good prosecutor. You have solid evidence against him. You just have to know how to use it to your advantage without leaving a hole for Scarlatti to worm herself through."

Aaron's sermonizing made a great deal of sense, which is why his words constantly echoed through her mind, until she'd reached the sunshine valley cemetery. Her worldly problems always seemed to shed at the entrance, until she returns. But Ebony fails to see the irony in the fact that she feels more at peace when she's visiting her mother's and father's graves. It was as if she belonged there with them.

Before dismounting, Ebony donned her Angela Cofer dark tinted sunglasses, and took a gander at herself in the rearview mirror. Then, she made the short walk to the juxtaposed tombstones that were only less than twenty yards away. The first thing she'd noticed were the two goblets that were filled with the flowers she'd pre-ordered from Tommy Wright and Company Flower Shop.

As she stood between the two graves, Ebony closed her eyes, and began the deep breathing exercise she'd learned while attending yoga classes. Once her mind was clear, she reverted to the good times she'd had with her parents, before that tragic day in June of 2005, which was eighteen years ago. Her father's killer had died in the courtroom with her father, but her mother's killer had never been discovered. And this same lack of justice had spawned on early hatred in Ebony toward any, and every police department, just as her late father had spawned her ambition to be a prosecutor.

Now, Ebony was thinking about the last moment she'd shared with her father, which was the day he was murdered. The school bus drivers were on strike again, and he had driven her to school.

"Here you are," Tyrone said, when they'd pulled up in front of the school.

"Thank you very much," an eleven-year-old Ebony replied, smiling. Tyrone held his hand out. "That'll be eight-fifty."

"You're charging me?"

"Yeah. Gas is not free."

"I should be charging YOU for how slow you were driving!" Tyrone laughed. "No, you didn't!"

"It's probably lunch time already," she added.

"Now, that's what you should be, a comedian."

"I'm not that funny," Ebony admitted. "Besides, they don't make as much money as a prosecutor."

"You just insist on being a D.A., huh?"

"It's all I dream about," she told him. "You told me that I should always follow my dreams."

Tyrone nodded. "I did. You know what? If that's what you want, I'm behind you one hundred percent."

"Really!" she beamed, smiling.

"Of course." Tyrone grabbed her bookbag off the backseat and placed it in her lap. "Now, get in there and make it happen!"

The sound of a passing car brought Ebony out of her thoughts. She looked back to see a green, older model Cadillac, making its way through the cemetery. She also noticed that the sun had begun to set, and she was perspiring from the mid-June heat. Taking one last look at the tombstones, she dabbed at the tears on her cheeks, then made the short trek back to her car, where she climbed behind the wheel, started the engine, and pressed auto drive.

"Destination?" the computerized system inquired.

"Home," answered Ebony.

She reclined her seat as the auto drive system did its downloading, which only took about ten seconds. Once the car began to move, Ebony put on her seatbelt, closed her eyes, and thought about what Aaron had told her earlier. But this was not the first time he'd called himself *coaching* her, which is something he'd been doing ever since Ebony has been with the district attorney's office. Aaron, who was thirteen years older than Ebony, has been with the Linkton County Sheriff's department for over eighteen years, with eleven of those years as a bailiff. Therefore, he'd sat in on a large number of trials, which is why Ebony assumes he feels that he knows enough to proffer advice and tactics.

But Ebony didn't think that there was a human being on this side of the planet, who could offer enough advice and tactics to overthrow attorney Rebecca Scarlatti, whom Ebony has heard so much about, but had never gotten a chance to meet until the inception of this trial. This made her think about the legendary Attorney Greg Bush, whose consecutive winning streak was broken when he'd lost a trial against the legendary Assistant District Attorney Tyrone Davis, which is still talked about to this day. The more she hears about how her father was the only Linkton County assistant D.A. to win as many cases as he's won, the more ashamed Ebony feels about dishonoring his name by being the total opposite.

"Destination: Home."

Ebony didn't realize she'd fallen asleep until now. She opened her eyes to see that her car was parked in the garage, beside Jason's Honda Cyclone, and the garage door was closing behind her. Ordering the engine to shut off, Ebony grabbed her cellular phone, briefcase, and pocketbook, then dismounted. Entering the house, she approached the eight-inch Sen-Tech screen mounted on the wall in the foyer.

After a second, it beeped, and SEN-TECH appeared on the screen in bold letters, acknowledging her presence.

"Locate Jason," she commanded, stifling a yawn.

"Locating Jason," a mechanical voice spouted as a computerized blueprint of the two-story house appeared on the screen, with a red light blinking at the bottom of the screen, which was the basement. "Jason located."

"Visitor count."

"You have one visitor."

"Gender?"

"Male."

Ebony turned and made for the stairs. She didn't have to inquire identification on the visitor, because she already knew that it was Benji, one of their neighbors. And she already knew that they were probably in drug-induced comas by now, which is why she was going to her bedroom to prepare for her run. Afterwards, she'll shower, then fix herself something to eat, knowing that Jason wouldn't have any kind of appetite. She just hopes that he doesn't go into one of his violent states tonight.

Chapter 2

"How are you employed, Mr. Shelby?" Ebony asked the rotund, white male who was seated on the witness stand.

"I am a private investigator," he answered.

"Self-employed?"

"Yes."

"And, how long have you been in this field?"

"Close to seven years."

"And, prior to this," Ebony spoke, studying her notes at the podium, "You were with the Bibb County Police Department for over nine years, correct?"

"Yes."

"Did you know Mrs. Brown, personally?"

"No, I did not."

"But you did get a chance to meet with her, prior to her death, am I right?"

"Yes."

"Could you tell the court how that came about?"

"Yes." He shifted in his seat. "Mrs. Brown contacted me by phone, and –"

"Let me stop you for a minute," Ebony interrupted. "For the sake of the court, I'll need you to include dates. On what date did Mrs. Brown contact you?"

"It was the fourth of August."

"Of last year?"

"Yes."

"You may continue."

The private investigator took a sip of his bottled water, before going on. "She asked if we could meet. Being that I'd just wrapped up a case, I was able to schedule a meeting with her for the following day, which was the fifth. After explaining her suspicion, she handed me the photo that I asked her to bring and filled out the necessary paperwork."

"And the photo was of whom?"

27

"Mr. Howard Brown," he answered, nodding in the direction of the defense table.

"Is that person in this courtroom today?" Ebony asked, knowing that she had to get this acknowledgement on record.

"Yes, he is."

"Could you point him out, and tell me what he's wearing?"

Shelby nodded at the table again. "He's right over there, wearing a dark-blue suit, and red tie."

Ebony regarded Judge Jackson. "Let the record reflect that the witness has identified the defendant, Mr. Howard Brown."

"Reflected," the judge replied.

"One moment, Your Honor."

Ebony approached the state's table, where Samantha Gordon was seated. Already knowing what she was coming for, Samantha handed Ebony a manila folder. Conversant with Scarlatti's demurs, Ebony, first, took the folder over to the attorney, who took her precious time sifting through its contents, before handing it back. Disregarding the simper on Scarlatti's face, Ebony turned to the judge.

"Your Honor, may I approach the witness?"

"You may," the judge answered, after pausing a moment to see if Scarlatti would object.

Approaching the witness stand, Ebony placed the folder in front of the investigator, then re-took her position behind the podium.

"Mr. Shelby," Ebony started, "What I just placed in front of you, is what's been marked as state's exhibit ten. Could you tell the court what that is?"

"It's a copy of my report from the Brown's case."

"A copy?"

"Yes."

"Could you open the folder for me?"

He did.

"On the top," Ebony continued," There's an eight-by-ten photo. Could you tell the court who's in this photo?"

"Mr. Howard Brown."

"How sure are you of that?"

"This is a replica of the six-by-nine photo that was given to me by Mrs. Brown on August fifth of last year," Mr. Shelby asserted, as if offended by the question.

"There's some type of document underneath the photo," Ebony went on, ignoring his inflection. "What is that?"

"It's a copy of the consent form that I had Mrs. Brown to fill out."

"And, what is it that she agreed to?"

"She agreed to pay me for a full week of surveillance on her husband, Mr. Brown."

"Did you hold up your end of the bargain?"

"I did."

"Make any discoveries?"

He nodded. "Of course."

"What were they?"

"I discovered that Mr. Brown was having an affair with his secretary, a Ms. Terri Bradshaw."

"After making this discovery," Ebony asked, "How did you document it?"

"Through photography," he answered. "Plus, I was able to record phone conversations between the subject, and his mistress."

"One second," Ebony said. Then, she approached her table where Samantha handed her a compact disc case. She turned to Mr. Shelby, holding the case up. "What I'm holding up is state's exhibit eleven. Are you familiar with this?"

"Yes," he answered. "It's a compact disc with phone recordings of conversations between Mr. Brown and Ms. Bradshaw."

"Are these conversations suggestive of infidelity?"

"These are intimate conversations," the investigator stated matter of factly. "My job is to bring back facts, not suggestions."

Ebony couldn't help but smile at his arrogance. "So, when I play this for the court, what exactly are we expected to hear?"

"Well –"

"Objection, Your Honor!" Scarlatti was on her feet, looking like a fashion model in her cream-colored dress suit, matching pumps, and black blouse. "Could you please ask the prosecutor to hold off on any details, and demonstrations of this particular evidence until after the witness is cross-examined by the defense?"

"I don't see why not," the judge answered, then looked over at Ebony. "Is there a reason why you can't postpone illustration of state's exhibit eleven?"

"No, Your Honor," Ebony answered, feeling as if she'd given in too easy.

"Objection sustained," the judge announced. "You may continue, Ms. Davis."

Thinking nothing of Scarlatti's objection, Ebony placed the disc on the state's table, then faced the judge. "Your Honor, permission to approach the witness?"

"You may."

Ebony approached, retrieved the folder from Mr. Shelby, then retook her position behind the lectern, opening the folder up in front of her.

"Mr. Shelby," Ebony spoke, sifting through the small stack of eight-by-ten photos of Howard Brown, and his blonde mistress,

"What I've extracted from your folder is a stack of eight-by-ten photos. How many am I holding?"

"Sixteen."

"Developed by yourself?"

"Yes."

"Ah, bailiff?" Ebony called out to deputy Aaron Taylor, who was standing between the jury and witness stands. "Could you assist me with the projector, please?"

Nodding his consent, Aaron crossed over to the projector, and positioned it in the center of the courtroom. Then, he activated it along with the 116-inch television across from the jury stand.

"Thank you, sir!"

Aaron nodded again, then returned to his post. Had it not been for the news cameras, Ebony would have, as she'd always done, took a moment to admire the way his uniform pants clung to his derriere. Just the thought of it sent hot flashes through her body, which was uncommon, because she'd never reacted to a man in this manner, let alone Aaron Taylor. Maybe this was the result of being divested of the male sexual organ for almost a week.

"Mr. Shelby," Ebony spoke, ignoring her thoughts. "I'm going to show you two of your photographs."

"I object to that, Your Honor," Scarlatti said, standing. "There's no need to go through these photos, when the jurors are going to have a chance to view them at deliberations."

"Your Honor," Ebony intervened, reluctant to give in this time. "This witness claims to be the developer of these photos. I only need him to verify two of them for the record."

The judge looked over at the defense table. "Ms. Scarlatti, I don't see anything wrong with this witness verifying his findings on record. Objection overruled."

Ebony almost sighed out loud. She couldn't believe that Rebecca had relinquished her contention so easily when she's widely known for her tenacity. Everybody knows that

"The Genie" would never pass up a chance to deflate any and every existing piece of evidence against her clients, which is why Ebony was a bit addled at this moment. But, instead of giving in to perplexity, Ebony proceeded on. She placed her first chosen photo onto the projector, which was of Howard Brown, and his blonde sweetheart, Terri Bradshaw, as they exited what looked like a hotel, holding hands, and smiling.

"Mr. Shelby," Ebony spoke, facing him. "Is this one of the photographs you've taken in the Brown's investigation?"

"It is," he answered.

"There are two people in this picture," she pointed out. "Could you please identify them for the court?"

"That would be Mr. Howard Brown and Ms. Terri Bradshaw," Shelby answered. "In this particular picture, they're exiting the Sunrise Hotel on Broad Street, on their way to Mary Ann's Diner, where they dined in. As you can see, the date at the bottom is August seventh of last year."

"And this one?" Ebony asked, replacing the photo with another photo that was a full headshot of a smiling Bradshaw.

"That's Terri Bradshaw again," he rejoined. "I always try to get at least one headshot of each subject for identification purposes, being that I periodically find myself testifying in divorce courts."

"I see." Ebony retrieved the photo and shut off the projector.

"And, how did you become a witness in this case?"

"Well," Shelby started, "I wrapped up my investigation for Mrs. Brown on the twelfth of August, which was on a Friday. We met on the following day. That's when I revealed everything to her, and she paid me for my services."

"Let me stop you there," Ebony cut in. "For the court, could you describe Mrs. Brown's reaction to this revelation?"

"On the surface," he answered, "She appeared unfazed by it. But I've been doing this for almost seven years. Plus, I have a degree in psychology. I would say that Mrs. Brown was, indeed, distraught."

"Objection!" Scarlatti said from her seat. "That would be mere speculation on the witness's part, Your Honor."

"Your Honor, I'll move on to the next question," Ebony announced.

"Good. Objection sustained."

"Mr. Shelby," Ebony continued, "You were telling the court how you ended up as a witness in this case."

"Yes." He cleared his throat. "Like I said, we concluded our contract on August thirteenth. This was Saturday. On that Sunday night, I caught the ten o'clock news, where they were doing a report on Mrs. Brown's demise, which was the top story. All that night, I thought about her dying in a house fire, but I dreamed of something totally different, which prompted me to take my findings to the homicide division. The investigators stayed in touch. When it was time for this trial, I received a subpoena from the district attorney's office. That's how I became a witness."

"Thank you, Mr. Shelby," Ebony said. "No further questions, Your Honor."

The judge looked to Scarlatti. "Cross?"

"Yes, Your Honor."

Ebony returned to the table with the folder, in which she handed off to Samantha, upon taking her seat. At this time, all eyes were on Scarlatti, who was on her feet, but chose to remain by her table.

"Mr. Shelby," she started, "You testified that you were able to obtain recordings of conversations between my client and, supposedly, his secretary, am I right?"

"Yes."

"Was this done through wiretapping?"

"Yes."

"Did you obtain a proper warrant for this procedure." Mr. Shelby furrowed his eyebrows. "No, I did not." Scarlatti regarded the judge. "Your Honor, at this time, I would like to move for a motion for limine."

"And, what are you trying to exclude?" Asked the judge.

"State's exhibit eleven."

"For what reasons?"

"The investigator's failure to obtain a valid warrant for the invasion of my client's phone conversations, constituted a fourth amendment violation."

"Your Honor," Ebony spoke up. "State's exhibit eleven, along with state's exhibit ten, had become an essential tool to homicide investigators in determining the true nature and motive behind the death of Mrs. Sheryl Brown."

"That still doesn't justify the fact that the recordings were illegally obtained, Your Honor," Scarlatti stood her ground. "To go forth with state's exhibit eleven, would also violate my client's privacy rights, in which he is fully entitled to by the United States Constitution."

Judge Jackson looked as if he was really pandering this. Ebony was perspiring, while Scarlatti appeared to have all the confidence in the world in her argument. And she should feel that way, Ebony thought, because her argument was valid. But, for the first time since the trial started, Ebony began to feel as if she had this case in the palm of her hand. "She'll need a little more than magic to get Howard Brown out of this one," Aaron's words echoed through her mind, which caused her to glance over at him. And, to her surprise, he was already watching her. He gave her an avuncular nod.

"At this time," the judge finally spoke. "I'm going to grant defendant's motion for limine. State's exhibit eleven is excluded from this case, and any further proceedings."

***

After the investigator was dismissed, the judge granted an hour and a half recess. Instead of going for something to eat, Ebony took this time to retreat to her office to relax, though Samantha insisted on tagging along. When they entered Ebony's office, Ebony slumped down in her leather, soft-cushioned chair, as Samantha locked the door before taking a seat across from her.

"What's wrong?" Samantha asked, after a moment of silence between them.

Ebony, who'd begun rummaging through the top drawer of her desk, stopped what she was doing to regard the green eyed, red-headed woman, when she'd been extremely close to ever since she'd started. Samantha's the only one who'd openly accepted the fact that Ebony was the youngest in their department and didn't judge her for who her father was. Ebony considered her a friend, but she had no idea that they would subsequently become more than that over time.

"Something's bothering you," Samantha went on. "And, I don't think it has anything to do with the trial."

Ebony closed the drawer, and leaned back in her chair with her eyes locked on Samantha's but didn't speak.

"It's him, isn't it?"

Ebony nodded slightly.

"Did he—"

"No," Ebony cut her off. "Not lately. It's what he's NOT doing. He hasn't touched me in almost a week. Sexually, I mean. I guess I'm just sexually frustrated."

"You would usually call on me at times like this," Samantha pointed out, a hint of hurt in her voice. "Am I no longer needed?"

"I'll always need you, Sam."

"What about now?"

"Especially now."

As if that was her cue, Samantha got up, and rounded the desk. She turned Ebony's chair to face her before getting down on her knees and smothering her in kisses. She groped her B-cup breasts through the blouse. Already keratose from the lack of affection, Ebony cupped Samantha's face, and voraciously returned the kiss. After a moment of this, Samantha broke the kiss, but maintained steady eye contact as she slipped her hands underneath Ebony's skirt and began to slowly and seductively relieve her of her panties. Before she could get the undergarment past Ebony's knees, the office phone rang, drawing Ebony's attention to it.

"Ignore it," Samantha said, edging the panties around the pointed heels of Ebony's pumps, then putting them up to her face, and inhaling deeply.

"That's probably Hutchins," Ebony replied, thinking it was the head district attorney, calling to taunt her about how the success of this trial could help her career.

"She can definitely go to hell," said Samantha, who was now kissing on Ebony's inner thigh.

"I agree," Ebony said, but still grabbed the handset from its cradle. "Linkton County District Attorney's office, Assistant District Attorney Ebony Davis speaking."

"Can you talk right now?" An unfamiliar male's voice boomed through the earpiece. "I mean, I've been watching the trial on TV, and I know all –"

"Who is this?" Ebony cut him off.

"I can't reveal my name right now," he purported. "But I do need to talk to you. It's important."

"I'm listening," Ebony said, gently pushing Samantha's head from between her legs.

"Not on the phone."

"Is this pertaining to the Brown's case?"

He was quiet for a moment. After drawing a breath, he said, "No. But, meeting with me would probably be in your best interest."

"Probably?"

"Yes."

"I'm hanging up now."

"I used to work for your dad," he spoke quickly.

The mentioning of her father got her full attention, diminishing her thoughts of hanging up on this stranger, who could very well be some demented individual trying to lure her in for whatever sick reasons he has in mind. But Ebony decided to test the water.

"My dad didn't own any businesses," she replied, looking down at Samantha, who was sniffing her panties again, with her eyes closed as if she were in pure bliss. "Perhaps there's a big misunderstanding. I don't think you know my –"

"You speak as if he's still alive," he cut her off. "You were only eleven when he passed."

Ebony took umbrage. "And, what's that supposed—"

"It means that I know more about your father than you do," he cut in again. "Things that I shouldn't speak on. Things that would probably scare you. So, like I said, this meeting would probably be in your best interest." He paused before adding, "It could also bring you closure on the death of your mother."

Chapter 3

Court was back in session. Everyone was seated, save for the jurors, who were slowly filing into the courtroom, and the stenographer, who appeared to be doing an overhaul of her machine. But Ebony's mind was on the call she'd gotten from the stranger, earlier. His assertion of knowing her father was plausible, but what he'd said about her mother had sent her mind spiraling out of control, making it hard for her to make the rational decision of meeting with him, or not. As far as she knew, he could be someone she'd sent to prison, and was out for revenge. Even if that wasn't the case, Ebony was still trying to figure out how he's aware that she had not gotten any closure on the demise of her mother, after eighteen years. Could he be her mother's killer? Is that why he's so anxious to meet with her! Did he plan to harm her? Is that why he insisted that she come alone? Is that why?

"State, you may call your next witness," the judge announced, pulling Ebony from her thoughts.

"Um," she stammered, slowly rising to her feet. "Your Honor, the state calls Ms. Terri Bradshaw to the stand."

The judge looked over at Deputy Taylor. "Bring in, Ms. Bradshaw."

Aaron exited the courtroom, returning with the blonde-haired woman, who was clad in a dark-blue, unprofessionally short skirt, with her hair pulled into a bun. The skirt, accentuated by the matching heels, gave her the ambiance of a call girl, as she sashayed to the stand. Just by looking at the young woman, Ebony could see why fifty-seven-year-old Howard Brown had fallen for her; she was beautiful!

"Please raise your right hand," Aaron instructed.

While Bradshaw was being sworn in, Ebony noted that, not once, had she looked in Brown's direction. Brown's currently out on bond, so Ebony assumed that they were still seeing each other. But, looking at this picture in front of her, gave her a whole different outlook on that assumption. Perhaps, this could work in her favor.

"State, you may proceed," the judge stated, after Bradshaw had taken a seat.

"Thank you, Your Honor," Ebony replied, as she made her way to the podium. "Ms. Bradshaw, I am Assistant District Attorney Ebony Davis, and I'm going to ask you some questions pertaining to what we've already discussed over the phone a few months ago. Do you remember our conversation?"

"Yes, I do," Bradshaw answered, her voice displaying a hint of youthfulness.

"During this conversation," Ebony went on, "What did I ask of you?"

"You asked if I could come to court, and answer questions."

"Did I specify on what questions would be asked?" Bradshaw shook her head. "No."

"Did I coach you on what, or what not to say?"

"No."

"Did I promise you anything?"

"No."

"Where are you employed, Ms. Bradshaw?"

"I'm currently a receptionist at the Linkton County Health Clinic."

"And, where were you employed in August of last year?"

"I was a secretary at West Group Appliances," she answered, casting a quick glance over at the defense table.

"Are you familiar with a Mr. Howard Brown?"

"Yes," Bradshaw answered. "He's co-owner of West Group Appliances."

"Do you see him in this courtroom?"

"Yes," she answered, maintaining steady eye contact with Ebony, to keep from looking his way.

"Could you point him out and tell me what he's wearing?" Ebony asked, coercing the muscles in her face to remain, though she was definitely grinning on the inside.

"He's wearing a dark-green suit," she rejoined, without pointing, or even risking another glance.

"Let the record reflect that the witness has identified the defendant, Mr. Brown," Ebony spouted.

"Reflected," the judge replied.

"How old are you, Ms. Bradshaw?" Ebony continued.

"Twenty-five."

"And what kind of terms were you and Mr. Brown on?"

"We had become close."

"How close?"

"We went out occasionally."

"You went out to lunch occasionally?" Asked Ebony.

"Well," Bradshaw replied. "That's how it all started. Then, we ended up going to fancy restaurants, where we had to dress casually. He would buy my dresses for me."

"Were you two ever intimate?"

"Yes."

"Did you know that Mr. Brown was married?"

"I did."

"And you were okay with it?"

"At first," she answered. "When he'd declared his love for me, I guess things changed."

"Did you ask him to leave his wife?" Ebony asked, remembering the conversation she'd heard on the disc from Mr. Shelby's investigation.

"No," Bradshaw answered. "But I did kind of give him an ultimatum."

Ebony raised an eyebrow. "Kind of?"

"Well, I actually told him that it was impossible to love the both of us."

"And, what was his response?"

"He told me that he was no longer in love with his wife," she purported. "Said that they were done, and he would soon be able to love me wholeheartedly."

"Were those his exact words?"

"Yes."

"When did he tell you this?"

Bradshaw shot Ebony an agitated look. "I don't remember the exact date."

"Was it last year?" Ebony asked, repudiating her visage and inflection.

"Yes."

"Can you, at least, give me a month?"

She shrugged. "He's told me this on several occasions. But the first time he'd told me this was in July."

"Are you sure?"

"I'm positive," she answered, a hint of attitude in her voice.

"It was the night of our office party, which was the twenty-third of July. He followed me back to my apartment after the party, which is when he expressed his feelings for me."

"And this is when you *kind of* gave him the ultimatum?"

"Yes."

"The same night he'd made the promise that he would soon be able to love you wholeheartedly?

"Yes."

"Who are you referring to?"

"Howard Brown."

"Has he ever told you this over the phone?"

"Of course. That's when we do most of our talking."

"Have you ever met Mrs. Brown?"

Bradshaw nodded. "A few times. These were on the days that she accompanied her husband to the office. She was a very sweet lady."

"Did you feel bad about sleeping with her husband?" Ebony went out on a limb.

Scarlatti lunged from her seat. "Objection!"

"No further questions," Ebony spoke up, making for her table.

"Cross?" The judge asked Scarlatti.

"Yes, Your Honor."

Ebony was already seated by the time Scarlatti had made it to the lectern. She was already feeling as if she'd revealed a motive for Howard Brown to murder his wife. To love Terri Bradshaw wholeheartedly. But she was anxious to see what kind of tricks "The Genie" has up her sleeves.

"Ms. Bradshaw, Scarlatti started, "I am Attorney Rebecca Scarlatti, counsel for the defendant, Mr. Howard Brown. Now, you testified that my client promised he would soon be able to love you wholeheartedly, am I correct?"

"Yes."

"And, he first told you this on the night of an office party?"

"Yes."

"Was there alcohol at this event?"

"There was."

"Did you drink any?"

Bradshaw seemed to linger before answering. "I did, but not that much, because I had to drive."

"Did Mr. Brown consumes any alcohol?"

"He did," she answered, "But not enough to impair his ability to function properly."

Ebony was smiling to herself. For Bradshaw had spoiled Scarlatti's intoxication tactic, before she could cancer the juror's minds with it.

"So," Scarlatti continued, "According to you, Mr. Brown was sober that night of the party, when he revealed his feelings for you?"

"Yes."

"The same night be allegedly promised to soon love you wholeheartedly?"

"Yes."

"Could anyone else attest to this?"

"No. it was just the two of us."

"He'd also made this same promise over the phone?"

"Yes."

"Do you have any recordings to corroborate your assertion?"

"Why would I record our conversations?" Bradshaw asked, as if it was the dumbest thing she'd ever heard.

"Could you please answer the question, Ms. Bradshaw?" Scarlatti asked, maintaining her bearings.

"No, I do not have any recordings of our conversations."

"Nothing further, Your Honor."

Ebony was no longer smiling to herself. She was so preoccupied with the way that Terri Bradshaw had naturally thwarted Scarlatti's first attack, she didn't see the second one coming. And, any seasoned prosecutor would have foreseen such a blow, which had definitely put a huge dent in Bradshaw's testimony. But, it wasn't over just yet, because Ebony still has a few more cards to play, before the conclusion of this *showdown*.

   ***

"Locate Jason," Ebony said to the monitor in the foyer of her home, then watched as the blueprint of the house appeared, showing that Jason was, as always, in the basement.

"Jason located," the computerized voice announced.

"Visitor count."

"You have zero visitors."

Depositing her briefcase in the hall closet, Ebony climbed the stairs to her bedroom, where she traded her work clothes, and shoes, for a pair of lime-green spandex shorts, tank top, and running shoes. After trying her hair into a ponytail, she grabbed her cellular phone, inserted her earbuds, then exited the room, while searching through her music playlists.

Though she intended to proceed out the front door, and immediately start her warm-up stretches before beginning her daily run, as Ebony approached the door to the basement, something inside her was telling her to go down, and check on Jason. Or, maybe she wanted him to see her in her spandex, knowing how keratose he would become when seeing her in anything that showed off her curvaceous figure. Perhaps, she was hoping to recapture those moments.

Turning the knob, Ebony pulled the door open, and slowly descended the wooden stairs to the basement that was dimly lit by a red light bulb, in which she's always hated. The rap music playing at a low volume had reached her ears halfway down the stairs, but the pungent smell of body odor, mildew, and feces had met her at the top, causing her face to take on a mask of contortion. Stepping onto the dark, soft carpet, she paused to look around as her eyes adjusted to the abnormality of the lighting condition.

Ebony didn't come down her often, but the place didn't seem any different than it did on her last visit. Jason's high school football trophies were prominently on display atop the stereo system; large posters of his favorite musicians, actors, and athletes lined the walls, along with the large flat-screen television; and there didn't seem to be an inch of a shift in the mahogany coffee table, and the sofa , which Jason was fast asleep on, that were the only means of furniture.

44

But, that smell! Ebony could understand the effluvia of body odor and mildew, but the feces smell was utterly out of place. As she looked down at her sleeping boyfriend, who had one hand tucked down, the front of his shorts, she wondered if he'd defecated on himself. With an ounce of doubt in her mind, she directed her attention toward the small door of the half bathroom, which was closed. Eyes already adjusted to the lighting, she headed in that direction. Reaching the door, she immediately pushed it open, and almost gagged when the stench assailed her nostrils unabated.

"Flush!" she demanded the computerized septic system, only to receive the beeping sound that normally antecedes the actual flushing process. "Flush, damn it!"

Receiving the same result, she pulled the door shut, and marched over to the sofa. Seeing the remote on the table, along with empty beer cans, bottles, a pack of cigarettes, a lighter, and a plate conveying a razor and crush residue, she picked it up, and shut off the stereo. At that instance, Jason awakened. His wide eyes searched the room frantically before landing on Ebony.

"How long has that toilet been broken?" Ebony plunged in before he could, seeing that his visage had changed from apprehensive to agitation.

"How the fuck would I know?" He replied, giving her body a once-over that could have been anything other than randy.

"Because, you're always down here!" She raised her voice. "You don't smell that? Does that stuff have your nose, *'AND'* you brain fucked up?"

"You better watch your mouth!"

"This is *'MY'* house!" Ebony stated, dropping the remote onto the table. "If anything, you better start respecting me!"

Ebony didn't know what had come over her. Maybe it was the way he'd regarded her body as if it meant nothing to him anymore but she knew that she was in trouble when Jason slowly sat up. She nervously watched as he extracted a cigarette from its pack and lit it. Tossing the lighter back onto the table, Jason rose to his feet, and took the two necessary steps to close the gap between them, towering his 6'1, 197-pound frame over the 5'7, 154 pound frame of Ebony's. She expected to be immediately assailed, but Jason exhaled a cloud of smoke into her face instead, which sent her into a minor coughing spell.

"What was that?" He asked. "I couldn't hear you from way over there."

With smoke-induced watery eyes, all Ebony could do was stare up into his. She didn't respond.

"I thought so," he taunted, before turning his back on her as if to resume his nap.

"I said," Ebony spoke through clenched teeth, stopping Jason in his tracks, "You better start—"

Smack!

Jason's body had not done a full turn when his right arm shot out like a bolt of lightning, and the back of his hand struck the side of Ebony's face. Her phone slipped from her grasp, as she fell backwards onto the soft carpet. At that moment, as she stared up at Jason with one hand holding the right side of her face, and the other supporting her in an upright position. Ebony decided that this perpetual abuse has to come to an end. And, Jason was definitely going to pay dearly for all the mental, emotional, and physical pain he'd caused her.

Chapter 4

That following day, at 12:56 p.m. Ebony pulled her Cadillac into Hester Park, looking around as if she would actually spot the guy who'd called on yesterday, insisting that they meet here. The park was semi-packed as always, so she had no choice but to park, and report to the designated spot.

The temperature was up in the upper eighties, which is why Ebony chose light-fabric capri pants, tank top, and a pair of sandals. With her dark Angela Cofer sunglasses on her face, Ebony ambulated with a little more confidence, knowing that her .380 caliber was tucked inside her pocketbook, just in case this guy planned to do more than just talk to her. She just hoped that he wasn't so bold as to try something in such a public place, in front of all these people.

Ebony made it to the large, encircled water fountain, and immediately took a seat on its marble-stoned edge, placing her pocketbook beside her. After making sure that her bag was open for easy access to her gun, she began surveying the area. It's not like she didn't know what she was looking for. If there were any truth to what this guy had professed over the phone, then Ebony knew that she'd be looking for a male, who was traveling alone.

While conducting her surveillance and trying her best not to look out of place, her eyes landed on a Caucasian couple that were strolling by, both holding onto a hand of the small child walking between them, which reminded Ebony of how she'd always longed to be a mother. It was just too bad that Jason didn't share her sentiments. He insisted that she take birth control, and threatened that if she ever comes up pregnant, he was going to beat the baby out of her.

Ebony was brought from her reverie by movement to the right of her. She looked to see that a man who appeared to be in his mid-forties, had sat down at about four feet away. He was clad in dark-brown shorts, matching T-shirt, and ball cap, with a pair of dark sunglasses on his face. He appeared to be handsome, though Ebony couldn't see but the left side of his face, being that he was looking straight ahead.

"It's not polite to stare at people," he spoke at a length, without looking in her direction.

"It's you," Ebony asserted, recognizing his voice.

"Are you wired?" He asked.

"Why would I be—"

"Did you bring protection?" He cut her off.

"Do I need protection?" She asked, not knowing if she should reveal this to him, being that he could still have ulterior motives.

"You should always carry protection," he told her, still not looking in her direction. "Especially being who, and what you are. Your dad made more enemies than he could keep up with." He paused to glance at her momentarily before looking off again. "What happened to your face?"

"That's none of your business," Ebony replied, hating the fact that he was able to see the swelling on her dark complexion, through the dark lenses of his sunglasses.

"I had genuine love for your father," he declared this in a defying tone. "I didn't agree with most of the things he did, or had me do, but the loyalty and love was always there."

"What things?" Ebony asked, only remembering her father being a phenomenal prosecutor, and the greatest dad in the world.

"Alfonso Walker," he replied.

"Is that your —"

"He's locked up in the county jail," the guy cut her off. "It's looking really bad for him. I need you to pull some strings to get him out."

"How could I possibly —"

"You're a prosecutor," he reminded her. "You can make it happen."

"Maybe," she replied, dubiously. "And, even if I could, the big question is, why should I? I mean, who is he? What does he have to do with the death of my parents? You did say this meeting was about my parents, right?"

"Of course," he replied, standing, looking down at her. "But you can't put a puzzle together without all the pieces. Alfonso Walker is a huge piece to this puzzle."

"And how do I know you're not scheming?"

"Your dad was a gambler," he told her. "I assume you've at least inherited *'THAT'* trait."

With that, the 5'10, 190 pound man whose name she still didn't obtain, swaggered off in the direction in which he'd come, leaving Ebony more confused than she were before coming here. Now, she has to decide if she's going to endeavor to find the right strings to pull in order to *save* this Alfonso Walker character from whatever he's facing.

Chapter 5

It seemed as if Monday had come around a little too fast for Ebony. Sunday dinner with her grandparents was its usual mundane event, with her grandmother doing all the talking, while the hatred that Ebony has for her grandfather lingered in the air like a substance that could be cut through with a knife. Also, it was Jason's second week not accompanying her, which used to be something he'd always look forward to every week. Plus, ever since Friday, he'd been spending his nights in the basement. But, this was fine by Ebony, because the love she had for him was no more. Now, she has to come up with a way to sever all ties with him so she could go on with her life.

"Your witness, Ms. Davis," Judge Carl Jackson now announced, after Attorney Rodney Kilgore was sworn in by Deputy Taylor.

"Thank you, Your Honor." Ebony got up, and approached the lectern, clad in her dark-blue, pin-striped pants suit, with her hair combed down her sides intentionally to conceal the right side of her face, where the swelling was close to invisible. "Mr. Kilgore, I am Assistant District Attorney Ebony Davis, and I only have a few questions for you. My first question is what kind of attorney are you?"

"Civil," he answered.

"So, you specialize in the private rights of citizens?"

"Yes."

"Were you employed in this same exact field on the thirteenth of August of last year?"

"Yes, I was."

"And did you receive a call from a Mrs. Sheryl Brown on this date?"

"Yes, I did," he answered, casting a glance at the defense table.

"Pertaining to what?" Ebony inquired.

"She was looking to file for a divorce," Kilgore replied, "And asked if I would represent her."

"Did you take her on?"

"I did."

"Do you remember how she sounded when you two were talking?"

Ebony ventured, hoping Scarlatti wouldn't object.

Attorney Kilgore looked to the ceiling, as if trying to retain. "I didn't know her prior to the call, so I can't say if she sounded like her normal self or not. I didn't ask, but she did go on to tell me why she wanted the divorce. And, as she explained everything, I detected a subtle emotional buildup. She was very upset, which is quite common for anyone going through such an ordeal."

"But she did call you on the thirteenth of August, to hire you to represent her in divorce court?"

"Yes."

"Nothing further," Ebony stated, heading for her table.

The judge regarded Scarlatti. "Cross?"

"No, Your Honor."

"You may be excused," he told Attorney Kilgore. "State, call your next witness."

"Your Honor," Ebony spoke, as she remained standing at her table, "The state calls Linkton County Fire Inspector Robin Ayers to the stand."

"Bring in Ms. Ayers," the judge said to deputy Taylor, who was escorting Attorney Kilgore to the exit. Then, he turned to Ebony.

"How many more witnesses do you have, Ms. Davis?"

"I have this next one," she answered, "And the retained pathologist."

"How long do you –"

"I can't approximate, Your Honor," Ebony cut him off. "But they should be in and out."

"Very well."

At that moment, deputy Taylor returned with Robin Ayers, who was a few shades lighter than Ebony, clad in a gray pantsuit, with her hair pulled into a bun. While she was being sworn in, Ebony's eyes locked onto Ayer's left hand that was rested on the bible that Taylor was holding. With the aegis of the courtroom's lights, the diamonds in her ring seemed to radiate a bright, almost mesmerizing glare, which caused her to think about Jason. But she quickly dismissed that thought as she made for the podium.

"Is it Miss or Missus?" She asked the investigator.

"Missus," she answered, displaying a bright smile.

Ebony nodded. "Mrs. Ayers, I am Assistant District Attorney Ebony Davis. Could you please tell the court how you're employed?"

"I am a fire inspector for the Linkton County Fire Department."

"How long have you been in this field?"

"I have almost four years in now," Ayers replied, a hint of glee in her voice.

"As a fire inspector," Ebony went on, envious of this woman's jovial department. "What is it that you do?"

Ayers cleared her throat, "My job is to assess fire damaged property to determine the cause of the fire."

"In August of last year," Ebony asked, "Did you do an assessment on a fire damaged home on Eastwood Court?"

"I did."

"Were you able to determine the cause of the fire?"

"Yes."

"Could you divulge this to the court?"

"Sure," she answered. "I was able to determine that the fire was induced by a highly combustible substance known as zodine, which is an uncommon household product."

"So," Ebony went on, leaning on the podium, "You wouldn't find this particular product in the average home as you would shampoo, toothpaste, and soap?"

"No."

"Well, where would you find this substance that you claim to be highly combustible?"

"Anywhere diesel engines are used or built," she answered. "During my investigation, I deduced that zodine is partially merged with diesel fuel, to create a homogeneous substance which sustains, and preserves diesel engines. Also, the hazard level of zodine surmounts that of the diesel fuel, which is why its handlers must wear protective gear, and refrain from excessive inhalation of the substance. Any fire with just a drop of zodine would be tantamount to a hydrogen bomb, which is why our firefighters had a tough time extinguishing the Brown's home."

"So, a fire such as this one would be considered arson?"

"Absolutely," Ayers responded. "But I assume that when a corpse is involved, It's considered murder."

"Nothing further, Your Honor," Ebony asserted, heading for her table.

"Cross?" The judge asked Scarlatti.

"Yes, Your Honor." Scarlatti stood, but remained at her table. "Inspector, you said that zodine is a highly combustible substance that is found anywhere diesel engines are used or built, correct?"

Ayers nodded. "Yes."

"Were there any diesel-operated machines on the Brown's property?"

"I don't think so."

Scarlatti cocked her head. "You don't think so?"

"I didn't assess anything outside the remnants of the house."

"But, as a fire inspector," Scarlatti went on, "After concluding the source of the fire, wouldn't it be a show of professionalism to scout the entire area, to see if you could locate the substance, especially if it's a rarity of some sort?"

"Yes."

"But, you didn't?"

"No, I didn't."

"Nothing further." Scarlatti retook her seat.

"Re-direct?" Asked the judge.

"No, Your Honor," Ebony answered. She couldn't believe that Scarlatti had easily pushed Ayers into admitting to unprofessionalism. On record!

"Will you be summoning your retained witness at this time?"

"Yes, Your Honor."

As the fire inspector was being escorted out, Ebony was starting to doubt her decision to retain this witness. Although this was a tactic she'd used numerous of times, it just didn't seem right at the moment, being that Rebecca "The Genie" Scarlatti was seated in the defense chair. But, Ebony was going to go forward with this witness. If Scarlatti finds a way to discredit him, which is incontestable, then she would have to trust in her closing argument, and the intelligence capacity of the jurors.

"State, your witness," the judge prompted, once Mr. Day had taken a seat on the witness stand.

"Thank you, Your Honor," Ebony stood, regarding the pathologist. "Mr. Day, keep in mind that you are still under oath. Now, with respect to states exhibit nine, which is your analysis report, you diagnosed Mrs. Brown as having no carbon monoxide in her bronchial passages, or lungs, correct?"

"I reported no carbon granules deposited in her bronchial passages, or lungs," he restated. "And no carbon monoxide in her blood, or other tissues."

"But, aren't these things usually found in victims who succumbs to such a death as Mrs. Brown's?"

"No," Mr. Day answered. "These things would only be found if fire was the actual cause of death."

Ebony made a mock expression of surprise. "So, fire was not the cause of death in this case?"

"No, it wasn't," the pathologist replied. "The body was charred beyond decomposition, but the bones, and most organs, were merely scorched. While examining the skeletal of Mrs. Brown, I discovered that her cranium had been mortally breached from the left, and rear, by a solid object of some sort."

"Is it possible that Mrs. Brown had accidentally started the fire?"

"No."

"Why not?"

"Because she was not alive when the fire started."

"And, what would that imply?" Ebony asked, hoping to get him to say what she needed him to say.

The pathologist glanced over at the defense table, then back at Ebony. "It means that someone had murdered Mrs. Brown before torching the house with her inside of it."

Ebony turned to the judge. "Your Honor, at this time, the state rests."

"Cross?" Judge Jackson asked Scarlatti.

She seemed to study Mr. Day with furrowed eyebrows for what seemed like an eon before answering. "No, Your Honor."

***

After the pathologist was dismissed, the judge granted a two-hour recess. Ebony, and Samantha, grabbed some sandwiches from the cafeteria, and made for Ebony's office, which is where they were now, enjoying their lunch in silence. As she ate, Ebony kept thinking about how Scarlatti had passed up the chance to discredit the pathologist. And what was the look she'd given him? It was as if she was searching for something to say but failed. Could this be what Aaron Taylor was trying to get her to see? Is Rebecca "The

Genie" Scarlatti going to need more than magic to get her client out of this one? Ebony was hoping so, because she really needed this win.

"Snap out of it," Samantha said from across the desk, obviously seeing that Ebony was pensive. "It's a little too late to be worried about the outcome of this trial. You may not be kicking Scarlatti's ass, but I'm willing to bet anything that she considers you a worthy opponent. And, you may have put the nail in Brown's coffin with the pathologist's testimony. He's guilty. The jurors should have determined that before the first witness was sworn in."

Ebony chuckled. "You're one hell of a prosecutor."

"Hey!" Samantha replied, smiling. "We get paid to assume everyone's guilty until proven guilty."

Samantha's statement immediately made Ebony's mind revert to her father. One night, she had overheard one of his phone conversations, where he actually said something about criminals being guilty until proven guilty. Now, she was thinking about the visit she'd had with the stranger, whom she'd totally forgotten about. That's when she remembered what she needed Samantha to do.

"Sam," she finally spoke, "I need you to dig up all the information you can on a Linkton County inmate for me."

Samantha sat down her sandwich, then grabbed her pen and notepad off the desk. "Name?"

"Alfonso Walker."

"The one who has a trial coming up next week?" Samantha asked, not bothering to write the name down.

"He has a trial coming up next week?" Ebony was hoping that Samantha was wrong about this.

Samantha shot her an incredulous look.

"What?" Ebony asked, dumbfounded.

"It's good to know you don't pay me any attention," Samantha accused, with a hint of attitude. "I've been telling you about this case for over two weeks. This is the same case that Briggs wants me to assist him on."

Now, Ebony remembered. "The double homicide?"

"Yes," Samantha answered, placing her pad and pen back onto the desk, and retrieving her sandwich.

"Are you sure this is the same guy?"

"He's the only Alfonso Walker being held at the Linkton County jail."

Ebony wiped her mouth with a napkin. "What kind of evidence do they have against him?"

"Hell," Samantha replied with a mouthful of food. "What kind of evidence do they *'NOT'* have against him?"

***

Back in the courtroom, as the jurors filed in to take their seats, Ebony was thinking about what Samantha had revealed about Alfonso Walker's case. He had murdered two men in front of a slew of witnesses, in which several of them are deponing against him. Plus, he was apprehended shortly after the crime, a few blocks away, still in possession of the weapon he'd used. With all of this, Ebony didn't know how she was going to be of any assistance to him. He didn't accept the state's offer of life without parole, but chose to take his chances in a trial that would result in the death penalty if he loses.

"Now that everyone is settled," the judge prompted, "We can resume with this proceeding." Before recess, the state was at rest, am I right?"

"Yes, Your Honor," answered Ebony.

He regarded Scarlatti. "Defense, are you ready to proceed?"

Scarlatti stood. "Yes, Your Honor."

"You may call your first witness."

"The defense calls Mr. Tommy Coalson to the stand."

The judge nodded to Deputy Taylor, who made for the exit. And, as he was passing her table, Ebony couldn't help but get a glimpse of the slight bulge in the front of his pants. It may not have been an erection, but Ebony's imagination begged to differ, which sent hot flashes through her body. Maybe it was time to treat herself, instead of cheating herself. But, who...

Deputy Taylor returned with Tommy Coalson, a Caucasian male, who appeared to be in his fifties, clad in a gray, two-piece suit, with a military-style crew cut full of natural white hair. As he was being sworn in, all Ebony could think about were the lies he was about to tell to help his childhood friend, and business partner, out of the jam he's in.

"Direct examination?" The judge asked, once Coalson was seated.

"Yes, Your Honor," Scarlatti, in a burgundy pantsuit, and her hair held high like the local celebrity she was. "Mr. Coalson, I am Attorney Rebecca Scarlatti. Do you know the defendant, Mr. Howard Brown?"

"I do," he answered.

"And, how do you know him?"

"We're childhood friends," Coalson admitted. "Plus, we're both co-owners of West Group Appliances."

"So, it's safe to say that you two know each other pretty well, huh?"

"You can say that."

"Hang out a lot?"

"We hang out enough," he answered. "Most of the times, it's at business meetings, social gatherings, or family outings."

"Did you two hang out on August thirteenth of last year?"

"Yes."

"On what day was that?"

"That was a Saturday."

"For the court," Scarlatti went on, "Could you tell us what this day was like with Mr. Brown?"

"What was it like?"

"Yes," Scarlatti answered. "What time did you get together?"

"I really can't say exactly," said Coalson, "But it was after twelve in the afternoon. It's not a ritual but, whenever we can, on Saturdays, we'll power walk around the track at Hester Park for over an hour. That's where we'd meet up at, as always. After our walk, we sat on a bench, and discussed everything under the sun. Then, we drove out to Blue's Bar and Grill, where we ate, drank, and talked some more. It was a little after three when we arrived there."

"And how long did you stay?" Scarlatti questioned.

Coalson looked as if he was trying to retain, then said, "I really can't remember, but I made it home around seven-thirty."

"So," Scarlatti began, "You were with Mr. Brown from twelve-something in the afternoon, until six-something that evening?"

"That sums it up, yes."

"Thank you. Nothing further."

"Cross?" The judge asked.

"Yes, Your Honor," Ebony answered, standing as Scarlatti headed back to her table. "Mr. Coalson, you testified that you and Mr. Brown are childhood buddies, am I right?"

"Yes."

"You were always on good terms?"

"For the most part."

"Always had each other's back?"

"Of course."

"Confided in each other?"

"Sure."

"Shared secrets?"

"I'm sure we've shared a few secrets along the way," Coalson answered. "Some that I may have forgotten."

"Are you married, Mr. Coalson?"

"Yes, I am."

"Between your wife and Mr. Brown," Ebony ventured. "With whom are you susceptible to share your darkest secrets with?"

Coalson was pensive for a moment. "I guess it would be Mr. Brown."

"Do you think he feels the same way about you?"

"I would say so, yes."

"If Mr. Brown murdered someone," Ebony ventured again, "Do you think he would –"

Scarlatti was on her feet. "Objection, Your Honor! Prosecutor is out of line!"

"Your Honor," Ebony spoke up, "I'm trying to substantially establish the comity between Mr. Coalson and the defendant for the record. My question was not intended to be inappropriate, nor speculate to any degree."

"Objection overruled," the judge rendered.

Ebony almost smiled to herself, as Scarlatti seemed to slump back down into her chair. But, knowing that this was only just a minor victory, Ebony resumed. "Mr. Coalson, my question was if Mr. Brown were to murder someone, do you think he would confide in you?"

Coalson shrugged. "I really couldn't say. I mean, I would hope so."

"Let me take you back to August the thirteenth of last year, Mr. Coalson," said Ebony. "While you and Mr. Brown were together, do you recall him having his cellular phone?"

"He did not have his phone that day," he answered. "He said something about rushing out of the house and forgetting to grab it."

"Has he ever done this before?"

"Not to my recollection," Coalson replied. "But I assume he has. It could happen to anyone."

"Nothing further."

The judge looked over to Scarlatti. "Redirect?"

"No, Your Honor."

"You are excused," he told Tommy Coalson. "Defense, call your next witness."

Scarlatti asserted. "Your Honor, the defense calls Mrs. Cathy Churchill to the stand."

"You did good with your line of questioning," Samantha commented Ebony in a low tone, as Taylor led Coalson out. "The part about keeping secrets may win you a victory beyond reasonable doubt."

Ebony drew a breath. "I sure hope so."

At that time, Mrs. Cathay Churchill, a Caucasian female in her mid-fifties, was escorted to the witness stand. Her large, ankle-length chinchilla coat exuded wealth, but the bright-red lipstick, and multi-layer of makeup on her face, were a little too much for anything outside of a circus arena. As she was being sworn in, Ebony noticed that her gaze seemed to linger on Howard Brown. And Ebony was highly conversant with the look in the older woman's eyes.

So, Ebony thought, Terri Bradshaw wasn't Howard Brown's only play thing.

"Direct examination?" The judge prompted.

"Yes, Your Honor." Scarlatti approached, and stood behind the lectern. "Mrs. Churchill, for the record, we've already spoken prior to this proceeding, am I right?"

"Yes."

"What did we talk about?"

"We talked about the fire that destroyed the Brown home."

"Did I ask anything of you?"

"Yes," Churchill answered. "You asked if I would come here and testify about what I know about the fire."

"Are you ready?"

Churchill casted a glance at Brown before answering. "I guess so."

"Before we go into the fire," Scarlatti started, "I need to know if you're familiar with the defendant, Mr. Howard Brown."

"Yes, I am."

"And how are you familiar with him?"

"Well," she began, "Before the fire, we were next door neighbors for over ten years."

"Were you on good terms?"

"Of course!" Churchill seemed to take umbrage. "We were visiting neighbors. We've went out on several occasions."

"Are you married, Mrs. Churchill?"

"Yes, I am."

"What is your occupation?"

"I am a housewife."

"So, you're pretty much always at home?"

"Yes."

"Were you at home on August thirteenth of last year?"

"Yes, I was."

"When the fire broke out at your neighbors' home?"

"Yes."

"Could you tell the court what you were doing at the time?"

"Sure," Churchill answered, adjusting herself in the chair. "I had my great-grandson that weekend. My husband had went off to bowl with some of his friends. While my great-grandson was playing video games in the sitting room, I was in the kitchen, preparing supper. I had all the windows open, being that it was the middle of August. That's when I was hit with a strange smell, which put me in the mind of trash being burned. Before long, I was engulfed in a black cloud of smoke. I knew that it was coming from outside, but

I still ran to check on Simon. He was okay, though I was coughing from it. I felt as if I was going to suffocate inside that house, so I hauled Simon and myself outside. That's when I saw that the Browns' house was on fire."

"Do you remember what time it was?" Scarlatti asked.

"I remember it being within the four o'clock hour," she answered.

"That's when I usually start preparing for supper."

"Did you call the fire department?" Scarlatti asked.

"No." Mrs. Churchill shot her an incredulous look. "Sen-Tech automatically notifies the proper authorities in the event of an emergency."

"Thank you, Mrs. Churchill," said Scarlatti. "Nothing further, Your Honor."

"Cross?" Judge Jackson asked as Scarlatti made for her table.

"Yes, Your Honor." Ebony stood, but remained at her table. "Mrs. Churchill, if you could take a wild guess, what would you say is the proximity of yours, and the Browns' house?"

Mrs. Churchill looked genuinely confused. "I don't get what you're saying.

"I'm trying to figure out the distance between yours, and the Browns' house."

"Oh!" Mrs. Churchill closed her eyes as if she was trying to draw a mental picture. Reopening her eyes, she said, "I really can't say.

If I took a wild guess, I'm sure it would be way off, considering that I'm no good at measurements."

"Don't feel bad," Ebony said with a smile. "I'm not good at it myself. But, let me ask you this. If someone at the Browns' house were to scream at the top of their lungs, could you hear them from behind the walls of your own?"

"Well," she answered. "I assume that my windows will have to be open, and the house would have to be completely quiet. I mean, I'm only assuming."

"Thank you. Nothing further."

***

Once court had adjourned for the day, Samantha had volunteered to turn the evidence in while Ebony made for her office to grab her things. After gathering her pocketbook, and briefcase, she locked her office up, caught the elevator to the ground floor, then exited the building. As always, since Howard Brown's trial had begun, the drone of spectators, and reporters were gathered out front. And she was not surprised to see Attorney Rebecca Scarlatti and Howard Brown, in the midst of them as questions were thrown back and forth to the both of them. Ebony approached Aaron Taylor, who was standing off to the side, watching the small spectacle.

"Enjoying the show?" she asked, stopping beside him.

"Not really," he replied, regarding her with a smile. "Actually, I was waiting on you. Ready?"

"Like yesterday," she answered.

"Ms. Scarlatti," Ebony heard a reporter say as she and Aaron circumvented the mob. "This prosecutor is known to have the worst luck when it comes to winning cases, but it seems as if she's found her momentum. Care to comment on her performance?"

"I must say that I am genuinely impressed by her performance," Scarlatti offered.

"Wow!" Aaron said, as they cleared the crowd, heading for the parking garage. "You heard it from the horse's mouth."

"Flatter me in front of the media, huh?" Ebony responded, not knowing what to make of Scarlatti's compliment, but thought about what Samantha had said about Scarlatti considering her a worthy opponent.

"I think she was sincere," Aaron proffered. "Hell, I'm also impressed by your performance. Once you find your footing, I believe you'll be just as good as your dad was."

After saying goodnight to Aaron, Ebony climbed into her car, and drove out of the garage. As she traveled down Fair Street, she was unaware of the grin on her face while mulling over Aaron's assertion of her being as good as her father was. *Is that even possible?* She thought.

Coming to a halt at a traffic light, Ebony grabbed her pocketbook off the front-passenger seat, and rummaged through it for a stick of chewing gum. Before she could find her pack of red wings, a car's horn sounded from behind her, giving her the impression that the light had turned green. But, when she looked up, she saw that the light hadn't changed. This made her glance into her rearview mirror at the dark-brown car behind her. She couldn't make out the occupant's features for the sunglasses, and ball cap he was wearing.

The occupant blew his horn twice. This time, when Ebony looked up, she saw that the light had turned green. Relinquishing her quest for her chewing gum, she tossed her pocketbook back onto the seat, and slowly accelerated through the intersection, glancing into her rearview. The car followed, and the occupant seemed to be playing some kind of tune on its horn. It was obvious that he was trying to get her to pull over, but Ebony wasn't sure if she wanted to do that, being that she had no idea as to whom it was.

Then, she realized that if she didn't stop, and see what it was he wanted, he could follow her to her home, which is something she did not want. That's when Ebony made her decision. As she came upon Burger King, she initiated her right turn signal, and saw that her follower had done the same. Turning into the restaurant's parking lot, she found a parking spot, parked, and waited patiently. Seconds later, the car rode past her, which was almost a blur in her rearview mirror. Momentarily, a male figure approached the right side of her car. As he opened the front passenger door, Ebony removed her pocketbook, and briefcase, off the seat, placing them on the rear seats.

"Any good news?" He asked, as he took a seat, closing the door back.

"I don't know what you expect to hear," Ebony said, though she really wanted to curse him out for following her. "Your friend murdered two people in front of several witnesses. Plus, he was caught with the gun, shortly after committing the crimes. You came to me for help, but there's only one person who could help him."

"Who?"

"God," Ebony replied.

"You should've been a comedienne," he said, before directing his attention out the passenger window.

"Trust me," Ebony spoke. "I was not being facetious. Considering all the evidence he has against him, his chances of getting acquitted are slim to none. I mean, what am I supposed to do?"

"Get me a copy of the witness list," he said, now regarding her through the dark lenses of his sunglasses.

"Get you a copy of the witness list?" Ebony asked, incredulous. "I'm not even the prosecutor on his case. And, even if I could obtain a copy of the witness list, why should I? You haven't told me anything substantial about my parents. You haven't even told me your name. If you want me to help you, you'll have to play by my rules. Deal, or no deal?"

A smile slowly spread across his face. "You are definitely his daughter."

"Deal, or no deal?" She repeated.

"Deal," he accepted.

"Name?"

"Richard Carter," he answered. "You dad called me Rick so you can call me Rick. I was arrested for armed robbery in 2005, and your dad was assigned to the case. He visited me in jail one day, offering to get my case placed on dead docket, if I agreed to work for him. I didn't know what kind of work he would have me doing, but I didn't want to plea out to twenty years, and definitely didn't want the life sentence I was facing if I lost trial. At that point, I didn't give a damn about what I had to do to get out of that situation."

"So, you took him up on his offer," Ebony stated. "What did he have you doing?"

Rick drew a breath, then pulled a small, ancient tape recorder from the pocket of his shorts. "This belonged to your dad. When I got the news on what happened in the courtroom, I rushed out to his house on Wilkins Street, to make sure there were no self-incriminating items, or documents, lying around."

"A house on Wilkins Street?" Ebony questioned.

"He bought it after your mom filed for divorce," Rick told her. "I didn't have a key, but I was good at picking locks, and breaching alarms. There were no documents to speak on, but I found a few guns, a briefcase full of money, and this tape recorder. I got rid of the guns, kept this recorder, and left the briefcase on your grandparents porch.

"I remember that," Ebony said, remembering the day, which was two days after the demise of her parents. Her grandparents had taken her to see a psychologist. When they returned home, there was a briefcase on the porch, sitting by the front door. Once her grandparents had gotten it inside, and surveyed the contents, they seemed to come alive with joy. "Was there a note?" She now asked, remembering them reading something that brought tears to their eyes.

"It was a typed letter," he responded. "I made it seem as if it had come from your dad, telling them to look after you, and to make sure you went to college. I didn't count the money, so I can't say how much it was."

"What's on the tape?" Ebony asked, upset that her grandparents hadn't told her anything about the money.

"A conversation between your dad, and Sara Jennings. I'll explain everything afterwards," he said, then pressed play.

RECORDER:

Sara: "How's that?"

Tyrone: "Feels good."

Sara: "Am I still the best?"

Tyrone: "For now."

Sara: "I can settle for that."

Tyrone: "This doesn't have anything to do with next week, does it?"

Sara: "The trial? Of course, not. I won't even mention that. But I am thinking about taking on   another profession."

Tyrone: "Like what?"

Sara: "I'm still thinking. Indeed something less stressful. Hell, I would sell drugs if I knew I wouldn't get caught."

Tyrone: (Laughing) "Yeah, right."

Sara: "All white people didn't grow up in the suburbs with silver spoons in their mouths. And I'm not as innocent as I appear. I've done things."

Tyrone: "Like what?"

Sara: "I used to date a drug dealer, years back. I've done and witnessed horrible things that I can't really speak on. He's the one who'd come up with the bright idea of sending me to law school. First, I had to wing myself away from heroin."

Rick stopped the tape.

"Is that the public defender who was found overdosed on heroin in the parking garage?" Ebony asked, now remembering the story. Rick nodded.

"That was her, but she was not a heroin addict."

"That's what she said on tape," Ebony begged to differ.

"She was only trying to get your dad to admit to setting up another prosecutor. She planted the tape recorder but, somehow, your dad discovered it. He had me and two other guys attack her in the parking garage. Once she was unconscious, I shot her up with heroin, and left paraphernalia in her car. Do you believe me now?"

"My dad had you doing stuff like that?"

"Your dad was a crime boss," Rick told her. "He had a slew of workers, and we all had criminal backgrounds. Do you know why he's never lost a case? Because, he thought like a criminal. Hell, he 'was' a criminal. Find that hard to believe?"

"A little," she answered, still trying to process this revelation. "What about my mom? What do you know about her death?"

"Do you think you can get the witness list?" he asked, purposefully changing the subject.

"His trial starts next week," Ebony replied. "A friend of mine is working with the prosecutor on the case. Maybe I can obtain the list without tipping her off. But, if I can't make it happen ..."

Chapter 6

It seemed as if Ebony had slept in intervals. Mental pictures of her father being the type of person that Rick had portrayed him to be, had kept her up most of the night. It was funny, because she could actually imagine him in a large, round-brimmed hat, and long trench coat, like the crime bosses she'd seen in old mobster movies. But, it was scary, because she was sure that she hadn't heard half of the heinous crimes he'd orchestrated.

"All rise!" Deputy Taylor announced, as the judge entered the courtroom. "The Honorable Judge Carl Jackson presides."

"You may all be seated," the judge spoke, taking his seat. "Defense, are you ready to proceed?" "Yes, Your Honor," Scarlatti answered.

"You may call your next witness."

The attorney got to her feet. "Your Honor, at this time, I will like to call the defendant, Mr. Howard Brown, to the stand."

Ebony attentively watched as Howard Brown, in his gray, expensive-looking suit, got up, and nonchalantly strolled toward the witness stand with a gait befitting someone half his age. To be almost sixty years old, he seemed well-preserved with his handsome features, and toned 5'10, 165 pound frame. Once he was sworn in, Rebecca Scarlatti took locus behind the podium. "Mr. Brown," she started, "I'm going to take you back to August thirteenth of last year. Do you remember what you did on this date?"

"I do," Brown answered, with a nod.

"For the court," Scarlatti went on, "Could you give a brief account on your activities, and whereabouts on the date in question?"

"Sure," Brown focused his attention on the jurors, as he spoke."

"It was a Saturday. I woke up around ten-thirty that morning. After having breakfast with my wife, I got dressed and made for Hester Park, where I met up with my colleague, Tommy Coalson. As always, we…

As Ebony listened, she couldn't help but infer that Brown was speaking as if he'd been rehearsing his testimony, Plus, he was telling his side of the story in the same exact manners Coalson had, which undoubtfully meant that it was all meticulously arranged. But what could she do? How could she validate this?

"…. I can't say what time we left there," Brown was saying, "But I made it home a little after seven."

"Did you discover anything upon returning to your abode?" Scarlatti asked.

"Yes," he answered,, voice cracking.

At this time, he was looking down, slowly shaking his head from side to side. Ebony saw it coming, but she didn't expect his crocodile tears to be accommodated by an award-winning act of waling, as he buried his face in his hands. That's when Ebony realized that she had a genuine hatred for this scumbag, who'd murdered his wife in cold blood, all because he couldn't accept the consequences for his infidelity.

As everyone looked on, a female jury member handed a Kleenex to Deputy Taylor, who examined it before handing it to Howard Brown. Bravo! Ebony thought as she watched him attempt to pull himself together, with a fraudulent, pitiful look on his face. Shifting her gaze, Ebony tried to read the visage of every juror, but couldn't. Maybe they were unmoved by Brown's phony display of affection.

"Can you go on?" Scarlatti now asked.

"Yes," Brown answered, dabbing at his eyes that were now as clear as a sunny day.

"I was asking, if you'd discovered anything upon your return to your home," Scarlatti went on.

"I did," Brown drew a breath, before going on. "I discovered that my house had been burned to the ground, and my—" He drew another breath. "My wife was inside at the time it happened. She didn't make it."

"Who were on the scene when you arrived?"

He shook his head slowly. "It was a circus. There were firemen, fire inspectors, police officers, and neighbors."

"Is that when you found out about your wife?"

"No," he answered. "I was told that the fire had just been extinguished, so everything was still hot. I gave the fire inspector the number to my sister's house in Covington, which is where I spent the night. She called me the following night, with her assessment."

"Your Honor," Scarlatti regarded the judge. "At this time, the defense rests."

"Cross?" he asked Ebony.

"Yes, Your Honor." Ebony approached the lectern, as Scarlatti returned to her seat.

"Mr. Brown, how long have you been married?"

"A little over twenty-eight years," he answered.

"Do. Excuse me, did you have a prenuptial agreement?"

"No."

"On the date in question," Ebony started, "Did your wife tell you of the findings of the private investigator she'd hired to follow you?"

"No."

"She didn't show you any photos of you and Ms. Bradshaw?"

"No."

"Did she say anything about a divorce?"

"No."

Ebony paused, seeing that she wasn't getting anywhere with her line of questioning. This was her chance to discredit Brown's testimony, but she couldn't think of a way to trip him. Then, she thought about something she'd seen a prosecutor do in a movie she'd recently watched. But, unlike television, a stunt like that would definitely ruin her chance of winning this case. To hell with it! She thought, regarding Brown with narrowed eyes.

"Mr. Brown," Ebony now spoke, subtly altering her tone to match that of the prosecutor she'd seen on the movie. "I think your wife *DID* show you the photos of you and your mistress. I think your wife *DID* say that she was divorcing you. No prenuptial agreement? I think that would be sufficient to crush her skull and set her on fire."

Scarlatti lunged from her chair. "Objection! She is badgering my client!"

"Nothing further, your Honor."

Ebony sauntered back to her table, smiling to herself, hoping that she'd planted the seed in the jurors' mind. As soon as she'd taken her seat, Samantha lightly kicked her foot under the table. Out the corners of her eyes, she could see a hint of the smirk that Samantha was doing a good job of quelling, which made her feel even better about what she'd done.

"Are we done with the defendant?" the judge asked.

"Yes, Your Honor," they both answered in unison. Scarlatti retaking her seat.

"You may step down, Mr. Brown," the judge asserted, then waited until Brown was back in his seat, before continuing. "Ladies and gentlemen of the jury, what we are about to do now is called closing arguments. This is where the state and the defense will come up, one at a time, and argue their case to you. The state will start it off, followed by the defense. Then, the state will close it out. State, you may proceed."

Standing, Ebony crossed the courtroom, and positioned herself in front of the jury box. As always, before beginning her opening, or closing agreements, she took a moment to study the face of every jury member.

"Ladies and gentlemen of the jury," she spoke slowly, and deliberately. "I'm not going to say much right now, because you will hear from me again. This should not be a hard case to decide. You've heard all the evidence. You've seen the pictures. I mean, what else could I possibly say or do that would further prove that Howard Brown is guilty of murdering his wife of twenty-eight years? It doesn't take a …"

After closing arguments, the judge charged the jurors then sent them to the jury room to deliberate. Ebony and Samantha took this time to journey to the cafeteria, where they were now sharing a table. Samantha was consuming a tuna fish sandwich, and Ebony was tending to a chicken salad, as her mind played back segments of Brown's trial. To say that she was worried about the outcome would be an understatement.

"Sam," Ebony now spoke, looking across the table at her friend. "I need your honest opinion."

Samantha regarded her, saying nothing.

"If you were a jury member in Brown's trial," Ebony went on, "Without being bias, what would your verdict be? Be honest."

Before Samantha could reply, the Head District Attorney, Barbara Hutchins, approached the table. "May I join you ladies?"

"Sure," Ebony responded, gesturing to one of the two empty chairs.

"You did a good job at closing," Barbara commented Ebony as she took a seat, placing her manicured hands in her lap. "In fact, I'm surprised at how you've handled yourself, being that this is your first high profile case. Are you still wondering why I handed this case to you?"

"I figured you wanted to humiliate me," Ebony said, consuming a portion of her salad.

"No." Barbara seemed unfazed by the accusation. "It was time you came out of the shadows. To prosper you need exposure. This is what you signed up for." She paused. "I'm about to retire but, before I relinquish my throne, I'm gonna make sure you're at least half as sharp as your father was."

***

It was after 5 p.m. when everybody were summoned back to Judge Jackson's courtroom, which could only mean that the jury had come to some kind of consensus. But, that wasn't the cause. The judge promulgated that the jury needed more time to deliberate and, being that it was beyond quitting time, he was going to adjourn for the day, and give them all the time they would need tomorrow.

Upon leaving the courthouse, Ebony was surprised at how the reporters had swarmed her and Samantha, in front of the building, inquiring about their sentiments on the impeding verdict. Being that they'd thrown Samantha into the equation, she took it upon herself to navigate the interview, in which she'd done with expertise. After parting ways, Ebony made the drive to the Linkton County Jail to see the guy that was putting her job, and possibly her Freedom, on the line for to help *beat the system.*

Ebony had already gleaned what information she could about the configuration of the jail's visitation procedures. She knew that non-attorney visits were monitored via audio and video whereas visitors were escorted to a trailer outside the building that was outfitted with booths, and camera-mounted screens. On the other hand, attorney visits were conducted more discreetly. Inside the building, Ebony was escorted to a secluded area that had four booths. Entering one, she took a seat in an uncomfortable plastic chair, and rested her elbows on the protruding concrete slab in front of her. She stared through the thick, clear glass that had a multitude of pencil-sized holes in the center of it, awaiting Alfonzo Walker.

But, she didn't have to wait for long because moments later, a dark complexioned, 5'6', 210 pounds man with a shaved head, and clad in an orange jail-issued uniform, was escorted into the booth by two officers. After securing the door, they opened a slot in the door for him to stick his hands through, in order to remove his manacles. Once the officers had made off, he took a seat on the steel stall, regarding Ebony with an inscrutable look.

"Alfonso Walker?" she asked, speaking through the holes in the glass.

"That would be me," he answered, a broad smile on his face. Then, the smile quickly vanished. "But I would appreciate it if you called me Bull."

Ebony narrowed her eyes. "Are you trying to intimated me?"

"No, ma'am," he answered with sincerity. "I would never—"

She cut him off. "Then, I suggest you save the tough guy act for your cellmates. Now, I've already talked to Richard, which I know you're aware of he's told me somethings that has me considering helping you, but I'm not one hundred percent committed. I mean, I can't think of one good reason why I should jeopardize my career for someone I know nothing about. What's in it for me?"

Bull was quiet.

"That was not a rhetorical question," she pressed.

"Your dad was a very powerful man," Bull finally spoke. "Not to take any glory from him, but he didn't attain this power on his own. He had a group of soldiers working under him. I was one of 'em. We did everything from intimidating to eliminating. Drugs were involved, in which I was the head of operations. Your dad made good money and paid us good money. He'd also left a lot of money behind. Did Rick tell your about the house on Wilkins?"

"He did," Ebony answered. "I also know about the briefcase full of money."

Bull waved his hand dismissively. "That wasn't even a quarter of the money left behind."

"Rick claimed he never counted the money."

"He didn't."

"But, you did?"

"Nope," Bull answered. "Rick didn't tell me about the briefcase until after he'd dropped it off to your grandparents."

"And, you take his word for it?"

"Rick may not be anything close to a Christian," he told, "But he stands firm when it comes to loyalty."

"And, you?" Ebony inquired with raised eyebrows.

"I have my faults," he admitted, "But a dog never bites the hand that feeds him."

Only the hand that 'STOPS' feeding him, huh? Ebony thought, but said, "You still haven't answered my question. What do I get out of helping you?"

"We didn't bother keeping up with you," he replied. "We didn't know what had become of you until the beginning of this trial you're working on. I knew who you were when the news reporter said your name, before they'd made a reference to your dad. I had no mind to contact you until they'd mentioned how successful you were at winning cases. That's when I figured that Rick and I could build you a team and help boost your status."

"By making me a criminal?"

"More like a crime boss," he answered, then glanced back as if to make sure the officers hadn't returned to collect him. "It worked for your dad. He wasn't undefeatable because he was a good prosecutor. But, I guess you have a hard time believing that."

"Pretty much," she answered. Although for some strange reason, she believed everything he and Rick had told her thus far. "So, you can make me undefeatable?"

"In time, yes," he replied. "I can also make you rich. I lost contact with your dad's plug, but I know a guy."

"Plug?" Ebony cut him off. "I know you're not talking about…"

"Of course."

She was now shaking her head from side to side. "I am not trying to get involved with that."

"You'll have people working under you," he told her. "You won't have to set up a payroll account, but they'll definitely need to be paid for their services. Besides, you won't' even have to touch the stuff. I'll handle everything. Like I said, I was the head of operations for your dad. That's how I know he'd left behind way more money that what was in that briefcase. And, that was probably someone's payoff, in which they never got the chance to receive."

"And how much money do you believe he'd left behind?" Ebony inquired, thinking about the fifteen thousand that her parents had left in her trust account, and the insurance policy she'd heard nothing about.

"Over half a million," answered Bull.

Ebony was stunned but defied to let it show. And, where would he leave such an amount of money?"

Bull shrugged. "I don't know. I mean, if I were you, I would try the house on Wilkins."

Ebony drove home thinking about the area that Wilkins Street was located in. Growing up, Ebony remembered it as a flourishing neighborhood, where only Linkton County's upper class residents dwelled. But, as the county bloomed over the year with communities being reconstructed, that area seemed to have been overlooked, which is why it was now crawling with Linkton County's minority. Ebony even remembered cases where there were gang related shootings in that particular tract. But the violence was the least of her worries. Bull was insistent that she check out the house on Wilkins, and that's exactly what she was going to do.

Now, she pulled her car into her garage, parking beside Jason's. Entering the house, she didn't even bother locating Jason on the Sen-Tech monitor, being that he'd pretty much made the basement his home. And, she still hadn't come up with a way to get him out of her house, though she'd periodically entertained the thought of having the authorities escort him out. But that would only make the headlines, which is something she did not need at the moment.

After placing her briefcase in the hall's closet and ordering the Sen-Tech system to set the alarm, Ebony made for her bedroom. Entering, she was surprised to see Jason sitting on the edge of the bed, clad in silk, posh pajamas with the shirt open, reveling his perfectly chiseled stomach and chest. Ebony was instantly turned on, but maintain her composure, as she sat her pocketbook down on the dresser, and began taking off her jewelry, starting with her earrings.

"I got the toilet in the basement fixed," Jason announced.

"Thank you," was all Ebony could say, as she kept her back to him, and tried not to regard him through the mirror.

Though she wasn't looking directly at him, Ebony could still see his movements in the mirror. And she definitely saw him get off the bed, and slowly approach her from behind. At this time, though she didn't feel a bit afraid, she was fumbling with the clasp on her necklace, a gift from Jason for her 29th birthday, with trembling hands.

"I'll get it," he said, relieving her of the necklace, and placing it in her hand.

"Thank You!" Ebony placed the necklace on the dresser, then commenced to remove her watch.

"I miss you, baby," he whispered in her ear, then began kissing her softly on her neck, which sent her hormones into overdrive.

***

Jason had sexed Ebony for hours, which resulted in her having to force herself out of bed the following morning. But the momentary body aches were accepted in good faith. During the long course of foreplay, all she could think about was giving birth to a beautiful little girl. Jason didn't know that she'd surceased taking birth control pills, almost a week ago, and she wasn't going to be a fool to tell him. But her dreams of becoming a mother had shattered when he'd brandished a Magnum Plus condom, before penetrating her. Well, Ebony thought afterwards, at least he'd endeavored to reclaim something he'd once cherished. Maybe he was trying to reconcile. Maybe she would forgive him for his past opprobrious deportment, in hopes that he would become a better man. Maybe he would.

"All rise!" Deputy Taylor brought the courtroom into order, as Judge Jackson entered. "The Honorable Judge Carl Jackson presides."

"You may be seated," the judge asserted, taking his seat. "Is everyone here?"

"Yes, Your Honor," answered Taylor.

"Bring in the jurors."

It was after twelve in the afternoon, and the jury was ready to revel their verdict. To say that Ebony was nervous would be an understatement. She probably would have felt a whole lot better if Samantha was seated beside her, but her friend had some misdemeanor cases to handle in another courtroom. Now, as the jurors filed in to take their seats, Ebony did her best to appear reticent, as she casually looked about the room. Rebecca Scarlatti and Howard Brown were engaged in conversation as if nothing was going on around them. The authorized news team seemed to be watching her every move and District Attorney Barbara Hutchins, who was seated on the back row, looked every bit of her sixty-three years, with enough make up on her face to glamorize four women. Catching her gaze, the D.A. nodded. Ebony returned the gesture.

"Will the foreman please stand?" the judge spoke, getting Ebony's attention, and summoning the foreman, an older white female, to her feet. "I understand that the jury has reached a verdict."

"We have," she answered, waving the verdict sheet in her hand.

"Could you please read your verdict out to the court."

"Sure," she held the verdict sheet up to read from it. "We, the jury…"

Chapter 7

Wednesday/ June 21, 2023

Fulton County Superior Courthouse

Atlanta, GA

12:39 P.M.

"According to the indictment," the Caucasian female judge, who appeared to be in her mid-fifties, spoke as she regarded the documents in front of her. "On November eighteenth of 2022, Mr. Anthony Hudson committed the act of aggravated assault again a Cynthia Graham, outside of First National Bank on Forsyth Road, before entering said bank, accompanied by two other subjects, and committing that act of murder against officer John Coston; aggravated assault against Wayne Stokes; kidnapping against John Coston, Wayne Stokes, Melody Edwards, Aisha Cummings, Lily Aldridge, Rachel Wallace, Casey Meadows, Johnathan Meadows, Amy Fischer, Steven Lambert, Manny Hobbs, Natasha Brown, and Kimberly Brown; armed robbery against above mentioned establishment, and all thirteen occupants; and murder against Bryon Jenkins, who was an accomplice." She flipped to the next page. "Mr. Hudson is also charged with arson, possession of firearms, and possession of stolen currency, which were taken from the First National Bank." The judge looked over to the defense table. "How does the defendant wish to plead?"

"Not guilty, Your Honor," answered the white male public defender that Anthony had met twenty minutes prior to entering the courtroom.

"Does the defendant wish to undergo an in court polygraph testing?"

"No, Your Honor."

She regarded the prosecutor. "State, what's your offer?"

The prosecutor, a black male with large, black framed eyeglasses, got to his feet, standing at 6'3. "Your Honor, the state is offering the max, which is life without parole for each count of first-degree murder; twenty years for each kidnapping; life for each armed robbery; twenty-five years for each aggravated assault; ten years for possession of firearms; ten years for arson; and five years for possession of stolen currency."

The judge regarded Anthony and his attorney with a look of uncertainty. "Is the defendant interested in the state's offer?" The attorney looked at his client.

"Don't you dare ask me that dumb ass question!" Anthony snarled in a low tone.

"If you don't take the offer," the lawyer told him, "We'll have to prepare for trial."

Anthony smiled. "Well, I hope you're ready to jump through hoops."

The attorney frowned at Anthony, before regarding the judge. "No, Your Honor, my client is not interested in the state's offer."

"Okay," she replied, shuffling through papers. "What is the state seeking?"

"Your Honor," the prosecutor spoke up. "The state is seeking the death penalty for both counts of first-degree murder. As of today, the district attorney's office will be filing a Notice of Aggravating Circumstances, in reference to the indictment."

"Very well," she looked over to the defense table. "Mr. Hudson, once we get the indictment prepared and signed. I'll have the bailiff bring it out to you for your signature."

Anthony nodded, then stood, ready to be escorted out by the bailiff. Before he could step from behind the table to greet the approaching officer, the public defender stood, and placed a hand on his shoulder.

"Mr. Hudson, he spoke in a conspiring tone. "I think you're making a terrible mistake. You know what they have against you. These people are not bluffing about seeking the death penalty. I think you should really consider taking the plea."

"I think you should really consider kissing my ass," Anthony replied then allowed the court officer to escort him out.

Thankful that he was separated from the other inmates, once Anthony was back in the holding cell, he took a seat on the steel bench and let his mind wander. And for reasons unknown, he was thinking about the day of the bank robbery that landed him in this predicament. He still couldn't believe he'd let his greed for money surmount his better judgement. In the beginning while the plan was being formulated for the robbery, his only concerns were getting his cut, and making life better for his son, and fiancée. He still couldn't figure out at what part of the heist did he commit to eliminating his accomplices and making off with everything. This wasn't something he'd intended from the start. Perhaps Marvin had sensed it, which is why he'd made the statement about greed being a man's downfall.

Now, Antony was seething all over again. This always happens when he thinks about how Marvin had miraculously escaped his demise. Images of Bo's head exploding at close range, played in Anthony's head, supervened by Marvin's tossing the gasoline can at him, causing temporary blindness. After being struck with some kind of solid object, Anthony remembered waking up in a recovery room of Grady Memorial Hospital, shackled to a bed, and guarded by four Atlanta police officers. That's when he wished that Marvin had murdered him, in lieu of leaving him with seven stitches in his head, and the rest of his life in prison. Well, at least that state was willing to accommodate him on the last part.

It had taken almost ten minutes for the bailiff to show up with the indictment. Fifteen minutes after signing it, Anthony was whisked away from the courthouse in a Fulton County Sheriff's squad car, and back to the Fulton County Jail, where he was strip searched before being allowed to return to his housing unit on the seventh floor. Being that they'd taken him to court without notice, he didn't' get a chance to inform Janelle, nor his mother of the proceeding. For it would have been relieving to have had their physical support today but, considering the prosecutor had mentioned the death penalty, he figured it was best that they weren't present. But, that only meant he would have to be the one to call and break the news to them. Though he was a bit exhausted, Anthony figured he'd call Janelle now and wait until after to deliver the crushing blow to his mother.

"These calls cost," Janelle complained, upon accepting his collect call. "I'm already behind on the light bill."

"Is that how you answer the phone when people call you?" he asked, trying to lighten the mood.

"Only when I know the call's gonna cost me seven dollars for fifteen minutes."

"Besides all that," Anthony said, determined to change the subject, "How are you?"

Janelle sighed, "I guess I'm okay. Your son is still bad as hell. He misses you."

"I wish you would bring him to see me."

"We're not going over this again, Anthony," she replied. "He doesn't need to see you like that. "I don't think it's healthy for him."

Playa Ray

"I don't think keeping him away from his dad is healthy, Janelle."

"I'm not keeping him away from you," she purported. "I didn't tell you to go out and rob a damn bank or murder a whole bunch of people! Every time you go to jail, I hold you down. How much longer do you think I can do this, Anthony?"

"You talk as if you're ready to give up on me," he observed, knowing that's where this was headed.

"I'm not saying that, Anthony."

"I went to court today," he attentively changed the subject.

"What did they say?"

"We're preparing for trial," he replied, now realizing that telling her about the impending death penalty would be a bad idea at the very moment.

She asked, "And, when will the trial be?"

"I don't' know yet," he answered. "But could you hold off on leaving me until we see how this gonna play out?"

She didn't respond.

"Where's my baby?" he asked.

"I haven't picked him up from school yet," she told him "And he got into a fight with one of his classmates yesterday."

"Did my baby kick his ass?"

"It was a girl, Anthony!"

"Well, did he kick 'HER' ass?

Janelle was quiet.

Despite how he was feeling, Anthony as smiling. "I'm just playing baby. Look, let me call momma, and see if she'll give you some money for the phone bill."

"She's already helping me with Alex," Janelle reminded him. "Plus, she has her own bills to worry about."

"I don't' see no harm in asking," he responded. "Once I see what's what, I'll write you a letter, or have my momma call you. Okay?"

"Okay."

"I love you."

"I love you too, Anthony."

As soon as Anthony hung the phone, a loud commotion broke out amongst the large group of inmates, who were standing around the television mounted on the wall. They were watching the news coverage of the murder trial in Linkton County. Anthony had no interest in the case that involved old white man, who'd murdered his wife, until his roommate Big Country, had avidly talked his head off about it at nights, He was telling him how he'd betted other guys in the unit hat the white man would beat the trial, because he had money, and a foreign attorney. That's when the case had become like a soap opera to Anthony because he, along with pretty much every other inmate in the dorm, had faithfully tuned in every day.

"If you owe me, pay up!" Big Country said, standing on top of one of the steel tables.

Anthony shook his head as he joined the crowd to catch the conclusion of the trial. They were showing footage of Howard Brown, and his attorney, being swarmed by reporters as they exited the courthouse.

"As you can see," a disembodied feminine voice spoke, "Howard Brown is leaving the courthouse a free man, after being found not guilty for the murder of fifty-nine-year-old Sheryl Brown. His wife of twenty-eight years. This also brings another victory for Attorney Rebeca Scarlatti, a senior partner at Burns and Associates, who was highly known for her miraculous triumphs in high profile cases. The Italian born attorney is also known as a globetrotter, who's battled it out with some of the most prestigious prosecutors. In the Browns' case, the presiding prosecutor was Assistant District Attorney Ebony Davis, daughter of the late Tyrone Davis, a former assistant district attorney who was murdered in this exact building, in 2005. Ebony Davis has been…"

The wheels in Anthony's head were turning. He couldn't believe what he'd just heard. As the camera zoomed in on Ebony Davis, who'd just exited the building, he studied her features as he'd always done. Now, he knew why she'd always looked familiar to him. Anthony cracked a smile for the third time today as he made his way back to the phones.

"Hello," his mother answered, in a sleepy voice, after accepting his call.

'Did you know that he had a daughter?" Anthony plunged in.

"Who?"

"Tyrone."

"You mean—"

"Yes, him, momma," he cut her off. "Did you know that he a daughter?"

"I knew he had a child," she answered. "But I didn't know if it was boy or a girl. Why?"

Chapter 8

"I can't believe how the city just let this neighborhood go to waste like this," Ebony said from the passenger's seat of Rick's car.

It was Saturday and though she was still a bit disconcerted about how the media had made her out to look like an inept prosecutor, after Brown's trial. Ebony knew that she had to take it on the chin and move on as she'd done with her other losses. But, she could not get over the fact she had developed a personal hatred for Rebecca Scarlatti, and Howard Brown.

When Rick had contacted her on that following day, Ebony explicated to him Bull's theory about there being a large amount of money still hidden somewhere in the vicinity of her father's house on Wilkins Street. Ebony thought that Rick would be incredulous as she was to this but, to her surprise, he admitted her father was way too intelligent *'NOT'* to bury over half a million dollars. But the ultimate question was, *'WHERE'* would he bury over half a million dollars?

"This is where they let the poor black people move to after kicking them out of their homes to build malls, and coffee shops," Rick offered to her statement.

"Coffee shops?" Ebony asked, now regarding him through her dark-tinted sunglasses. "Is that what they really built?" Rick shrugged. "I have no idea. Hell, they built a bagel shop on Lawrence. I don't even think black people eat bagels."

Ebony laughed, which is something she had not done in quite some time. Despite the twelve-year difference, she has come to find Rick attractive in a bizarre way. His dry sense of humor seemed to add to his charm, which did something to her, sexually. But she knew better than to act on it. For that would definitely be unprofessional, being that Rick had basically become her subordinate.

"This is it right here," Rick announced, pulling up in front of a white and blue house.

The house wasn't shabby, but one cold tell that it hadn't been properly maintained by the leaves that visibly cluttered the gutter and littered the yard. Plus, the grass was in dire need of a full-scale lawn service. Although, the place appeared uninhabited, the white curtains hanging in the windows begged to differ.

"Do you think someone lives here?" inquired Ebony.

"Of course." Rick killed the engine. "Don't let the outside fool you. It's all a sham."

"And how would you know?"

"It's obvious."

Ebony didn't get it but asked. "If someone does live here, how are we going to search the place?"

"First, we'll have to get them to jump ship."

"And how do you suppose we do that, Captain?" Ebony questioned, with much sarcasm, making sure to put emphasis on 'Captain.' "Should we make them walk the plank?"

Rick regarded her through the dark tint of his own sunglasses.

"If that's what it takes. But we'll try Plan A, first. Just follow my lead."

As they dismounted, Ebony took a few second to survey the neighborhood. The weather was exceptional, so people were lounging on their front porches, and children were playing in yards, or riding bikes up and down the street that ended in a cul de sac. One guy was riding a lawnmower over grass that looked as if it needed no attention. The aroma of burning charcoal and grilled meat filled the air. Despite the area being considered the bottom of the barrel of Linkton County, Ebony felt that here was some kind of tranquility amongst it resists. Then, her eyes landed on a group of young men crowed on the steps and porch of one house that sat near the end of the street. And they like all the other people who were out and about were attentive watching the strangers.

"T.V. thugs," said Rick, who was now standing beside Ebony.

Ebony shot him an inquisitive look.

"They look more menacing on T.V," he explained.

With that, Rick proceeded up the carless driveway. Ebony took one more glance at the group of men, before falling into step behind him. Once they'd reached the front door, Rick stepped aside as if to let her do all the negotiating.

"I thought I was follow your lead," she spoke in a low tone.

"You are," he replied. "Ring the doorbell."

Ebony pressed the button, but no sound came back to them from the inside. The sound of the lawnmower could still be heard, but it wasn't loud enough to drown out the average chimes of a doorbell. Deducing that it didn't work, Ebony rapped on the door with her knuckles. This time, they heard foot steps that got louder as they neared the door.

"Who's there?" an older, grumpy-sounding voice, asked.

Rick took the initiative. "We're here about the ad."

"What ad?"

"The one in the Homes Trade magazine," Rick maintained his ploy. "The one where you're asking for thirty-five thousand. I mean, if you're not ready to sell, then there's another house that my girlfriend wants to look at. We'll just be on our way.

It was quiet on the other side of the door. Just when Ebony decided that she'll give a try, they heard the sound of locks being disengaged. Seconds later, the door opened to an older man who looked to be in his mid-fifties, with a full, salt and peppered beard that connected with the same length of hair around the sides, and back of his head, but contrasted with the large, bald at the top. He was wearing dingy gray jeans, matching sweater and nothing on his feet. As the old man eyed them suspiciously, Ebony began to wonder what Ricks next move would be. Whatever it was she was hoping that he wasn't going to assail the guy, at least not in front of the whole neighborhood.

"Now, where did you see this ad?" he finally asked.

"In the Homes Trade magazine," Rick answered. "Are you the owner of the house?"

The man seemed to linger as he studied Ebony as if trying to place her. She was silently praying that her ball cap and sunglasses would encumber him from recognizing her as the prosecutor he'd recently seen on the news, which would probably blow Rick's plan out of the water, because she definitely didn't have thirty-five thousand dollars to defray the house.

"Well," he finally replied. "I suppose I am the owner."

"Was it bequeathed to you?" Ebony inquired, thinking that he may have been a friend of her father's.

"What does it matter?" he snapped. "Look, I don't' know who posted that ad, but his house is not for sale."

With that, he slammed the door in their faces. Ebony looked to Rick who only responded by stepping off the porch and heading for the car. Catching up to him, Ebony casted another glance around and, sure enough, they were still being watched.

"Now, what?" Ebony asked once they were back inside the car.

"I can't move without your permission." Rick responded, starting the car.

"My permission?" she asked. "What would you need my per—?"

The look on Rick's face pretty much answered her unasked questions. Her heart felt as if it had dropped to her stomach, as she thought about what he was asking for her permission to do. But does he intend to harm the old man? She wondered. Well, of course, she concluded. And she now realized that she hold the guy's fate in her hands. She also realized that this is only the beginning. This is just one of the many executive decisions she'll have to make in the near future.

She directed her attention back to the house, to avoid the look that Rick was giving her. Just as she did, she saw a fluttering on of the curtains in the front room as if the man had been watching them and drew back so not to be seen. Now, she was wondering if the money was worth the man's life. But what if the money isn't anywhere on the property? What if the money didn't not subsist? What if…

"All right," Ebony finally spoke, still watching the house. "You have my permission."

***

After being taken back to the park to retrieve her car, Ebony made for the grocery store, making sure to take her time shopping as she mulled over what she'd gotten herself into within the past two weeks. She still couldn't' believe that she'd ordered the hit on that poor old man. But for some odd reason, she didn't feel a bit compunctious. Perhaps this was a trait she'd inherited from her father. He's the one who'd sparked her premature aspiration to become a prosecutor. She'd always thought she could make him proud by following his footsteps, but never in a million ears would she have thought that his footsteps led down such a dark path.

Getting home, Ebony pulled her car into the garage. Before she could cut the engine, Jason entered the garage via the adjacent door, clad in tan slacks. He also wore a matching polo shirt, and cream-colored dress shoes. He was moving faster than usual, which was notably odd to her. She wasn't afraid but, as he approached the driver's door, she studied his eyes, which were surprisingly clear, indicating that he wasn't under the influence of any drugs or alcohol. But she still remained skeptical as she killed the engine by remote. Jason pulled the driver's door open as Ebony released the latch on her seatbelt.

"Welcome home," he said, in a normally composed tone, leaning in and giving her a peck on the cheek. "Gone on in. I'll get the groceries."

"Are you sure?" Ebony asked, wary of his sudden act of benevolence.

"When you put up the briefcase and pocketbook," he replied. "Meet me in the dining room."

Ebony did not bother to contest. For whatever he was up to, she was soon to find out. She grabbed her pocketbook and briefcase off the front passenger seat, dismounted and made for the entrance. Getting to the door, she paused to look back at Jason, who'd been standing in the same spot, ogling her body. When his eyes finally raised to meet hers, Ebony realized that hey conveyed a different look from what she'd seen while he was approaching the car. And, she was highly familiar with this look. This was the look she hadn't seen in weeks. It turned her on, and she wondered if he'd seen it in her eyes. Not willing to give him that pleasure at the moment, she turned, and proceeded on into the house where her nostrils were hit with sundry aromas of cooked foods. This made her smile to herself because for the past few days, Jason had been slowly making his way back into her graces. Perhaps, he knew that he was on his was out the door, she thought to herself.

After depositing her briefcase and pocketbook, Ebony entered the bathroom adjacent to her bedroom to drain her bladder. As she sat on the toilet, her thought reverted back to Rick, and what she'd given him permission to do. And, for some reason, she was more worried about Rick than she were the old man. But why was she worried about Rick? She was sure that he'd demonstrated his ability to handle himself in the streets, numerous of times, so he could handle an old man, right? Maybe that wasn't it. Maybe her newly developed sentiments for him were reprehensible for her worries.

Ebony pushed her thoughts of Rick to the back of her mind, as she exited the bathroom. To give Jason a little more time with the groceries, she approached the dresser and began taking her hair out of its bun, combing it downwards to let it cascade over her shoulders. That's when she realized this was well past time for her to get her split ends cut. Making a mental note to do so next week, she exited the bedroom making for the dining room, where he had two lit candles sitting in the middle of the table. She also noticed that he'd removed four of the six dining chairs, leaving the two that sat at the long end of the table.

"You can choose any seat," Jason asserted, upon entering the dining room, carrying two plates of food.

"Did you put the groceries up?" Ebony asked, taking a seat.

"The refrigerated items." He placed a plate in front of her, and the other at the opposite end of the table. "I'll be right back."

He left the room. Ebony looked down at her meal that consisted of spaghetti, and two pieces of garlic bread. To her, spaghetti was Jason's best dish. She could vaguely remember her mother's spaghetti, but she was almost sure that it didn't amount to Jason's. This had her antenna up, because she couldn't retain the last time Jason had prepared a meal for her.

What is he up to? She thought to herself.

At that moment, Jason re-entered the room, carrying two bowls of salad, and a bottle of ranch salad dressing tucked under his arm. After placing the items, and relinquishing the salad dressing to Ebony, he left again. Ebony was beyond famished, but she didn't want to be rude by starting on her meal. However, she did take the initiative to *"douse"* her salad with her favorite dressing as she longed for the shredded cheese, bacon bits, and croutons that Jason had taken the time to adorn it with. As if that wasn't enough torture, the aroma that wafted off the spaghetti and garlic bread, did nothing to help the matter.

"Lemonade," Jason announced, upon re-entering. "I don't think I made it too sweet this time," he added, placing one glass in front of her before taking a seat at the other end of the table.

"So," Ebony spoke, taking her fork into her hand. "What's the occasion?"

Jason shrugged. "I'm just making dinner for my woman. It's not like this is the first time I've done this."

"It's the first time in a long time," she accused, forking spaghetti into her mouth, then biting into a garlic bread.

"You're right." He took a sip of his drink. "I guess I'm just trying to make up for all the times I've mistreated you. Any other woman would have left me by now."

"There's more," Ebony prompted, when he'd paused to dig into his spaghetti. "I'm listening," she added, starting on her salad.

"I just plan on doing right by you from now on," Jason purported.

Ebony knew that she was about to go out on a limb, but she had to know. "What about the drugs? The alcohol? Are you—"

"You can't blame the drugs and alcohol for how I've been acting," he said sternly, cutting her off. "That stuff keeps me calm. It's keep me grounded."

"That's what it has your mind thinking," Ebony rectified. "It has you blind. It won't allow you to see what other people see in you."

Jason narrowed his eyes. "And, what do people see in me?"

"I can't speak for other people."

"Well, what do '*you*' see in me?"

Ebony signed inwardly. For she did not expect for the conversation to go this far. How could she tell Jason what she really thought about him, and his addictions, without sparking an ugly confrontation?

"You have potential," she finally spoke, choosing her words carefully. "When you're consumed with these substances, you become someone else, which makes it hard for people to see your true potential. You lost a good job behind your additions. Kayla left you for that reason." Ebony paused. "But, that's the usual outcome of an addict.

"So, you look at me as an addict." This was a statement. "Did you look at yourself as an addict when you were nose deep in those plates with me?"

"I used it occasionally," Ebony protested.

"For recreational use, huh? Jason had a smirk on his face. "I guess that's what all government officials say when they get caught with their hands in the cookie jar, right? You're not considered '*junkies*' or '*addicts*' like the rest of us.

"Can we just enjoy our meal? "Ebony pleaded. What she thought was a special evening, was turning into the total opposite. And, it was all her fault, because she'd inadvertently struck a nerve by mentioning Jason's perpetual addiction, though she didn't mean any harm by it.

"Of course," answered Jason. "Like I said, I'm just trying to make up for the times I've mistreated you. A man can't change overnight, so you'll have to give me some time to prove to you that I *'CAN'* change."

"I think that's fair," Ebony said, before forking a chunk of salad into her mouth.

***

It was shortly after eleven p.m. when Rick pulled the stolen Ford Acropolis on Moore Avenue. Counting houses as he drove, he parked across the street from the sixth house to his left, immediately killing the engine. Unlike Wilkins Street, Moore Ave was deserted at this time of the night. This was the same street that Rick had actuated to enter Tyrone's home on the day he was murdered, over eighteen years ago. Being that there had been no geographical development of the area since then, he figured the pathway that led to the back of Tyrone's was still accessible.

"Which one is it?"

Rick looked over at this accomplice. Gerald was only seventeen but had the athletic build of a twenty-five-year-old pugilist. He'd pretty much watched Gerald grow up in his neighborhood, raised by a drug-abusing mother, who barely took care of him and his baby sister. When Ebony had given him permission to carry out the mission, Rich knew that he would need some assistance. When he'd returned home earlier, and spotted Gerald in his shoddy clothing and shoes, he knew he had a trusty sidekick for tonight. An offer of ten thousand dollars was sufficient for the boy to sneak out of his bedroom window and meet Rick a few blocks away from their locale

"It's on the next street," Rick answered his protégé's question. "Like I said, you can't underestimate him because of his age. Do as I told you and nothing extra. And keep those gloves and skull cap on at all times. Any questions?"

"When do I get paid?" Gerald wanted to know.

"As soon as we dispose of the body," Rick assured him.

A broad smile graced the boy's face, putting Rick in the mind of a five-year old boy at a toy store. For he was sure that Gerald had already spent a large portion of the money in his head. This reminded him of himself, when he'd begun exchanging bad deeds for lump sums of *dirty* money.

"Let's get in and out," Rick said, pressing the trunk release button with one of his gloved hands.

Dismounting, Rick looked around once more, pulled the brim of his ball cap lower, then made for the rear of the car, where he was met by Gerald. After pulling the portable hand truck from the trunk, Rich handed it to Gerald to carry, then led the way. There was no fence segregating the two houses they tread between but, as they neared Tyrone's house, Rick realized that it's fence would be a slight encumbrance.

"Leave that here," Rick said, once they'd reached the fence.

Being that the fence only stood at about three feet, five inches, Rick gripped the top of it with both hands, then hoisted himself over in one motion, landing with a soft thud on the unkept grass. The fence didn't make enough noise to prompt any attention, but Rick still scanned the nearest houses for any signs of someone peering out of their window.

Once Gerald had relinquished the hand truck and hoisted himself over the fence in the same manner as Rick had, they slowly covered the small distance of the yard, making it to the backdoor. Looking around once more, Rick spotted a yellow extension cord protruding from the bedroom window and leading to one of the conterminous houses. Considering this, he realized that the man was a squatter. He also realized that they now had another way in without breaching the kitchen window, or back door. For he would have assumed the bedroom window to be locked, had it not been for the cord.

"Change of plans," Rick spoke in a low tone. "We'll go through the bedroom window."

"What if he's awake?" Gerald questioned.

"We'll just have to wait until he falls asleep."

With that, Rick moved to the window. With the windowsill being just inches about his head, he had to stand on the tip of his toes and was able to peer inside the room. The curtains that were parted in the middle gave him an unobstructed view of the television that was on. Shifting his position, he could, with the aegis of the light from the T.V, see where the old man was reposed on his back, clad in a t-shirt, and boxer briefs. His eyes were partially closed, so Rick assumed he was asleep. He turned to Gerald.

"He's knocked out," Rick told him. "You'll go in first, but quietly. Don't touch him until I'm in. But if he wakes up before I get in, take him out. Understood?"

Gerald nodded.

"Quietly," Rick reminded.

He turned, and began lifting the window as slow, and quietly as possible. To his surprise, the window gave with a barely audible grinding noise. Plus, it remained in position when he gingerly removed his hands from it. After another glimpse at the sleeping man, Rick turned to Gerald.

"Let's make it happen," he said, bending, and interlocking his hands to assist his protégé.

Gerald placed one foot into Rick's hands, gripped the windowsill, then carefully pulled himself up, and into the opening with the zeal of a professional cat burglar. Once Gerald was in, Rick peered in to monitor his movements. And, just as he was instructed, Gerald took locus beside the bed, towering over his target. This made Rick smile to himself, because the boy seemed to have the natural instincts of a killer. Or was he motivated by the money?

Whatever it was, Rick liked it.

Rick made sure to survey the area once more, before pulling himself into the window. Thankful that there was nothing underneath the window, he eased himself onto the floor, then slowly got to his feet. He took this time to survey the room, which seemed to boast the same furniture that Tyrone had left behind, though a bit dilapidated.

Approaching the bed opposite of Gerald, Rick looked down at the sleeping man for a half a second, before looking over at his protégé, who was regarding him with a half-expectant look on his face, obviously anticipating Rick's appropriation to proceed. Rick nodded and, in an instant, Gerald climbed on top of the man, wrapping his huge, gloved hands around his neck, and using his 6'1, 170-pound frame to hold him down. On contact, the old man eyes popped open, displaying apprehension on a full scale.

The old man endeavored a scream, but it was hampered by the pressure applied to his larynx. Rick clinically watched as the man ineffectively thrashed his 5'9, 150-pound body upward against Gerald's, in an attempt to throw him off. Even his attempt to claw Gerald's face seemed futile, as he feebly lashed his arms out. Rick saw tears stream laterally down his face, as his enlarged eyes remained transfixed on his murderer. Momentarily, his arms dropped down beside him, indicating that he was about to *give up the ghost.*

"Wrap him up in the bedspreads," Rick ordered, once the man had expired.

Despite the posthumous excreta that now stained the man's underwear, Rick helped Gerald roll him up in the sheets and comforter, then unplugged the extension cord, leaving them in total darkness, save the dim light from the moon and stars that flooded through the window.

"Why'd you do that?" Gerald questioned.

"We'll drag him out the backdoor," Rick replied, disregarding the query. "Since I know my way around the house, I'll take the lead."

The bedroom door was already standing wide open. Rick grabbed the man's legs, and Gerald did the upper body. Leading the way, he backed out of the room, looking over his shoulder, and using the night sky's light coming through the windows, and his body's contact with the walls to guide him to the backdoor. Only sitting the body down long enough to unlock and open the door, and gain outside to close it back, they moved quickly to the fence.

"We'll have to toss him over," Rick announced. "On the count of three."

With all the strength they could muster they hefted the cadaver over the fence on the third swing, thankful that the spreads remained intact. Once they were both over, they hoisted the body on the hand truck, strapped it down, then made the short trek through the pathway, which wasn't all too strenuous for the air induced tires.

Moore Ave stills seemed deserted when they'd returned to the car where Rick activated the trunk by remote. Once they'd placed the body into the trunk, Rick had Gerald to put the hand truck on the rear seats before they climbed up front. Starting the car, he made a U-turn and headed for the main road.

"Put your seatbelt on," Rick said. He was not trying to give the police an ounce of a reason.

Gerald complied while asking, "Do I get paid now?"

"The task is not fully complete," Rick replied. "We still have to dispose of the body."

"And the car too, right?"

Rick smiled. "You watch too much CSI: Atlanta."

"That's my favorite show!" Gerald professed, with pride.

102

"Is that what you want to be?" Rick tested. "A crime scene investigator?"

Gerald shrugged. "I haven't decided yet. I just want to make a lot of money and take care of my sister."

"Well, you just made ten thousand dollars in one night," Rick reminded him. "Could you see yourself doing this for a living?" Rick questioned.

"Killing people?"

"I think so."

Rick pondered this as he drove. He knows that he and Bull will have to assemble a team of goons for Ebony, and Gerald was an example of what they'll be searching for. He had the build, and definitely the courage for this line of work. This was Gerald's first kill, and Rick could still see the reticent look on his face during the whole ordeal. This was something to revere, because it had taken him approximately four kills before he's acquired that kind of equilibrium.

Finding the wooded area he'd chosen for the mission, Rick turned onto the dirt road that ran the length of it and drove, listening to the tires crunch and grind on the soil beneath them. Reaching his point, Rick pulled the car into the opening in the woods, driving five yards before stopping and shutting off he engine and lights.

"Wait here," Rick told Gerald, then unstrapped his seatbelt, and pushed the driver's door open.

Before getting out, Rick retrieved a chrome Colt .45 handgun from under the driver's seat. Leaving the driver's door open he circled around the rear of the car until he reached the passenger's side. Gerald looked up, but didn't seem fazed, nor alarmed to be looking down the barrel of the weapon. Even after Rick had fired two slugs into his chest cavity, Gerald's visage near wavered.

Chapter 9

If you're serious," Ebony's grandfather, Terrence, was saying to Jason, "I can put a few words in to my friend. His nephew runs the company now."

"Oh, I'm very serious," Jason replied, taking a sip of his tea. "Besides, if I don't' hurry up and find work, Ebony's gonna kick me out."

At the mentioning of her name, Ebony, whose mind was elsewhere, looked up to see Jason grinning at her. Repudiating the annoying look, she glanced across the table at the man she hated more than anyone in the world. And she knew that he was cognizant of her feelings, because he could never maintained steady eye contact with her. Only holding her gaze for a split second, he dropped his head and feigned to be interested in his dinner. Ebony turned to her grandmother, whom was seated beside him.

"Momma," she began, "Why haven't the gutters been cleaned out?"

Sixty-seven-year-old Regina Davis regarded her granddaughter. "We have to find someone else to do the yardwork. Mr. Hunt injured himself last week."

"How?" Ebony asked. She'd known Mr. Hunt ever since she'd come to live with her grandparents when her parents died.

"I think he fell off a ladder." Regina looked as if she was trying to retain, then turned to her husband. "Isn't that what happened, Terrance?"

"That's how it was told to me," he rejoined, keeping his attention on his food. "He was trimming branches off a tree when it happened. Broke one of his legs."

"I'm sorry to hear that," Ebony offered, then turned to Jason. "I don't think Jason would mind tending the yardwork until you find somebody else."

"No, we can't just—" Regina went into a laconic coughing spell clutching her chest.

"Is it your heart, momma?" Ebony asked, highly aware of her grandmother's heart condition.

"It's always my heart, baby."

Ebony could see the pain in her eyes. "Do you need your medication?"

"I'm out."

Ebony wheeled on her grandfather. "How is she out?"

Terrance regarded Ebony without making direct eye contact. "Dr. McAdams ordered her something stronger. It hasn't gotten here yet."

"And, how long has she been out?"

"Since this morning," he answered. "We're hoping they come tomorrow."

"I'll make sure to call that doctor when I get home," she promised, slicing through her meatloaf with her fork. She was about to help herself to a piece, when a chilling thought entered her mind. Slowly lowering her fork to her plate Ebony regarded her grandmother with narrowed eyes. "Momma, how long have you ever went without your heart pills?"

Regina shrugged her frail shoulders. "I don't know, baby. I don't think I've never went without them."

"What if there's an emergency?" Ebony was heated now. The mere thought of her grandmother dying because of a late delivery of something that pretty much kept her alive, had her mind in a vortex.

"Child, there won't' be no emergency," she assured, with a dismissive wave of her hand. "If it's God's will, I'll be okay until my medicine gets here. But, if he calls me home before then, just make sure you take care of your granddaddy."

Ebony cogitated her grandmother's words on the drive home, and wondered if she could sense her death like she'd heard about in stories told by associates in high school, and college. Perhaps, some older people *'CAN'* sense the proximity of their dissolutions she thought. But Ebony wasn't ready to lose the person she loved more than anything in the world, which would definitely be intrusive.

"You okay over there?" Jason inquired, pulling Ebony from her reverie.

She regarded her boyfriend from the passenger's seat. "Yeah, I'm okay."

"I haven't given you a massage in a while," he confessed. "Would you like that?"

Ebony drew a breath. "Not tonight, but I appreciate the offer."

There was a pregnant pause before Jason asserted. "That was the most I've heard you say to your granddaddy. What's the beef between you two?"

"Our relationship has always been strained," she offered, directing her attention out the passenger's window.

Neither one of them spoke for the duration of the ride, in which Ebony had slipped back into her thought of her grandparents. Her stomach churned at the thought of losing her grandmother. Perhaps, this is why Regina had giving her this subtle forewarning, so she could mentally prepare herself for the tragedy, which she didn't get the chance to do in the quietus of her parents. Taking this into account, she promised herself that she would be ready for whatever God has planned for her grandmother. But why couldn't he just take Terrance instead? She thought.

"I'll be up in a minute," Jason said, after parking his car in the garage, and shutting off the engine.

Ebony said nothing. She dismounted as the garage door was closing, and caught a glimpse of an unfamiliar green Cadillac with tinted window, ride by at a slow pace. Thinking nothing of it, she entered the house, heading straight for her bedroom, where she placed her pocket book on the dresser, extracted her cellular phone and plopped down on the edge of the bed.

"Skyfone," she spoke into her cellular. "Call Dr. Mc Adams."

"Calling Dr. McAdams," the computerized voice came back at her, supervened by a waltz ringtone.

"Dr. McAdams," the doctor answered, monetarily.

"This is Ms. Ebony Davis," she announced assuming formality.

"Well, hello, Ms. Davis!" he said with familiar delight. "How are you?"

"I'm okay for the most part," Ebony let on. "Am I disturbing you?"

"Not at all. How may I help you? Is Mrs. Davis all right?"

"I don't know yet." She cleared her throat. "She's out of medication."

"Which medication?" There was alarm in his voice.

"Whatever you have her taking for her heart condition."

"One moment," he said, before Ebony heard him pressing button on his phone. "Ah, yes. She should have run out today. But I've ordered her something newer, and stronger, to retard the increase in her condition. She should have received it yesterday."

"It had never arrived."

"Maybe it was a miscalculation on my part." McAdams took the blame. "We're dealing with a new pharmacy out in Wisconsin, so I'm not yet sure on how long it takes for them to fill an order. If you want me to, I could call and inquire on it tomorrow.

"That would be decent of you," Ebony replied. "But what is she supposed to do in the meantime? What if there's an emergency?"

"I've already briefed Mr. Davis on what to do in the event of an emergency," the doctor told her. "But I guess you're wondering if she'd be okay until the arrival of the medication.

Ebony said nothing.

"To be honest," Dr. McAdams continued, "I really can't give you a substantial answer, being that we're dealing with an erratic heart disease. No one, not even the best cardiologist in the world could determine when it'll claim it's victim. But we're all aware that eventually, it *'WILL'* claim it's victim no matter what, or how many medications they're on."

"Then, why prescribe medication to such patients if they're just going to die from the disease anyway?" Ebony questioned. Her concern for her grandmother was at an all-time high now.

"We follow procedures as we're trained to do, Ms. Davis." There was a hint of attitude in his tone. "There are protocol, policies we have to follow in order to preserve lives, which is our top priority. Now, like I said, if you want me to, I'll call and check on your grandmother's prescription tomorrow."

"Yes, I would like that," Ebony deferred, knowing there wasn't a thing she could do or say to change the situation. She had to let the doctor do what he was trained and well paid to do.

"Ms. Davis," he spoke, all attitude gone from his voice, "I know you're worried about your grandmother but, right now, you have to put it in God's hands. Pray for her."

"Thank you, doctor."

Ending the call, Ebony placed her phone on the nightstand beside the bed and drew in a deep breath. She didn't really believe in God, so McAdams advice incontestably fell on deaf ears. So there was nothing left to do but prepare herself for the inevitable. But, right now, she needed a strong drink to ease her mind before her bath.

As she left the bedroom, enroute to the kitchen, she wondered where Jason was, and what he could possibly be doing. Ebony figured that he shouldn't be in the kitchen, fixing anything to eat, because he'd complained about being stuffed before leaving her grandparents' home. But what is he doing? She thought. Could he still be out in the garage?

Nearing the basement, which was right before the kitchen, she saw that it's door was ajar and stopped in front of it. She wanted to continue on to the kitchen, but her feet wouldn't budge. Suddenly, the urge she'd had for a strong, alcoholic drink, had dissipated. Another urge came at her unabated, which is why she'd mechanically pulled the door open and begun descending the stairs.

The wooden stairs creaking beneath her feet was all Ebony could hear as she slowly moved lower into the subterranean part of the house that was dimly lit by the ever present red lightbulb. She paused at the bottom of the steps, to allow her eyes to adjust to the lighting condition. Once she was able to visually discern what was what she spotted Jason sitting on the sofa, with his head back, and eyes closed, which was a state she had become all too familiar with, since they'd been together. Looking to the coffee table, she found its source.

On impulse, Ebony moved forward until she was standing over the table that contained a plate with a razor and a powdered substance on it, sorted out in two lines. Beside the plate was a rolled-up dollar bill. As she stared at the drug, her urge for it augmented, which was strange to her, because she had abdicated her addition almost a year ago. But, here she was, craving for something that had almost become a bane to her career.

Suddenly, thoughts of her grandmother's imminent demise flooded her mind, reducing her to a much more vulnerable state. She had to prepare herself for it but didn't know if she could do it on her own. Jason wouldn't be enough to console her in such a situation she needed something substantial.

Without giving it another thought, Ebony dropped to her knees. As if sensing her intention, Jason lifted her head, regarding her with an unreadable expression. But Ebony was already committed. She picked the rolled bill up and slid the plate closer to her.

Chapter 10

Monday

"You may all be seated," Judge Carl Jackson said, after taking his seat on the bench. While everybody were retaking their seats, he shot a concerned look over at Ebony, who was the only somebody wearing sunglasses. "Are the lights too bright for you, Ms. Davis?"

"Pretty much," Ebony replied, now seated. "I woke up with a migraine."

"Take anything for it?"

"Some Tylenol," she lied, hoping he would just let it go. "It's not as intense as it was when I awakened this morning."

"Will you be able to function professionally?" he inquired with a raised eyebrow.

"I'll manage."

The judge looked as if he was incredulous of her response, then scooped up the documents in front of him. Clearing his throat, he said, "This is the State versus Michael Strong, which is a bond hearing requested by Mr. Strong, through his attorney to determine whether or not Mr. Strong meets the criteria for a reasonable bail. For the state is Assistant District Attorney Ebony Davis. Representing the defendant is Attorney Gregory Stuart, from Linkton County Public Defenders Office. Mr. Stuart, why should your client be granted a bond."

"Well, your Honor," the Caucasian male attorney started, as he got to his feet at the defense table, in which he shared with Michael Strong, a black male clad in a jail-issued uniform. "My client is only charged with possession of a firearm, and residential burglary. Despite neither of these charges being any of the seven deadly sins, it's my theory and the theory of the founders of the United States

Constitution, that my client should be granted a reasonable bond, which would irrefutable secure his rights under the Fourteenth Amendment that entitles him to the equal protection of the laws.

Judge Jackson shifted his gaze to Ebony. "Ms. Davis, is the State at issue with defendant's request for a reasonable bond?"

"Of course," she responded not bothering to get to her feet. "The Fourteenth Amendment does entitle Mr. Strong to the equal protection of the laws, but there's nowhere in the U.S. Constitution that it necessitates the judicial system to set him bail of any sort. It only admonishes against setting *'EXCESSIVE'* bails. And possession of a firearm and resident burglary may not be considered 'deadly sins, as the defense attorney put it, but these particular charges has elevated Mr. Strong to recidivist status under Section 17-10-(a). If that's not enough, Your Honor, the handgun that Mr. Strong was in possession of when he was apprehended, was registered in an assault in which local authorities are still investigating."

"Your Honor," Attorney Stuart intervened, "My client is not charged with assault. This is mere speculation on the prosecutor's part. But if the assault does exist, my client is not complicit to it, being that he had found the handgun in the house that he was accused of burglarizing."

"Is that all from the defense?" the judge asked.

"Yes, Your Honor."

He turned to Ebony. "State?"

"That's all, Your Honor."

"Considering the argument of both parties," Judge Jackson went on, "I'm going to rule in favor of the defense and set bail in the amount of twenty thousand dollars for each charge. Defendant may be released once twelve percent of the combined amount is paid. Next case."

As court resumed with other bond hearings motion hearing, and plea arrangements, Ebony did her best to maintain her equilibrium, as a million and one things occupied her mind. She still didn't know if Rick had successfully carried out his mission on Saturday. However, she did make sure to tune into the news channel while getting ready for work this morning, to see if there were any indications of it. But the top story was about two bodies found in a fire damaged car on Sunday.

Plus, she didn't know how she was going to obtain witness list in Bull's case. She could ask Samantha to make a copy of it, but they would only implicate her in whatever tragedy was to befall the deponents. And Ebony didn't know how her friend would act after realizing she'd aided such tragedies. Being that Bull's jury selection had started today, Ebony knew that she was pressed for time.

Judge Jackson called an hour recess at twelve-fifty. Ebony wanted to grab something to eat from the cafeteria, but her anxiety seemed to have devoured her appetite. Therefore, she journeyed to her office, where she flopped down in her soft-cushioned leather chair. Looking down at her office phone, she saw that she had two messages. Before listening to them, she opened her bottom drawer, pulled a breakfast bar from her pocketbook, tore the wrapper open, and took a large bite out of it.

Message One. "Tfixedhe computerized voice promulgated, before Rick's voice came with laconic message. "The same Burger King."

Beep

Message Two. "This time, an unfamiliar feminine voice breached the speaker, in an all-business tone. "Hello, Ms. Davis, I am Carol Jenkins. Whenever you get the chance, please call me My number is ...."

Ebony replayed the message in order to log the phone number into her cell phone. After tagging it with the woman's appellation, she stored the information, then erased the messages from her office phone, before dialing Dr. McAdams' office number, in which he answered on the third ring.

"Dr. McAdams."

"Ebony Davis."

"What a coincidence," he offered with delight. "I had just spoken with Mrs. Davis a few minutes ago. She informed me that her medication had arrived earlier. Being that she admitted to having minor complications overnight, I'll go by and check on her once I leave my office for the day."

"Thank you, Doctor."

"No problem."

Ebony rung off, feeling bad that she didn't call and check on her grandmother last night like she had intended to. Well, she would have, had she not been under the influence of crush for the most part of the night. She thought she would only do one of the two lines she'd encountered on the plate, but Jason, after watching her vacuum the first line up her nose, pulled out a small, plastic resealable bag contain more of the drug, and tossed it on the table. Last night, Ebony Regina Davis relapsed.

With her mind back on Bull's trial, Ebony consumed the rest of her breakfast bar tossed the wrapper in the trash bin beside her desk, then exited her office with just her cell phone, and keys in hand. She didn't know why she was about to do what she had in mind, but she just couldn't sit around almost an hour doing nothing. Stepping off the elevator, she marched with a purpose toward Judge Torri Richardson's courtroom.

During jury selections, only court officials, defense attorneys, the accused, and a large panel of prospective jurors were allowed in the courtroom, which was why there were a large group of people waiting outside of the courtroom, whom Ebony surmised were family members of the victims and witnesses to Bull's atrocities. There were also uniformed and plain clothes officers amongst the swarm. Ignoring them, Ebony doffed her sunglasses, approached the double doors, and waved her hand to get the attention of the bailiff standing at the rear of the room, which was a few feet away from the entrance. Recognizing her, the bailiff, whose name Ebony failed to remember, approached and used her key to unlock the door.

"I just want to sit in for a while," Ebony whispered answering the officer's incisive expression. "Thirty minutes. Take a few notes."

The officer nodded, allowed Ebony to enter, then locked the door back. Immediately, Ebony's eyes shot over to the defense table, where Bull was seated with a white, court appointed attorney. They locked eyes for a moment, before she looked over to the State's table, where Samantha was seated with Assistant District Attorney Corey Briggs. They were both looking back at her. Judge Richardson, along with every other person in attendance, were also regarding her. Ebony nodded at the judge, then quickly took a seat on the last bench, being that the others were filled with civilian for jury selection.

Resuming, Judge Torri Richardson, a white female in her mid-fifties, directed her attention back to the witness stand where a white female of the same age sat patiently. "Juror twenty-six if you are selected to serve on this panel, would you be able to maintain a fair, and impartial mind while listening to both sides, and base your decision solely on the evidence present in this case?"

The prospective juror shrugged her shoulders. "I guess I could do that."

"Ma'am, we do not need you to guess, "Judge Richardson chided.

"This is not Jeopardy. We did not summon you here to make a decision based on your personal theories. If selected to serve on this panel, it is not, and never will be, your imperative to make assumptions."

While the judge was mildly chastising Juror twenty-six, Ebony looked over at Samantha and Briggs, who were sitting a little too close for her taste. Ebony was cognizant of Corey's affinity for Samantha and figured that he was aware of their relationship, which is why he would periodically ask her to assist him on cases. Ebony wanted to believe that he did this intentionally to irk her but, right now, she had to keep her mind on business.

Now looking over at Bull, who was clean shaven, and clad in a dark-blue dress suit, Ebony finally realized that there was no way she was going to obtain the witness list without tipping Samantha, or maybe even Briggs, off to what was afoot. And being that this was the plan that Rick had come up with, she didn't even think to fabricate a contingency plan.

***

"Did you get it?" Rick asked, as soon as Ebony slid into the passenger seat of his car that was parked in the lot of the same Burger King they'd assembled at on the day that Rick had followed her from work.

Closing the door to retain the AC blowing from the vents, Ebony looked over at Rick, and was able to see her reflection in his mirror-tinted sunglasses, being that he was regarding her in anticipation of the answer to his query.

"No, I did not," she responded, almost defensively, regarding him through her own sunglasses. "There's no way I can get that list without tipping my hand to the prosecutors on the case. I'm friends with the assisting prosecutor, but I don't think it would be wise to let her in on this."

"You're right," Rick directed his attention out the driver's side window as if in deep thought. Then, he said, "I handled that."

"The old man?" Ebony almost whispered, as if she could be heard by anybody other than Rick.

"Yeah," he rejoined, still looking out the window. "You don't watch the news?"

"Of course, I wa—"Ebony paused, trying to recollect what she'd seen on the news earlier. "I saw the news this morning," she told him. "There was nothing pertaining to that."

"It was the top story."

She remembered. "The burning car?"

Rick nodded.

"But they found two bodies. Was there someone else in the house with him that night?"

"Nope, just him." Now Rick turned to face her. "I went back yesterday, and cleaned the house of anything that could link him to it."

"What if the house was in his name."

"It wasn't"

"Did he tell you that?" Ebony was being sarcastic.

"He was a squatter," Rick answered, ignoring, or lost to her acidity. "I disconnected the extension cord he had running to the neighbor's house. Whenever you're ready to search it, let me know."

"There were two bodies," she said, reluctant to let this go. "Who was the—"

"That's not important," he cut her off. "We still have Bull to worry about. If you can't get him out, the deals off. You do remember the deal, right?"

Ebony directed her attention out the passenger window to avoid his gaze. Of course, she remembered the deal. If it wasn't for the deal, she wouldn't be sitting here now. If it wasn't for the deal, two people wouldn't have been found dead in a burning car over the weekend. If it wasn't for the deal she would…

Ebony turned to Rick. "He has a wife, and a seven-year-old daughter."

"Who?" Rick inquired.

"The prosecutor."

Rick seemed to pique up. "Oh yeah? Do you know where he lives."

"Of course," Ebony answered, before removing her sunglasses, and evaluating him with narrowed eyes. "But whatever you do, the little girl is not to be harmed."

"I was thinking something along the lines of kidnapping, torturing the wife."

"Which probably wouldn't work," she told him.

"Why not?"

"He hates his wife."

On the drive home, Ebony felt as if she'd sold her soul to the devil. Two people were found dead over the weekend at her hands. Now, a mother and her child were about to be put in a dangerous compromising position, on the strength of her. And, for what? Because of the deal she'd made with Rick and Bull, to help her become an infamous prosecutor like her father was, and find out who's killed her mother would she be responsible for the lives of other innocent people along this journey? Of course, she thought. Ebony knew that she was walking a path that was not only pernicious to others, but to herself also. But the big question was, would it all be worth it in the end?

Chapter 11

Tuesday

It was 7:28 a.m., and dawn had already set upon the residential street lined with modern homes on both sides. Some were surrounded by picket fences, but all seemed to have two car garages attached to them. The aroma of lilacs wafted through the slits of the cracked tinted windows of the SUV that Rick was sitting in. He was parked in front of the house next to the house Ebony had given him the address to, which is where he'd been since 6:43 a.m., with the engine off. With his seat slightly reclined, Rick kept his eyes on the soft-pink and white house, which did not have a fence of any kid lining the yard, and was only periodically distracted by a passing vehicle, some middle, class shithead on their way to their place of business, or to cheat on their spouse.

After talking to Ebony in the Burger King's parking lot yesterday, Rick had immediately formed a plan to get Bull out of his situation. Rationing the plan was easy, but the pre-arrangements had been exhaustive, and time-consuming, which was why he'd made it home at almost two in the morning. Three and a half hours was all he was allowed to sleep, before being awoken by the alarm he's set on his cell phone.

At 7:20, Rick saw the first sign of life at the targeted house, when a light flicked on in one of the upper rooms casting a dull glow through the thin curtains of the window. According to Ebony's report the husband, wife and daughter, leaves the house around the same time, with the husband on his way to work, and the wife taking the daughter to school on her way to her own job. Rick just hoped they didn't leave at the exact same time, which would complicate matters, and force him to take drastic measures.

Now at 7:52 a.m., Rick's attention was directed at the garage, as the sound of the door's motor reached his ears. The door lifted, revealing a gray BMW 750XT, and a black BMW wagon. Only the 750 was occupied. The driver, whom Rick figured to be Corey Briggs, backed out of the garage, and waited at the edge of the driveway until the garage door was secured into place, before driving off. Rick simpered at Corey's sense of security for his family, which he would find out today was not enough.

Turning the ignition with one of his gloved hands, Rick pulled the SUV into the driveway, parking directly in front of the garage. Cutting the engine, he grabbed his dreadlock wig off the passenger seat, and donned it, checking himself in the rearview. After a quick survey of the area, he complemented his look with a black sun visor, and dark sunglasses. Before he could evaluate himself in the mirror again, he was alerted by the muffled sound of a car's alarm being disarmed, in which he automatically knew had come from within the garage. He listened. Two car doors slammed in tandem. The engine came to life. Almost ten seconds after, the door to the garage began to rise.

Quickly, Rick grabbed his handgun and roll of duct tape off the front passenger seat, then dismounted, looking around once more. Once the door was high enough, he ducked up under it and approached the driver's side of the BMW. The women shrieked at the sight of him, almost losing the cigarette hanging from her mouth, and conveyed the same fearful look as her daughter.

"Shut it off," Rick demanded, holding the gun up for her to see, but not pointing it directly at her.

She cast a frantic, but furtive glance at her rearview mirror, as if her mind was telling her to throw the car into reverse, and make a break for it. But, Rick was hoping that she wasn't as stupid to believe that she could bulldoze the Chevy truck that was blocking her path. Perhaps she'd recognized this, which is why she killed the engine, and looked at Rick as if awaiting further instructions.

With the gun now down by his side, and out of view of anyone who may pass by, Rick said, "Close the garage door!"

She pressed the button on the remote attached to the car's visor. Once the door was secure, Rick climbed into the backseat of the BMW, leaving the rear door open for the disgusting smell of the cigarette smoke.

"The first thing I need you to do," Rick stated, "Is put out that nasty cigarette. You're killing your daughter before she has a chance to live." He waited for her to defuse the cigarette in the ashtray, before going on. "The second thing I need you to do, is call your job, and inform them that you won't make it today."

***

As Corey Briggs pushed his BMW along the highway, he mentally rehearsed his opening statement for the Alfonso Walker's case. He was kind of relieved that the trial didn't began yesterday, due to the amount of time it had taken to select a jury. It's not that he wasn't ready because he was beyond fully prepared. It was just that he was hoping to drag the case out for at least a week. Being that he was still in the process of wooing Samantha Gordon, which is why he'd lobbied her to assist him on this high profile case. He figured it would be enough time to at least get her to consider going out with him. It's not like she wasn't aware of his marriage to Kathy, because everyone at the office was.

Plus, he would be able to flirt freely with Samantha, without catching evil stares from the damn ever present Ebony Davis, who's always staring daggers at him whenever he even speaks to Samantha. He was highly inquisitive about the proximity of their friendship, but he would question it once he'd gotten his foot in the door with

Samantha. Who knows? Maybe, they'll let him in on one of their girl-on-girl nights. Corey smiled at the thought of bending Ebony over and ramming every inch of his manhood inside her anus, until blood drips from her eyes. Maybe that was a bit too much. He shook the thought and reverted his mind back to the trial as he exited the expressway.

"Incoming call from Kathy," the car's automated Bluetooth system apprised, interrupting his thoughts.

"Answer," he said, wondering why Kathy would be calling him at this time, which was rare. "What is it, Kathy?"

"I have your family," a male's voice boomed through the car's speakers, slow, and deliberately.

"Excuse me?" Corey wasn't sure if he's heard correctly.

"You're the prosecutor on Alfonso Walker's case." The man went on. "If you know what's best for you and your family, you'll find a way to lose the trial."

"L-lose the trial?" Corey stammered, at a lost for words as he drove with both hands locked onto the steering wheel in a death grip. Right now, he was experiencing a fear he'd never known.

"I'm taking your daughter with me," the man spoke again, bringing tears to Corey's eyes. "Your wife will be at home when you arrive. You'll get your daughter back when Alfonso Walker is acquitted."

Corey began to panic. "I can't g—"

"I have the ears of a wolf," the man cut him off. "If I hear anything about the authorities being involved. I'll bury her alive."

Wiping tears from his eyes, Corey tried again. "I can't guarantee Mr. Walker will be acquitted. How about I just have the judge take me off the case?"

"You're the chosen one, Mr. Briggs," Said the stranger. "I advise you to pray to every God you can think of. This is not a game.

Chapter 12

Pulling into the parking garage of the Linkton Count Courthouse, Ebony spotted Samantha leaning against the trunk of her car, with her briefcase at her feet, as if she was waiting for someone. This angered Ebony, because the only person she could think of was Corey Briggs, being that his car was not in its usual spot. And the huge, school girlish smile on Samantha's face didn't make things any better. Seconds after Ebony had parked, Samantha materialized at the driver's door with the same grin on her face, and briefcase in hand. She pulled the door open as Ebony was gathering her things.

"Good Morning!" Samantha beamed in a sing-song tone.

"Mm-hmm," Ebony replied, dismounting with her briefcase, keys, and cell phone in hand.

Samantha's smile turned into a frown, as she slammed the car's door, and fell into step with Ebony, who was making off without her.

"Um, did I miss something?" Samantha inquired.

"Rough night," Ebony lied, then decided to test the water to see if Samantha would be honest. "You would usually be inside by now. Were you waiting for somebody?"

"No, I was making sure nobody steals my car," she sassed.

"Anyway, I checked my email when I got home last night, and there was an invitation from Albert. He's throwing a party at the mansion, on the fifteen of the month. That means we have three weeks to come up with the sexist evening gowns ever made."

Great, Ebony thought to herself. Her thoughts of Samantha falling for Corey Briggs, had been assuaged, only to be replaced by thoughts of Samantha's occasional fling with Albert Spires, the governor of Georgia. Anytime Albert would throw a get-togethers, and invite Samantha, he and Samantha would sneak off for their private session. In the governor's mansion, he has a particular room he'd take Samantha to, claiming he doesn't allow his own wife to step foot inside of it, which had Ebony wondering if his wife was sensible of his infidelity.

After acquiring cups of coffee from the cafeteria, Ebony escorted Samantha to her office, then made for her own, where she took locus behind her desk, sipped her coffee, and went over her court case calendar. Satisfied that nothing has changed, she decided to check her messages, being that she still had almost ten minutes before she was to report to the courtroom.

The machine announced that she had only one message. Ebony pressed play, and thought she'd erased this message yesterday. Then, she realized it was a whole new message from the stranger identifying herself as Carol Jenkins, claiming they needed to talk, and again leaving her phone number. Ebony had forgotten all about this caller. She didn't know the woman, but the woman seemed hell-bent on trying to contact her. Remembering that her number was stored in her cell phone, she grabbed it off the desk, and scrolled through it until she found the information. But, before she could press the call button, there was a knock at her door.

"It's open," she answered, thinking it was Samantha.

The door eased open, and in walked District Attorney Barbara Hutchins. As always, she appeared to have a canister of makeup plastered to her face, and she was clad in a gray pantsuit as if she was prosecuting a trial, which is something she rarely did.

"Am I disturbing you?" Barbara asked, closing the door and crossing the room.

"Not at all." Ebony placed her phone back on the desk. "Have a seat."

Barbara took a seat opposite Ebony, interlacing her wrinkled hands in her lap. "So, how are you?"

"You mean—"

"No," Barbara cut her off. "That's behind us. You win some, you lose some. I don't' know how your father could win them all, but that's neither here nor there. I was inquiring on your wellbeing. How are you?"

"Oh, I guess I'm fine."

"You guess?"

Ebony made a show of checking her watch. "I have to be in court soon, Ms. Hutchins."

"Barbara smiled. "Of course. And I'll be on my way to Judge Richardson's courtroom. I'll be sitting in on the whole Alfonso Walker trial. Did you know that I was on the scene of the crime?"

"No, I did not," Ebony lied.

"I'm accustomed to seeing such gruesome scenes," she went on, "But there was something troubling about the particular scene. If it was up to me, Alfonso Walker would be on his way to death row today, and executed tomorrow. But he'll get what's coming to him."

Ebony only nodded.

"Anyway," Barbara resumed. "We have a high profile case coming from Bibb County. You should have heard about it. It's the murder case involving that pastor. His lawyer moved to a change of venue, and it was immediately granted. I was told. Now, we have to find a way to work a trial date into our already saturated schedule.

"Let me guess," Ebony finally spoke. "I'll be the one prosecuting the case."

Barbara smiled as she got to her feet. "I don't see why not. Besides, if you plan on taking my place when I retire, you have to at least 'LOOK' qualified."

Ebony watched the head district attorney leave, and wondered why she was persistent about helping her build her credibility. It was obvious that Barbara Hutchins and Tyrone Davis had something other than a co-worker's relationship going on. Just the thought of those two together made Ebony cringe.

Forcing that objectionable image from her mind, Ebony immediately checked her watch, and realized she would have to remit returning the stranger's call in order to make it to the courtroom on time. Therefore, she entered the number into the On-Time calling gesture of her cell phone for eight o'clock tonight. Then, retrieving her briefcase, she exited her office. Thinking about Corey Briggs, and the dilemma she was sure he was aware of by now, she could actually picture him sweating Bullets, and stumbling over his words through the entire trial, knowing that the end results determined his daughter's fate.

Ebony smiled.

Chapter 13

Ebony pulled her Cadillac into the driveway of a red-brick house, parking behind an ancient old car that looked as if it had been out of commission since the late nineties. Not bothering to figure out the make of model of the vehicle, she directed her full attention on the house in search of any sign of movement through the curtains of either of the two windows facing her.

When Rick had given her the address to the house via her answering machine, he instructed her to just enter as if she owned the place. Basically, he was telling her to act normal, just in case there were people out and about when she arrive, but why was she lingering? Perhaps, she was afraid of what she may encounter beyond those walls. Did Rick abduct Corey Briggs's daughter, and bring her here? Did he touch her in places he has no business touching her? Was he touching her in those places right now?

Ebony quickly killed the engine, removed her gun from the glove compartment, and dropped it into her pocketbook. Then, she exited the car, moving toward the house with a purpose. She didn't even bother looking around to see if she was being watched, but nearing the front door, she feigned as if she was actuating her keys to gain entrance. Once she felt that her charade had lasted long enough, she pushed the door open.

The living room was bare, save for two ottomans, in which Rick occupied one. Beside him on the carpeted floor where his gun, sunglasses, sun visor, a roll of duct tape, and what appeared to be a wig of long dreadlocks. With one leg rested atop the other, and his arms folded over his chest, Rick was regarding her with a blank expression. Plus, he looked tired. His eyelids sagged a bit, which is something she found quite intriguing.

Closing, and locking the front door, Ebony held her arms out, palms up, in a questioning gesture. Rick tilted his head to the right, indicating the short hallway to the rest of the house. She studied him for a few more seconds, before heading in that direction. The first bedroom door she came upon was closed. Seeing that the other doors along the hall were open. She figured this was the one. She turned the knob, and pushed the door open.

Like the living room, the bedroom was only lit by the daylight breaching the thin curtains in the window. It was also bare, with the exception of a wooden chair sitting in a corner, it's back to her. Seated in the chair was Briggs little girl, her ankles duct taped to the front legs of the chair, and her wrists bonded to the arm of it. With her head down, chin buried in her chest, her dark hair hung loosely, obscuring any signs of her facial features. Ebony mentally coerced herself not to approach, but she watched the girl for any signs of life. After seeing the girl's shoulders slightly rise and fall from her breathing, Ebony eased the door shut, then re-entered the living room, where she took a seat on the other ottoman, placing her pocketbook beside her.

It's quite hot in here," Ebony spoke in a hushed tone. "No A.C.?"

"No electricity," Rick responded.

Ebony furrowed her eyebrows. "So, whose house is this?"

"Nobody's." He stifled a yawn, before continuing, "I've been in and out of this house for almost a year now."

"How did everything go?" Ebony changed the subject. "Where's the wife?"

"I guess everything went well," he said. "I left the wife duct taped to the driver's seat of her car, in their garage. I let her hear the whole exchange between her husband and I. I told him to blow the trial, and he could have his daughter back. Call the cops and she dies.

"But, what if one of them panics? What if they call the cops out of fear?"

Rick turned, and locked eyes with her. "Then, I'll have to make good on my word. Let's just hope this prosecutor loves his daughter like you say he does."

Ascertaining that Rick had not fed Cindy Briggs since she'd been in his possession, Ebony made trips to McDonald's and a gas station, by obtaining food and bottled water for both. Rick and the little girl, who was surprisingly acquiescent as Ebony fed her, being that Rick didn't feel like cutting and reapply the tape. While nourishing her, Ebony whispered words of encouragement, and ran her hand over her fine, sleek hair that was disturbed by the bandana tied around her head to cover her eyes. Before leaving, Ebony ordered Rick to cut Cindy loose then escorted her to the bathroom, where she had to assist, and watch as Cindy disencumbered her stomach contents. While Rick was reapplying the tape, Cindy again dropped her head as if she'd already accepted her fate without an ounce of hope of returning home safely. This churned Ebony's heart. She wanted to hold the little girl and assure her that everything would be alright. But, another part of her wasn't so sure. What if Corey Briggs couldn't pull it off?

On the drive home, Ebony's mind was transfixed on Cindy, which only intensified her longing for a child of her own. She was surprised at how she'd instantly become attached to the seven-year-old. She felt some kind of chemistry between them. At this time, Ebony made her mind up. Either Jason was going to give her what she wanted, or she would welcome insemination through a sperm bank.

"Incoming call from Samantha," the disembodied voice of her car's Bluetooth system announced.

"Take call," Ebony responded, as she pulled to a stop light. "Yeah, Sam?"

"Girl, you are not going to believe this!" Samantha's voiced with conspiratorial enthusiasm.

"I'm listening."

Samantha went on, "I don't' even know how to explain it. You should have seen Briggs in trial today. I've never seen him like this."

Ebony was smiling. "Like what?"

"It's like he was…" Samantha seemed to trail off. "I don't know. It's like he was nervous or scared. He was sweating profusely and stumbling over his words. You may not believe this, but I think he's attentively trying to lose the trial."

"And why would you think that?"

Samantha's voice came back in almost a whisper. "All the evidence came up missing."

Ebony mouthed a 'yes'! as she pumped her fist in the air. She was amazed at how her plan has proven effective. Briggs was actually doing what he had to do to get his child back, no matter the consequences. This was power beyond power Ebony could already see herself dominating the judicial system. If she didn't get the D.A.'s position when Hutchins retires, she was definitely going to supplant Barbara's successor by any means necessary.

"Look, baby," Ebony spoke, pulling into her driveway, and activating the garage door. "I just got home. Talk to me about this tomorrow."

Samantha signed "All right, love!"

"Love."

Ebony entered the house via the garage and made for her bedroom. Jason wasn't there, but she knew exactly where he was, and what he was doing. After placing her pocketbook and cell phone on her dresser, Ebony began undressing, preparing for her shower, while fighting the urge to venture down to the basement, which is where she was sure to get a quick *fix* before starting dinner. She was already late getting home, which was why she'd abandoned her nightly run—so Jason may have already eaten. But she would inquire before heading for the kitchen.

Now down to her panties and bra, Ebony made for the adjoining bathroom. Before she could cross the threshold, the ringtone from her cell phone would reach her ears. She stopped in her tracks and retraced her steps back to the dresser. The name and number staring up at her from the screen of her cell phone, belong to Carol Jenkins, the stranger who'd been trying to reach Ebony for two days now. Remembering that she'd inserted the number into her On-Time calling feature, Ebony pressed answer, then put the phone to her ear. She heard ringing, which indicated that the recipient hadn't picked up yet.

"Hello?" Carol's voice final came through.

"Ebony Davis."

"Oh! Hi!"

"What'd you need to talk to me about?" Ebony prompted, ready to get this over with.

Carol giggled. "You three are too much alike. I swear."

"Excuse me?" Ebony inquired.

"I'm Carol Jenkins."

"I'm already familiar with your name," Ebony told her. "What do you want?"

"I, um…" Carol lingered. "I was seeing your dad back in ninety-six."

Ebony was quiet. For she did not know how to respond to this.

"It didn't last no more than four months," Carol went on. "I only knew of his wife, your mother. I didn't know her personally." She paused to take a deep breath. "I only called because Anthony asked me to contact you."

Ebony found her voice, "And, who is Anthony?"

"My son," she answered. "He is also your brother."

Chapter 14

Friday

It's been three days since Ebony had spoken to Carol. The revelation had caused Ebony two nights of unrest. Carol and her father had an extramarital love affair in ninety-six. Ebony turned three in ninety-six. Her mother and father had pledged their vows in ninety-six. This made her wonder if her father and Carol were seeing each other before he pledged his troth to her mother. Carol never verified it, but she did claim that the mention of her pregnancy may have induced their separation. Tyrone, according to Carol, had become angry, saying he would not take on responsibility of another child, and even went as far as threatening to cause her to miscarry if she didn't undergo an abortion.

Carol's delineation of her father's deportment didn't sit well with Ebony. It was bad enough that she was still trying to digest the fact that he was a bigger criminal than most of the criminals he'd sent off to prison. But an unfaithful husband? A man who would neglect a woman carrying his unborn child? Over a month ago, Ebony would have vigorously contended such allegations about her father, but after learning what she'd learned from Rick and Bull, Carol's story didn't seem so farfetched, which is why, on the following day, she pulled Anthony Hudson up on her office computer. Though pictures didn't always depict a person's full features, Anthony's picture on Georgia Criminal Files seemed as if it was taken by a high professional photographer, with high quality equipment, in lieu of a county intake officer.

Anthony's dark skin could have easily been passed off as coincidental, but his facial features were unmistakable. The parallelism he shared with Ebony and her father, was bone chilling, but Ebony wasn't sold on Carol's side of the story, and Anthony's photo, alone. Being that Anthony is currently incarcerated and facing the death penalty, it was incontestable that he was in dire need of her assistance. As far as Ebony knew, it could be a con. If Anthony did prove to be her half-brother, then the only ties they would have to each other would be their father. And Tyrone Terrence Davis was long dead.

"Your Honor," the Latina attorney, Ellen Martinez, spoke bringing Ebony from her thoughts. "I don't' see any reason why my client's prior offense should be mentioned, which would be totally out of context. Her prior offense has no connection to her recent one. It is also not a felony, in which the state could use to recidivate Ms. Washington. Where fore, the defendant prays that the court will grant the gag order in good faith."

Ebony watched the other women retake her seat at the defense table beside her client, a white female in her early thirties, who was clad in a jail issued uniform. As always, whenever they'd get the chance to battle it out, Martinez did not look in her direction. In fact, she made a show of sifting through the documents in front of her, to keep from doing so.

"Thank you, counsel," Judge Jackson said, then turned to Ebony.

"State, do you dissent to the defenses request for a gag order?"

Ebony stood. "Of course, Your Honor. The State's mentioning of Ms. Washington's prior offense is routine. If I'm not mistaken, a defendant's criminal history is mentioned in trials except for when a gag order is enacted by the court to preclude a miscarriage of justice. Where fore, the defense has not demonstrated any substantial reasons to warrant such an order, which automatically renders the request null and void."

Before Ebony could sit, Ellen Martinez was back on her feet. "Your Honor, the reason for the request is to prevent the State from making a mockery of the defendant before a panel of jury members, which is, undoubtedly, the State's intention. The same intention that could, and would, strip my client of a fair trial."

"And, this prior offense would be the cruelty to children charge," the judge questioned.

"That would be two counts, Your Honor," Ebony answered before the attorney could. "And, despite the counsel's assumption, the State is not interested in besmirching Ms. Washington's name, but to show that she's not a first offender, and definitely not the angel that her attorney will try to make her out to be."

"Your Honor," Martinez spoke up. "Once the jury hears of my client being arrested for cruelty to children, without knowing the depth of these charges, they will automatically cast stones at her character, which would be totally unfair to her."

Judge Jackson held a hand up. "I think I've heard enough. Both arguments hold a great deal of truth, but I'm going to rule in favor of the defense and grant the gag order. State, you are hereby ordered to refrain from mentioning defendant's prior offense during the course of trial, once the proceeding take place. So ordered, this thirtieth day of June. State, call your next case."

"That would be the State versus Donte Hayes," Ebony responded, taking her seat. "Plea and arraignment."

"Very well." He regarded Deputy Taylor. "Bailiff, please escort Ms. Washington back to her holding cell, and bring in Mr. Hayes."

As Taylor made off to do as he was told, Ebony cast a glance over at Ellen Martinez, who was gathering her paperwork into her briefcase. The attorney was moving so fast, she inadvertently folded some of the documents at the corners. Once the stack was complete, she grabbed her briefcase, rounded the defense table, and marched past the State's table with her head down. But she didn't clear the table without casting a glance at Ebony from the corners of her eyes. Being that Ebony was attentively watching the attorney, she caught it. And, the look she saw in Ellen Martinez' eyes, was not friendly. Her eyes didn't convey what could genuinely be described as hatred. But Ebony could tell that they held some disturbingly ancient dark secrets.

***

Assistant District Attorney Corey Briggs' anxiety was getting the best of him, as he watched the jury members file into the courtroom to take their seats. His daughter had been abducted, and held hostage by some unknown thug, three days ago, and these twelve individuals, obliviously, held her fate in their hands. For he had done everything he could possibly think of to botch the trial; withheld evidence, excluded some of the State's expert witnesses at the last minute, and even gave the worst and succinct, open, and closing arguments he'd even given. If the jury finds Alfonso Walker guilty, then everything he'd done would be in vain.

Cindy would surely die.

That thought alone brought on a whole new level of trepidation. Truthfully, Corey wouldn't know what to do if his precious little girl were to succumb to a tragedy resulting from his profession. And it would definitely crush Kathy, who'd taken a sick leave from work and had been crying ever since he'd found her bound to the driver's seat of her car in their garage, when he returned home on Tuesday. They cried together that night, after Corey had to use physical force to keep her from calling the police. And they still didn't' know if their child was still alive, because her taker, who'd called from a different payphone every night, wouldn't permit them to talk to her.

Now, Corey directed his attention to the defense table. Alfonso Walker had been reticent throughout the whole trial, he'd noticed. Well of course he would be. He was complicit to the abduction of Cindy Briggs and was probably confident that he would walk out a free man at the conclusion of the trial. And Corey had already made up in his mind that if something happened to his daughter, he would visit every known address on Walker's file, and murder everything in the vicinity.

"Will the foreman please stand?"

Judge Torri Richardson's voice pulled Corey's attention toward the jury booth, where the foreman, a middle-aged white woman slowly rose to her feet with the verdict sheet in hand. At this moment, Corey was visibly sweating, and his body's temperature was hot, which had him feeling as if the heat was exuding from the body of Samantha Gordon, who was seated just inches away from him. He'd asked her to assist him on this case in order to get close to her, but his whole agenda changed when Cindy was kidnapped. Maybe, he would try again in the near future, once all this was behind him.

"I understand that the jury has reached a verdict," the judge went on.

The foreman nodded. "Yes, Your Honor. We have."

"Could you please read the verdict out for the court?"

The older woman lifted the verdict sheet to read from it. "We the jury..."

Chapter 15

Ebony pulled her car into the driveway of the house on Wilkins Street, parking behind a white Kia Zues that she figured Rick had purloined. Cutting the engine, and disengaging her seatbelt, she looked around to see who was watching her. It was Saturday, so people were, indeed, out and about. And yes all eyes seemed to be on her. But the eyes she was mostly concerned about belonged to the group of ever present men occupying the steps and porch of the house near the end of the street. *TV thugs* is what Rick had called them. She just hoped it wasn't a misnomer, as she grabbed her pocketbook that was heavier from the weight of her .380, and climbed from the car, clad in low-cut jeans shorts, a snug fitted tank top, and white Nike Reflexes.

With her ballcap pulled low, and sunglasses concealing her eyes, Ebony swaggered toward the front door, intentionally putting a little more bounce in her rump, hoping to appear more like a coquettish *ghetto queen* and less like a repulsive government official. Reaching the front door, she made as if she was negotiating the locks with her keys, then turned the knob.

When Ebony entered, closing the door back, she saw Rick sitting on the sofa with his shirt off, and one foot propped up on the coffee table. Plus, he was reading a book, in which he didn't bother to look up from. For some odd reason, this seemed to anger Ebony. How dare he not acknowledge her? She walked over and stood over him with both hands on her hips.

"Where's Cindy?"

"Who?" He still didn't look up.

"The little girl, Rick," she answered, voice intimidating a threat.

"I set her on fire." He answered, flipping a page in his book. "The same way I did the old man."

"You did what?" Ebony could not believe what she was hearing. She could not believe that Rick had harmed that precious little girl, when Briggs had kept to his end of the bargain. Now, she was tempted to draw her gun and...

"You find that shit funny?" she questioned, seeing the simper he was now regarding her with.

Rick closed the book and placed it in his lap. "You're displaying emotions for someone you don't even know. That could end up being your downfall. However, the girl was bait. You knew what her fate was if her dad didn't come through on his end of the deal."

"But, he did come through on his end of the deal," Ebony spoke through clenched teeth.

"And I came through on mine," he told her. "The girl made it home safe."

Ebony almost sighed out loud. "Really?"

"That was the deal." He grabbed the book and tendered it to her. "You should hold on to this. It was your dad's favorite book."

"Where's Bull?" she finally asked.

Rick shrugged. "I couldn't tell you. I didn't give him a specific time to be here but, knowing him, he's probably laid up with one of his girlfriends."

"And, how many girlfriends do 'YOU' have?"

Ebony couldn't believe she actually said that out loud, but she refused to let her visage reveal how surprised she were about it. Though Jason was periodically "servicing her engine" now, it still felt as if something was missing as if he wasn't hitting those right spots anymore. Perhaps, Ebony was looking for something more. But she only felt like this when she was around Rick. His demeanor is what made him nonpareil, compared to other men she'd dated, or been around. This same demeanor had won her over on the day they'd first met at Hester Park, and still seemed to trigger something inside her.

"I found a hollow spot in the floorboards of the kitchen, "Rick said, clearly repudiating her question. "And, before you get all skeptical. No, I did not pry."

"So, you think the money's under the kitchen floor?" Ebony questioned. After hearing what Bull had said about Rick, she would never have to question Rick's loyalty. It was Bull whom she was skeptical of.

"It seems more logical," he answered. "I mean, I couldn't actually see your dad digging a hole in the back yard. He was constantly receiving, and dishing out money, so he needed a spot he could get in and out of with less complications. Plus, he didn't' have to take the risk of being seen."

"So, it's under the floor," Ebony concluded, now regarding the motionless window fan sitting beside the sofa, as she realized how extremely hot the temperature was inside the house. "Why is it so hot in here?"

"There's no electricity," Rick told her. "I told you that the old man was a squatter. I disconnected the extension cord he had running to the house next door."

"To make it look as if he packed up and left willingly." Ebony, nodded, indicating that she understood.

Rick got to his feet, looking down into her eyes. "You ready to check out the kitchen's floor?"

"Lead the way," she responded, trying hard not to drop her gaze to his chest that glistened from perspiration.

Rick turned and made for the kitchen. As Ebony followed, she took this time to admire his back. Considering Rick's criminal background, his body showed no signs of his periodic prison terms, being that he had no tattoos, and didn't look as if he'd spent his time working out like most prisoners did. But, despite all of that, Ebony could see herself running her tongue along his spine and planting soft kisses on the cicatrix at the small of his back.

"This table hasn't been moved," Rick said, interrupting Ebony's thoughts as he indicated the dilapidated wooden kitchen table that was partly cluttered and surrounded by four chairs. "I found the hollow spot underneath it."

Ebony was wondering what galvanized him to search the floors for hollow spots in the first place but withheld her interrogation. Instead, she told him, "Well, let's see what we have."

Gripping the edge of the table, Rick pulled it, along with the chairs, toward the backdoor, disturbing the roaches that were feasting on the various unwashed dishes in the process. Regarding the spot, Ebony could see the indelible outline of the table on the multi-stained hardwood floor which corroborated Ricks assertion that it had not been moved since the last time her father moved it. But, what she didn't' see was any indication of how to manipulate the wood in order to get beneath it

"How do we get inside?" she asked Rick, who'd just rejoined her.

"With something we can jam through the cracks," he answered looking around. "Perhaps, a butterknife."

Rick stepped toward the sink. While he was fishing through one of the drawers for a butterknife, there was a knock at the front door. Ebony had already assumed it to be Bull, but she was still indecisive about how she was going to play her hand with him. As far as she was concerned, he could have ulterior motives. Well, it was better safe than sorry.

"Push the table back!" Ebony told Rick, who was now facing her with a knife in his hand.

Rick looked confused. "Push it back? It's nobody but Bull."

"Maybe," she replied, hoping she didn't have to explicate her sentiments to Rick. "Whether it's him or not, I still want you to push it back. We'll check for the money some other time."

Rick seemed to cogitate this for a brief second, before tossing the knife into the sink, and doing as he was told. Once the table was back into place. Ebony began realigning the chairs as Rick made for the front door. Still unsure of what to expect now that Bull's out, she placed her back against the sink, which put the table between her and the entrance of the kitchen. Moments later, Bull entered, supervened by Rick. As always, his head was shaved. But, he'd also taken in initiative to shave his facial hair, save for his eyebrows and lashes. Despite the weather, he was clad in a black t-shirt, black shorts, and matching tennis shoes.

"You are definitely Tyrone's daughter," Bull spoke, a broad smile on his face as he stopped short of the table. "To be honest, I didn't think you could do it. But I apologize for doubting you."

"I didn't do it all by myself," Ebony responded, seeing the lascivious look in his eyes as he evaluated her body. "I'm quite sure Rick had filled you in on his mission."

Bull nodded. "He did. What about the money your dad left behind? Did you find it?"

"We've searched the whole house," Ebony lied, disregarding the look that Rick was giving her. "If there's any money, then it's buried in the backyard. Are you ready to start digging?"

Bull's head snapped back as if he'd been struck. "Digging?" That wasn't a part of our deal."

"You don't have to remind me of our deal, Mr. Walker."

"Bull," he corrected.

She waved a dismissive hand. "Whatever, I got you out. That was my part. Your part is to build me a team and tell me everything your brain can remember about my parents. Until my team is properly established, you are my

142

indentured servant. Now, do you have a problem with our arrangement?"

"No, I do not," he answered, then looked back at Rick, who was leaning against the door jamb with his arms folded over his chest.

"You're right. She's definitely a force to be reckoned with."

***

On the drive home, Ebony's mind was on the large sum of money that could possibly be interred under the kitchen's floor of the house on Wilkins. If the money was indeed there, it's incontestable that they were extremely old bills, in which she'd have to convert into newer bills, and transfer a percentage to her bank account. She just hoped Rick wouldn't betray her trust by revealing this to Bull.

Entering the house, Ebony made for the bedroom, where she dropped her pocketbook on the dresser, doffed her tennis shoes and socks, and slid her feet into her house shoes. It was only a few minutes after four, and she would usually start dinner a little after five on Saturday. Therefore, feeling the urge to get high, she journeyed off to the basement to join Jason.

Making it to the basement, she turned the knob, pulled the door open, and slowly descended the stairs. As she neared the bottom of the stairs, moving further into the dim glow of the red lightbulb, she could hear the rap song "Magician" by Playa Ray, playing at a low volume on the stereo system. Getting to the bottom of the steps, she paused to allow her eyes to adjust to the lighting. She'd already known Jason was down there, but she didn't expect him to have company.

Seated on the sofa beside Jason, was Benji, who was six foot two, and 240 pounds with a muscular build. As always his head was clean shaven, and his red beard seemed to protrude four inches away from his face. As Ebony approached, Benji's eyes were transfixed on her body, whereas Jason's were closed. His head was tilted back, indicating that he'd just taken a hit of the powdered drug, and was trying to parry the subsequent drainage from his nostrils. The plate on the table was clean of the drug, but Ebony knew that there was more of it inside Benji's little black bag sitting on the floor beside his foot.

"Where the fuck have you been all day?"

Ebony's eyes shot from Benji's bag to Jason, who was giving her the look of death. And she was highly conversant with this look. Crush is a mixture of cocaine and morphine, which is a mood altering drug. Whatever a person's mood is before using the drug, it's amplified once their high kicks in. Perhaps, Jason was upset before stuffing his nose, Ebony concluded, and this was one of those times when she would endeavor to avoid him at all costs.

"You don't hear me talking to you?"

Ebony's delay in response must have infuriated him more, because he lunged from the sofa as if pulled up by invisible strings. With the coffee table between them, Jason leaned, bringing his right arm across it. Ebony saw it coming but did nothing to avoid it. In fact, her body seemed to automatically brace itself for the impact.

SMACK!

Jason's palm made contact with the side of her face. Ebony stumbled back a foot, disconcerted by the fact that Jason had done this in front of Benji. With one hand holding the left side of her face, and the other balled into a fist, she fixed him with a monstrous look tantamount to the one he was given her.

"Don't ever put your hands on me again!" Ebony spoke through clenched teeth.

Jason tilted his head to the side, "What the fuck did you just say?"

144

"You heard me," she stood her ground. "Don't ever put—"

Jason leaped over the low table like an Olympic gold medalist. On instinct, Ebony back peddled until Jason was directly in front of her. Then, she started throwing wild punches in which quite a few had caught him in the face. But her bravura was short lived. In one swift motion, Jason bent down, and snatched her legs from under her, causing her to land hard on her back. Before she could regain an ounce of the wind that was knocked out of her, Jason had her pinned down with his hands around her throat, thumbs pressing down on her larynx, encumbering air from entering or exiting her lungs.

At this time, Ebony had completely given up her will to fight. It was as if she welcomed her fate as she lied motionless, staring soullessly up into the abyss of Jason's eyes. Her eyes became watery, producing a filmy curtain. And turning everything into blur. She figured this was the first stage that led up to her demise. Now, she was wondering how long it would be before darkness overtakes her.

"Jay!" Benji's voice sounded distant. "Dude, what the fuck are you doing! You're gonna kill her, man! Chill the fuck out!"

Despite Beji's plea, Jason did not let up. He was in a drug induced trance, something Ebony was all too familiar with, due to her experience with the drug. Feeling as if she was losing consciousness, Ebony closed her eyes. She felt her body go numb. She felt the pain in her back go numb. She felt...

She heard Benji call Jason's name again. His voice still sounded far off but, for some reason, Ebony could feel him near. His proximity was confirmed when she felt the weight of Jason's body forcefully lift from hers, as his hands snatched from around her throat. As if she'd been divested of air for over an hour, Ebony voraciously filled her lungs with it, disregarding the burning sensation. Still lying inert with her eyes tightly shut, Ebony could hear Benji admonishing Jason in a hushed tone. But that was not enough for Ebony. She'd already vowed that Jason would pay for his opprobrious behavior towards her. Now, she he was more than determined to make sure he does.

Chapter 16

The following day, Ebony pulled her Cadillac into the parking lot of Century Publication, which was an ancient old monastery looking building, where one could find retro published items such as newspapers, magazines, and books of all genres. Yesterday, when Ebony inquired on information about her father, Bull had insisted that she meet him and Rick here. She still couldn't figure out why but, here she was parked in the not crowded lot, waiting for them to show up.

Well, she didn't have to wait for long because, shortly after she'd killed her engine, Rick's dark brown Audi Avenger entered the lot, riding past her. His windows were tinted, but not dark enough for her not to see, and recognize both occupants. Once the car had parked at a distance from her, Rick and Bull immediately dismounted, and made for the entrance of the building as if they hadn't seen her out there. Concluding this, Ebony donned her sunglasses, grabbed her pocketbook off the passenger seat, and exited the car, moving fast in an attempt to catch them before they entered. But as she neared the building, Bull and Rick stopped at the entrance and were now watching her. This made her slow her momentum a bit. As she approached, both regarded her with concerned looks, then exchanged glances. She already knew that the tumid left side of her face was the reason for the expressions.

"Don't ask," Ebony prompted, hoping to circumvent an conversation on what transpired last night. "Now, why are we here?"

"You wanted to know more about your dad," Bull answered. "So I'm taking you to the newspaper section. Rick and I are going to pull up some two thousand and five articles and show you some crimes that were orchestrated by him."

"We can pull those cases up on the internet," suggested Ebony.

"That stuff is monitored by the government," Bull replied. "You of all people, show know that."

Ebony nodded, feeling a bit asinine.

"Once inside," Bull resumed. "I suggest we do little to no talking, being that we don't' know if the place is bugged, or who's listening. When Rick and I show you a case, jot down what you can on whatever you want to know, and we'll fill you in on it later. Dig?"

"Let's go."

The three of them entered the building where they had to sign in and leave their I.D. cards at the front desk. Making it to Room 8, which was a mass room of numerous wooden shelves filled with age-old newspapers, and a desk occupied by a clerk, they browsed around until they came upon the papers printed in 2005. While Rick and Bull were searching different sections, Ebony retrieved her pen and notepad from her pocketbook, and waited patiently.

"Top Story," said Rick who was the first to present a paper to her, holding it so she could see the top page.

The headline read: *Alleged Victim of Linkton Count Prosecutor, Commits Suicide.* Not bothering with the date, Ebony shorthanded the headline just as Bull approached with a paper. Saying nothing, he pointed to the headline that read: *Storeowner and Two Others Found Dead After Store was Set Afire."* Ebony quickly jotted this down, feeling as if Rick would make an immediate return, and she was right. A few seconds after Bull had moved on to get another newspaper, Rick approached.

This went on for almost thirty minutes. Ebony had enough entries in her notepad to make her father seem reprehensible for every crime committed in Linkton, and all the surrounding counties. But, for some reason, Ebony was skeptical about most of them. Maybe it was because she couldn't see how her father was tied into the crimes. However, Rick and Bull did promise to elucidate everything for her.

It was after 3 p.m. when Ebony, Rick, and Bull left Century Publications migrated to Kentucky Fried Chicken, where Rick and Bull accessed the drive thru. Ebony didn't order anything, being that she was engaged to have Sunday dinner at her grandparents. Then, she followed them to a nearby park, where they were now seated at a picnic table under a gazebo.

"I remember that case very well," Ebony was saying. "In fact, I remember telling my dad that I didn't think Reid was a bad person. For some reason, I don't think he did it."

"Now you know the truth," said Bull, before biting into one of his biscuits. He and Rick were seated across from her.

"But why would my dad have Laura pull such a stunt?" Ebony wanted to know. "What transpired between him and Reid."

"We were never told," Rick answered.

"Hell, we didn't ask," Bull pitched in. "We were paid to pull off special details. Once those details were completed, we collected money, and waited for the next call."

"So, Laura didn't really commit suicide, huh?"

Rick and Bull exchanged glances.

"What about the storeowner who was set on fire in his own store?" Ebony moved on, feeling pressed for time.

"He sold drugs for your dad," Rick took the initiative. "Once his time was up, we were called in to pull that job off. The other two guys were his runners."

Ebony glanced down at her notepad. "The man who was gunned down in his front yard. Who was he?"

"Wayne Griffin," Rick answered. Your dad got him out of jail, in exchange for him to sell drugs for him."

"Did they have a dispute?"

Rick shook his head. "Nope. His time was up, also."

"And, what the hell does that mean?" she questioned looking back and forth from the two. "Did my dad stamp expiration dates on these people?"

They exchanged another glance.

"I'm listening," she promoted.

Bull took the bait. "Your dad was always recruiting. Maybe, he was being cautious, but he never had long term dealings with anybody. When he tells a person they're done, it's exactly what it meant."

"And he did this with all of his recruits?"

"Of course," answered Rick. "No one was exempt."

"What about you two?"

"Including us."

Ebony furrowed her eyebrows. "You mean to tell me that you two worked for my father, knowing he would kill you after the terms?"

"Tyrone wasn't a person to say 'no' to," Bull told her. "That's if you cared anything for your immediate family."

"I see." Ebony didn't need further elucidation on that statement. "Has he—"

"Yes," Bull cut her off. "A few have tried to escape their agreement."

Ebony drew a breath, looking down at her cell phone that sat beside her notepad. Noticing the time, she said, "We'll pick this up some other time. Right now, I have a dinner appointment to make." She stood, placing the notepad into her pocketbook. "Bull, I need you to get started on my recruits. Rick, I want you to assist him until I find you a different task."

"What about the money?" Bull inquired. "You know—"

"In due time," she cut him off, grabbed her cell phone, then headed for her car.

As she drove, Ebony notably replayed Bull's question about the money over in her head, trying to see if she could perceive ulterior motive in his inflection. She understood that she would have to pay her workers for their services, but Bull seemed a bit too anxious to get his hands on her father's *buried treasure.*

Thinking this, Ebony knew she had to expedite the recovery and interchange of the money, just in case Bull decides to go on his own scavenger hunt. And this would entail an immediate change of plans, which is why she pulled her car into the eatery and entered the restaurant. After ordering her food, and finding a table, she made her first of two calls that would solidify her change of plans.

"Hello?" her grandfather answered.

"Put momma on the phone." Ebony demanded, inflection void of pleasantries.

"Alright."

Monetarily, her grandmother's voice sounded through the earpiece. "Yes, baby?"

"How are you, Momma?"

"I'm fine, sweetheart," she answered. "Are you and Jason on the way? The food's almost done."

Ebony cleared her throat. "That's why I'm calling about, Momma. We won't' be able to make it."

"Is everything alright?"

"Yes, ma'am," Ebony responded. "A situation came up and it requires my undivided attention. I'm sorry."

"Baby, I understand," Regina told her granddaughter. "Do what you have to do. I'll
see you next Sunday."

"You'll see me before then, Momma," Ebony promised. "And I'll call you later tonight. Okay?"

"Okay, baby. Momma loves you."

"Love you too."

Concluding the call Ebony decided to tend to her meal, before placing her next call, hoping that Rick would be alone by the time she finished. While she ate, she thought about hers and Jason implicit arrangement. They hadn't spoken, nor made direct eye contact since yesterday. Once again, he'd made the basement his own private abode, only journeying to the main bedroom this morning to grab some of his things. Well, as far as Ebony was concerned, he could turn the basement into his very own catacombs, because, to her, he no longer existed.

"Talk to me!" Rick answered his phone.

"This call is confidential," Ebony spoke, hoping he would catch on. "Is Bull still with you?"

"Yeah, I still got that," Rick coded his response.

"When you drop him off," she said, "Meet me back at the house pronto."

"You got it."

Hanging up, Ebony left a five-dollar tip on her table, then made for the restroom, where she drained her bladder, and rechecked herself in the mirror. Back in the car, she drove with the music off, and let her mind wander with the soothing sounds of the A.C. in the background. She tried not to think about her father, and all things she'd ascertained about him, but couldn't help it.

Thoughts of her father brought on thoughts of his alleged offspring, Anthony Hudson. Ebony knew that she could easily walk away, and forget about him but, just the thought of having a half-brother had her thinking otherwise. Perhaps, having him in her life would fill a small portion of the void inside of her from the loss of her parents. But first, she must make certain that he is who he says he is.

Pulling into the driveway of the house on Wilkins, Ebony dismounted, and marched toward the front door without looking around to see who, or if anyone was watching her. She also didn't feign to use her keys to gain entrance. Entering the still humid interior of the house, she dropped her pocketbook on the table in the living room then entered the kitchen where she stood around taking in the sight of the unwashed dishes that were still crawling with various insects.

Realizing that she didn't know the exact time that Rick would arrive, and the nightfall would leave them in the dark, being that the house had no electricity, Ebony decided to take herself useful. On the counter, she saw a box of black trash bags. Placing two bags inside of one for the thicker layer, she gingerly began disposing of everything on the table. After tying the bag and setting it off to the side, she spotted some dishwashing liquid on the counter, and a decent looking dish rag draped over the faucet.

Getting over her wariness of the liquid, Ebony stopped the sink up to make dishwater, then cleaned the table, counters, and also the sink after draining the water. She thought Rick would have arrived by the time she was done, but he hadn't. Now, she found herself staring at the section of the floor underneath the table, as she considered the proximity of eventide. Not knowing what to expect beyond the flooring is what kept her from going at it alone, but she didn't' want to risk it getting dark and have to do it another day.

With her sweat dampened shirt sticking to her body from the uncomfortably high temperature, Ebony made her decision. She pushed the table toward the rear door, dragging the four chairs with it. Fishing a butter knife from the silverware drawer, she knelt down, looking for abnormality in the wood. Finding it, she jammed the knife between the boards and edged along the deep crack, gradually lifting one of the planks in the process. Before she could partially displace the three-foot piece of wood, a multitude of roaches scampered from beneath it, almost causing her to drop it.

"This place is in dire need of an exterminator," Ebony muttered, lying the piece of flooring to the side."

The light from the kitchen's window was inadequate for her to see down into the darkened gap, but she could tell that the soil underneath had been excavated. Placing the knife beside her, Ebony used both of her hands to lift the next piece which was a few centimeters longer, Tossing it aside, she peered down into the hole, and was able to see some sort of bag. Before she could remove a third piece, she heard the front door being opened and closed.

With her heart beating triple time, and her not knowing if it was Rick or not, Ebony thought about her gun, then realized that her gun was in her pocketbook, and her pocketbook was on the living room's table. Unnaturally, she didn't feel as if her life was in danger but, in the event that her guest wasn't Rick, she didn't want to expose the cavity in the floor, nor what it contained. So, still in her kneeling position, she retrieved the second board, and started to wedge it back into place.

"It's just me."

Hearing Rick's voice hampered her movements. She did all she could not to drop her head in relief. When Ebony looked up, Rick was standing over her with some small quaint looking lamp in his hand. She also noticed he changed clothes, indicating that he'd been home. Plus, he smelled of fresh soap, and reapplied cologne.

"You brought a lamp?" she asked, not trying to conceal the disbelief in her tone.

'It's one of those battery-operated lamps," he replied, flipping a switch, giving the room the proper illumination. "Unless you have the ability to see in the dark."

Ebony simpered at his sarcastic remark.

Chapter 17

"Please tell me you got eight hundred and twenty thousand."

The bills recovered from the cavity in the floor were stored in a duffle bag. After putting the floor back together, and the table and chairs back into place, Rick and Ebony took seats and began their own separate count to see if they'd come up with the same number. Now over three and half hours later, rubber-banded bills were counted and sprawled out on the kitchen table. Being that they'd been interred for a long period of time, the ancient bills boldly boasted the money smell that still permeated the kitchen.

"That's my count," Rick now replied, yawning as he stretched his arms into the air. "Now, what?"

"I'll keep the money here until I can get them switched over to newer bills," Ebony answered, trying her best not to look down at Rick's bare chest. "In the meantime, I need you to discard all of this old furniture and put new locks on the doors. Once I purchase the house, I'll have the utilities cut on, and a Sen-Tech system installed."

"Sounds like you'll be moving in."

"Eventually."

"Do we tell Bull about the money."

Ebony evaluated him a moment before speaking. "Not yet. He'll know when I think it's time for him to know. And I trust that you'll keep this between us," she continued before he could respond. "Right now, I have another dilemma. Not too long ago, I was informed that I have a half-brother."

Rick furrowed his eyebrows but said nothing.

Ebony resumed. "He's being held at the Fulton County Jail for multiple counts of armed robbery, kidnapping and two counts of first-degree murder."

"This came from your grandparents?" Rick finally asked.

"No," Ebony answered. Checking her watch to see that it was almost eight o'clock. "I was contacted by his mom who claimed to have had an affair with my dad in ninety-six."

"And you're going for this?" asked Rick. "It could be a scam."

"I pulled him up on file." Ebony was struggling to keep her composure. "I saw his picture. He's like a spitting image of my father. I can make a copy of it and show it to you."

Rick held his hands up in surrender. "I think I'll take a rain check on that. If you say he fits the bill, I can only take your word for it. I just hope you know what you're doing."

"So do I."

"A case like his must have gained some attention from the media," Rick observed. "Did it make the news?"

"It made World News," she answered.

"When?"

"Last November."

"Pedestrian robberies?"

Ebony shook her head. "No. It was the first National Bank in Atlanta I don't know if—"

"Hold up!" Rick encroached holding hand up for emphasis. "I think you've just revealed the scam."

Ebony was confused. "How?"

"If he robbed a bank," Rick started, "He definitely wouldn't be sitting in the Fulton County Jail. That's a federal offense."

Ebony smiled. "It seems like you're out of touch with current laws. As of May, of last year, legislators passed the bill, granting state courts discretionary jurisdiction to try federal offenses."

"Are you serious?" Now Rick seemed confused. "So, the state now has the choice to try a federal case, or toss it the big boys?"

"That's right."

"Well, I guess I am out of touch with current laws."

Chapter 18

Wednesday

July 5, 2023

"Why would you say that Janelle?"

It had been over three weeks since Anthony had seen Janelle. It's been almost the same amount of time since Janelle had opted to have her cellular phone disconnected in order to keep the gas on, which made it close to impossible to reach her, being that, for some reason, she no longer responded to his letters.

Now looking up the visitation monitor at his son's mother, who'd dyed her crop cut hair red, Anthony realized how much he missed her, though he was still torn between letting her go, and trying to salvage what fragment of relationship they had. Every time he thinks about trying to make it work between them, he was always constantly reminded of how she isn't making his situation any better, being that she doesn't write, send him money, nor bring his son to see him.

"It's a bit too complicated to explain right now, Anthony." Janelle now answered looking away.

Anthony switched the receiver to his other ear. "You keep leaving me in the dark. Stop beating around the bush, and speak your mind. When did we start—"

"I can't do this anymore," she cut him off, still looking away.

"And, what the hell does—"

"Stop playing dumb, Anthony!" She was now staring back at him from the screen of the monitor. "I'm tired of going through this with you. We can't have a decent relationship because you're always locked up. And each time, I'm always there for you, bending over backwards to make sure you have everything you need." After pausing to draw a breath, she said, "I can't do it anymore. I don't have the strength to."

"You picked a fine time to tell me this," Anthony pointed out. "Just kick a man when he's down, huh?"

"Don't give me that crap, Anthony!" Janelle bristled. "If that was the case, I would have kicked you the *'FIRST'* time you went down. So, don't even try that bullshit with me!

"So, why now, Janelle?"

"I'm not blind, Anthony," she responded. "I don't 'know much about the law, but I know the difference between residential burglary and murder. You won't get a slap on the wrist for killing another human being, Anthony."

"What about my son?" Anthony wanted to know. "Are you going to just take him away from me?"

Janelle looked away before speaking into the receiver. "I think it would be best for him."

"And, who in the hell sold you that bird brain ass idea?"

"It's common sense, Anthony," She now regarded him. "You're never getting out, and I don't need him idolizing you for your stupidity."

"Visitation will conclude in two minutes," the computerized voice sounded through the earpiece of the receiver.

"Think about this, Janelle." There was desperation in Anthony's voice, in which he hoped Janelle didn't catch. "You're making this decision on your own. What about me? What about Alex? How do you know that taking him away from his father would best for him?"

"As humans," she stared. We don't always make the best decisions. But we have to live with whatever decision we make in our lives. And this'll be another decision I'll have to live with. I wish you the best, and I'll—"

The screen went blank. Anthony closed his eyes and mustered up enough willpower to keep himself from snatching the receiver out of the wall, and assailing the monitor with it. For that would only get his visitation rights stripped away from him, which would be unfair to his mother, who was the only other person on his visitation list.

Exiting the small booth, Anthony made for his assigned dorm with a mind full of evil thoughts. How could Janelle just take his son away like that? He knew that there was no way he could absquatulate his situation. But did she have to remind him of that? And why haven't Ebony Davis contacted him after the conversation with his mother? Perhaps, she was incredulous to the thought of having a half-brother. Or maybe she was one of those *daddy's little girls,* who thought her father was incapable of lying down and having a child with anyone other than her mother.

With his mother now on his mind, when Anthony entered the dormitory, he made a B-line to the array of the phones mounted to the wall, surprised that one was unoccupied. As he lifted the receiver, and commenced to dialing his mother's number, his name was called over the intercom with the instruction to report to the seven hundred dorm, the same dorm he'd just returned from. He knew that it wasn't an attorney visit, because they would have promulgated it as such. Besides, his public defender has yet to make any kind of contact with him. Well, whatever it was, Anthony was bound to find out as he hung the phone, and exited to the dorm.

Re-entering dorm seven hundred, Anthony took a seat on the steel bench, being that there was no one there to greet him. He's sat for almost ten minutes, thinking of all kinds of reason why he was summoned to the multipurpose dorm, when in walked the captain, accompanied by an older white man in a white doctor's coat, and carrying a small case of some sort.

160

"Mr. Hudson?" the captain inquired as they approached.

"That's me," Anthony answered, not bothering to stand.

Stopping in front of him, the captain spoke again, "This man drove all the way from Linkton County to see you."

"Oh, yeah?" Anthony now regarded the visitor, who was evaluating him through extremely small eyeglasses. Hearing that he'd driven all the way from Linkton, the same county in which Ebony Davis resided, gave Anthony a string of hope.

"I'm Dr. Shannon," the older man spoke, "from the Linkton County Health Department, and I was requested from the District Attorney's office to obtain DNA samples from you. But, being that this is not an order from the courts, you have every right to refuse. Do you understand?"

"Of course," Anthony replied, suppressing a smile. "What all samples do you need?"

***

"At this time," Judge Jackson announced, 'I'm going to grant a one-hour recess. I want everyone back here at two forty-seven." He looked over to the State's table. "Ms. Davis? Do you know how long your appointment will take?"

"I have no idea," Ebony replied, gathering documents into her briefcase "If I see that it'll hold me over the one-hour deadline, I'll call the front desk, and have them to notify you."

"Fair enough."

Ebony gathered her things, and exited the courtroom, heading for the elevators. She figured that she wouldn't need more than an hour, but she planned to enjoy every second from the monotonous atmosphere of the courtroom. She was really hoping to run into Samantha after her appointment, so they could make off for a little fondling. Libidinous thoughts of Samantha, had Ebony in a state of elation, as she exited the elevator, and made for her office.

"Ms. Davis?"

Ebony was standing at the door to her office, about to insert her key into its lock, when her name was called. She looked to her right to see District Attorney Barbara Hutchins approaching, with a solemn look on her face, despite the multiple layers of makeup that created a slight mist of obscurity.

"Do you have a minute?" Barbara asked, once she'd approached.

"Not really," answered Ebony, who wasn't in the mood to confabulate with anybody other than Samantha. "I'm on my way to an appointment."

"Corey Briggs has requested a leave of absence," the head D.A. resumed, as if she hadn't heard Ebony's reply. "Said something about seeing a psychiatrist and working out some family issues. "She paused as if awaiting a response, in which she didn't get. "However, until he returns, I'll be divvying his caseload amongst the rest of you And, no, I'm not excluding myself. I'll be helping out. I'm coming to you now, because he has a motion hearing tomorrow for an impeding trial. You'll be handing that."

"I have cases of my own scheduled for tomorrow, Ms. Hutchins," Ebony finally spoke, incredulous that this old witch had sprang this upon her so suddenly.

"Those cases you have in that time slot have already been rescheduled."

"Plus, I don't know a thing about his case." Ebony pointed out, hoping to get her supervisor to reconsider.

Barbara smiled. "You and I both know that, sweetheart. But lucky for you, I'll be your assistant. Stop by my office and pick up the file before you leave for the day."

With that, Barbara Hutchins turned, and retreated in the direction in which she'd come. After watching her turn the corner, Ebony entered her office, exchanged her briefcase for her pocketbook, and was back out the door, thinking of the Corey Briggs. There was no doubt in her mind that Briggs's was still mentally suffering from the perilous breach of his family's welfare. Now, she was wondering if he would ever return. This made her smile because, if he doesn't return, he would be one less threat to her chance of acquiring the D.A.'s position when it became available.

It took exactly twenty-six minutes for Ebony to reach North Spring Bank. Finding a parking spot in the small lot, she pressed the trunk release button, before extracting her cell phone from her pocketbook. She looked at the purple attaché case that appeared undisturbed atop the removable piece of carpet that concealed the spare tire.

On yesterday, after dropping her grandparents off at home from the fourth of July dinner she'd treated them to, Ebony journeyed out to the house on Wilkins Street, to retrieve the old bills. She saw that Rick had already begun discarding the furniture, whereas the living room was stripped of it's contents. Finding two sets of keys inside the duffle bag with the money, she figured he'd changed the locks though she hadn't noticed upon entry. It also made her realize that a portion of the money could have been missing. Not wanting to doubt Rick's loyalty and not wanting to show up to her appointment with currency unaccounted for, Ebony took the initiative to make a final assessment. Everything was all there, which made her feel a bit of guilt for doubling Rick's loyalty, but all the more grateful, and passionate, toward the older man.

Now, with the attaché case in tow, Ebony entered the bank and was immediately welcomed by the air conditioner that reperceived her of the over eighty degree weather that already had her blouse sticking to her back from perspiration. The three cashier lanes were all occupied with customers, but her destination was the customer service desk, where sat a young blonde, who seemed to be chatting up a storm with her cellular glued to her ear. Headed in the that direction, Ebony's kitten heel sandals drew attention towards her as they click clacked on linoleum tiled floor

"I'm here to see, Mr. Perry," Ebony promulgated upon approaching the desk.

The blonde looked up as if offended by Ebony's encroachment. "Name?"

"Ebony Davis," she answered, removing her sunglasses, and hanging them on her blouse.

"I'll call you back, Stephanie," the blonde said into her phone, before ringing off, placing it atop her desk, then tapping on the computer's keypad. Once she'd pulled up what she was searching for, she regarded Ebony with a plausible smile.

"I guess you're in luck. He's available." She stood. "Right this way."

Mr. Perry's office was only a few feet away, but the blonde managed to turn the short walk into a fashion models tryout as she purposefully strutted in her fashionable six-inch heels, and light blue, snug fitted dress that came down to her knees, and showed off every curve of her five foot five frame. But Ebony enjoyed the display as she followed it, her eye affixed on the woman's curvaceous derriere, up until they'd reached the door. Tapping on the door twice, the blonde stuck her head inside, announce Ebony's arrival, then pushed it all the way open to let her enter.

The bank's assistant manager was already on his feet, behind his desk, when Ebony entered. He was about five feet seven, 145 pounds, clean shaven, with bright orange hair cut down to his scalp. His wire-rimmed glasses and pink bowtie that contrasted with his brown dress suit, gave him the appeal of a high school dean, in lieu of what the oak and brass plate on this desk insisted.

"Thank you, Betty," he said to the blonde, who nodded, then disappeared, closing the door behind her. He then regarded Ebony with a smile, and outstretched hand. "Ms. Davis."

She accepted his hand. "Mr. Perry."

"Please, have a seat," he said, gesturing to the sole chair in front of his desk. Once they were both seated, he nodded to the attaché case beside Ebony's feet. "Is this the currency you wish to exchange?"

'It is, Ebony detected the concern in his voice.

"I know we've never established an amount over the phone," he said slowly, "But is it possible that you have ten thousand or more in that case?"

Ebony nodded. "It's possible."

"How possible?"

"Highly possible." She knew where this was going, and she came greatly prepared.

Mr. Perry furrowed his eyebrows. "Now, you know that anything of that nature has to be reported to the IRS, Ms. Davis.

"Is that the bank's policy?"

He nodded. "Yes, ma'am. It's also required by law."

"Have you always abided by these laws and policies, Mr. Perry?" Ebony asked, penetrating his brown eyes with her very own.

"I don't make the rules," he answered, evasively, dropping his gaze to the picture frame on his desk that Ebony could only see the back of.

"You have a beautiful wife," Ebony commented. She'd already figured that the assistant manager was going to force her to play this card with him. In fact, this was what she'd come *greatly prepared* to do.

Mr. Perry shot her an incredulous look, as if he knew better than to believe that she was capable of seeing the photo from where she was seated. But he didn't' say a word.

Ebony resumed, "I was at the Bankers Association dinner party in February. Your wife had on this unforgettable blue Susan Parker evening gown, and matching pumps. She's a natural blonde, right?"

"Not my wife," he answered slowly shaking his head from side to side. "She's always—"

"You're right," Ebony cut him off, a half smirk on her face.

"What the hell was I thinking? She's always been a brunette. On that night, she was quite stunning in a gray Flannigan dress, and matching, low-cut boots. Am I right?"

He still seemed at a loss for words.

"So, who was the lucky woman in the Susan Parker display?"

Ebony continued, in a slow, and low theatrical tone. "Any guesses, Mr. Perry? Would you like to buy a vowel? You have five seconds."

"Are you serious?" he asked Ebony, who was looking at her watch.

"Times up, Mr. Perry," she announced, looking into his eyes again.

"Any idea? Could that person be Betty Walters?"

"That's our receptionist," he scoffed. "Of course, she was at the dinner party. And, what does that have to do with anything?"

"Before you started as a bank teller for Glendale Bankers in Missouri," Ebony posed, repudiating his question, "Did they do a thorough background check on you?"

"How'd you—"

"Did they? She cut him off, voice conveying authority.

He shrugged. "Of course. All banks are binded under federal law to conduct thorough background checks on prospective employes."

"To make sure these people are who they say they are, right?"|

"What are you getting at, Ms. Davis?"

"It would be quite a shame for this bank if the government came in here and red taped the place for violating Section Three of Federal Codes of banking and Procedures, wouldn't it?" she asked, tilting her head slightly to one side.

Mr. Perry narrowed his eyes. "I don't' know what kind of games—"

"Not only are you cheating on your wife with a transgender," Ebony cut in, "But you are very much aware that he's working at this bank under an assumed name, which makes you complicit to aforementioned violations."

"Betty's a good person," he muffed through clenched teeth.

Ebony smiled sardonically. "I'm quite sure he is, Mr. Perry. And I would feel deeply contrite to be the one who blows the whistle on the enormities going on within the walls of this not so prestigious bank."

"Okay," Mr. Perry spoke, leaning forward, and resting his hands on the desk. "Maybe you *'CAN'* prove the violation of the F.C.B.P. maybe you *'CAN'* get me terminated for knowing about the violation. But, there's no way in hell you can prove that I have anything going on with Ms. Walters outside of the workplace."

"Spoken like a true gambler," she acknowledged. "Are you willing to put your hard-earned achievements on the line? Are you really willing to bet everything on black?"

Again, he was at a loss for words.

"I thought so, "Grabbing the attaché' case off the floor, Ebony approached, and placed it on the desk in front of him.

"There's eight hundred and twenty thousand dollars in here. I want four hundred and twenty thousand dollars transferred to my account, and three hundred changed over to newer bills, twenties and fifties. I'll stop by and pick them up whenever time permits.

"What about the other one twenty?" Mr. Perry asked, as Ebony made for the door.

Getting to the door, Ebony turned to face him with one hand posed on the knob. "I'm a prosecutor—not a financial advisor. Hell, take your wife to Hawaii or something."

Upon re-entering the courthouse, Ebony checked her watch to see that it was 2:43. She wanted to see if she could see Samantha but was highly aware that she only had four minutes to return to the courtroom as the judge ordered. So, abdicating her thoughts of playing truant a little longer in order to see if she could score a quicky with Samantha, Ebony retrieved her briefcase from her office, then made for the courtroom. The only two people present were Deputy Taylor and the stenographer, who appeared to be packing up her things as she was leaving for the day. They both regarded her when she entered.

"Did I miss something?" a perplexed Ebony asked, as she approached and placed her briefcase atop the State's table. "Jackson had mentioned something about having mild chest pains when he arrived this morning," Taylor apprised as he approached Ebony. Shortly after calling the recess, I guess the pain had become unbearable, because he called me into his chambers, and made me the bearer of the bad news. Wcl, I guess it's good news to us subordinates, huh?"

"He cancelled court for the rest of the day?"

Ebony didn't know if she should flip chairs or jump for joy.

"There was no one to fill in for him on such a short notice," Taylor replied.

"I guess I'll see you guys tomorrow," the stenographer said as she made for the exit.

"Goodnight, Ms. Nettles," responded Taylor. Once she left, he turned back to Ebony. "Well I guess you can go home and get an early start on dinner."

"And I'm quite sure your wife would be delighted to have her husband home at such a decent time for once," Ebony said, though she'd always been under the impression that the fire between him and his wife had died out a longtime ago.

"Yeah, I guess so," he said, looking off.

Ebony made an attempt at a quick recovery. "Or, you can take me out to a late lunch. My appointment hindered me from doing so."

Taylor now regarded her with a twinkle in his eyes that she'd never seen before. "Are you sure he won't' mind?"

She smiled. "What he and your wife doesn't know, won't hurt them."

Chapter 19

Saturday

July 8, 2023

The over three hour drive to Atlanta would have taken a toll on Ebony, had she not gotten the proper rest she'd afforded herself the previous night. She was still a bit exhausted by the time she made the Howell Mill Road exit. After stopping for gas, she set her GPS system for the intended location and was back on the road. Almost twenty mutes later, she was driving through a resident neighborhood that was analogous to the one on Wilkins Street, back in Linkton County, sans the huge circle at the end.

Carol Jenkins' abode wasn't the worst looking house in the vicinity, but it definitely wouldn't make top ten on anybody's list of best looking homes. And the burgundy, older model Honda didn't make the picture any more desirable as it sat in the driveway with weather strained paint, and a spare tire at the rear that looked as if it had been stripped from a child's tricycle.

Pulling in behind the Honda, Ebony put her car into park, and sat watching the house to see if someone would peer out, after hearing her pull up, though her engine was barely audible to someone standing within two feet of her car. Seeing no signs of life, she took in the surroundings, wondering why no one was out on such a beautifully sunny day. Maybe Atlantans favored their air conditioners more, she thought, as she killed the engine, dismounted and made for the front door, with her pocketbook hanging from her shoulder, and a manila folder in hand. Reaching the door, she rang the doorbell and, for some reasons, was surprised that it actually worked.

"Who is it?" a feminine voice answered, moments later.

"Ebony Davis"

It was quiet on the other side of the door for almost half a minute, before Ebony heard the sound of security locks being disengaged. The door seemed to open in slow motion until Ebony was standing face to face with the woman, she assumed to be the one she'd gotten the call from. In a pair of gray jeans, and red t-shirt the woman stood at about five feet, with a stomach that irrefutably hung over her belt buckle. Ebony couldn't determine the length of her hair for the jet-black wig that sat perfectly atop her head, but she could clearly tell that this woman was well over fifty years of age. She was definitely total contrast of what Ebony had imagined, which now had her feeling that this woman was not the type of woman her dad would go for, ruminating how comely her mother was.

"You look much taller on T.V.," Carol offered, with a wide smile, revealing exceptionally white teeth.

Ebony matched her smile. "Well, you know those camera people can tweak the images to their own liking. Who knows? Me being six-foot ten cold be one of their twisted fantasies."

This made the older woman laugh. "You may have a point there. Come on inside."

She stepped aside to allow Ebony entrance. Upon entering, Ebony's eyes seemed to dance around as she inspected every nook and cranny of the living room that reminded her of the one at her grandparents, being that it was cluttered with stuffed animals, old toys, and probably pictures of Carol's entire family, including ancestors. But for some odd reason, it all made Ebony feel at home.

"Make yourself comfortable," Carol offered, upon closing the door back. "Would you like anything to drink?"

"Do you have any bottled water?" inquired Ebony.

"Sure."

As Carol made for the kitchen, Ebony took a seat on the sofa, placing the folder in her lap, and her pocketbook beside her. Being that she was seated directly in front of the air conditioner wedged in the window, the air caressed the back of her neck, giving her chills, but seemed to add to her comfort. At this time, the array of pictures on the coffee table had her attention. As if not wanting to get caught looking, she quickly surveyed the photos, looking for any sign of her father, or anybody else she may know. But, the only people recognizable to her were Carol and Anthony, of various ages. Switching her gaze to the small table beside the sofa, she found herself looking at a much larger picture of Carol, when she was much younger. Plus, she was accompanied by a man that had seen in some of the photos on the table. Now, evaluating Carol's figure in the photo, made Ebony change her thoughts about her father not going for this woman, she was definitely stunning!

"That's me back in ninety-four," Carol expounded upon re-entering the living room with a bottle of water. "I thought I'd hold on to that figure forever. Here you go, baby."

"Thank you," Ebony said, accepting the water.

"You're welcome." She took a seat on the other end of the sofa. "I assume you obtained my address from Anthony's file."

"I did."

"Well, it's nice of you to come by."

Ebony nodded, then took a sip of her water. Reverting her attention back to the picture on the small table, she asked. "So, who's this guy?"

"That's Leonard," answered Carol, "We had been on and off since high school. In fact, we had just broken up when I met your dad. After your dad went his way, I ran back to Leonard and explained the situation to him. I actually cried on his shoulder. I didn't think he'd take me back after I'd gotten pregnant by another man, but he did. And, not once did he mention anything about an abortion."

"So, he helped your raise Anthony?"

Carol nodded. "He did. Leonard couldn't produce, so he looked at Anthony as God's gift to him. He died when Anthony was eight."

"What happened?" Ebony asked, hoping that Leonard's demise wasn't another murder orchestrated by the notorious Tyrone Davis.

"Leonard was enlisted in the Army," she explained. "He was called to assist with patrolling the border in Syria when a suicide bomber drove a car loaded with explosives through their check point and detonated it. I remember watching the story on the World News. As they repeatedly showed footage of the explosion, I was praying to the High Heavens that my husband wasn't at that location. I prayed that he was stationed at another section of the border, or that it wasn't even his shift."

She paused for a brief moment, while fiddling with the wedding band on her finger. "I guess it was his time."

"I'm sorry to hear that," Ebony offered, with sincerity.

Carol waved a dismissive hand. "That's life, baby. Only God knows what he has instore for us."

Ebony only nodded her agreement "How did Anthony take the news?"

"He was devasted," the older woman answered. "Leonard was basically his father. He'd been with Anthony since birth; never leaving his side. There was never a time—"

"When did you tell him about Tyrone?" Ebony encroached taking another quaff of her water.

Carol drew a breath before answering. "The day after his twelfth birthday. I felt that he was old enough to understand then. Of course, he didn't believe me at first. I mean, why should he?"

"When did he start believing?"

"After moving to Atlanta," Carol answered. "I still kept up with Tyrone by watching his high-profile trials on T.V. This was something I was doing while we were messing around. Anyway, after seeing that Anthony wouldn't believe me, I started forcing him to watch Tyrone's trials with me. I can't say when he started to believe it but, somewhere along the way, he became obsessed with Tyrone. I couldn't pull him away from the TV whenever Tyrone was on it." She locked eyes with Ebony. "He even cried when he heard of Tyrone's death."

"So, my dad wouldn't take a paternity test?" Ebony wanted to know.

Carol shrugged her shoulders up and down. "I don't know. I mean, I don't think he would have. He'd already told me that he wanted nothing to do with my baby."

"There were other ways," said Ebony. "Unless technology wasn't as advanced as it is now."

"I really don't' have a clue as to how it was back then, opposed to now," she answered. "I couldn't tell you anything about—"

"When's the last time you'd spoken to Anthony?" Ebony interrupted.

"I think it was Wednesday," Carol rejoined. "He was saying something about a doctor coming to see him from Linkton County to get DNA samples. We automatically assumed it was your doing."

"It was."

"Did you find out anything?" Carol asked, now regarding the folder in Ebony's' lap for the first time.

Saying nothing, Ebony handed the folder over to the older woman. Though she was watching her facial expression for any signs of regret, Ebony could see Carol's hand tremble as she opened the folder up on her lap, and began reading the content of the one page document. For she just knew that the results were going to induce some kind of emotional response from the woman.

And just as she'd figured, tears finally cascaded down Carol's cheeks, which is what Ebony had anticipated.

***

"Man, my wife has to be the dumbest woman on Earth!" Big County asserted, upon entering the cell, pulling the door back to lessen the noise on the other side.

Anthony was lying on his bunk, reading an old urban street novel by Seven McCray, when his cellmate had entered. Though his eyes traveled along the words in the book, his mind wasn't fully grasping the story, being that it was preoccupied with thoughts of Janelle jutting him, and the visit he'd received from the DNA analyst. He figured that, in order for Ebony to send the doctor all the way from Linkton County, then she was actually considering his mother's story. This gave Anthony hope, because he really felt that Tyrone Davis was his biological father, and that, once Ebony gets confirmation, she would be willing to pull some kind of strings to help him out of his situation. He would just have to deal with Janelle and Marvin once he's back on the outside.

Although these thoughts were hindering him from enjoying his book, Anthony was kind of relieved to be interrupted by his cellmate. Big Country, who'd driven from his hometown in Savannah, Georgia, to be arrested for murder, had a keen sense of humor that would always lift

Anthony's spirts whoever he was down. So, gracious for the intrusion, Anthony closed his book, laid it on his chest, and regarded his 5'10, 282-pound friend with a feigned impassive look.

"What's the problem now?" Anthony asked, deliberately matching his tone with this visage.

"Remember when I told her to contact my lawyer, and ask about my new court date?" the big guy asked pacing back and forth in the small cell.

"I remember." Anthony answered.

"Well, she talked to the lawyer," Big Country went onto explain. "But she can't remember one damned thing the man said." He stopped to regard Anthony. "Can you believe that shit? She can't remember one brief conversation with my lawyer, but she can tell you everything about all the women I've cheated on her with."

"So, she went there again, huh?" Anthony asked, all too familiar with the petty altercations between the love birds.

"Did she!" Big Country's eyes had enlarged. "It's like she waits for me to call, just so she can throw it up in my face. I can't even call to check on the kids, without hearing the bullshit. When I call to wish her a happy anniversary, guess what I hear?

"Is that a rhetorical question?" Anthony asked, with raised eyebrows.

Big Country frowned. "I'm serious, man. This crazy woman just won't let up. I'm already facing life without parole. I figured she would consider that and, at least, have the decency to spare me the drama until we see how this gonna play out."

"I guess that comes with being a womanizer," Anthony offered with a grin. "You can't play both sides of the field. You're either gonna enjoy the fruits of God's creations, or pluck one from the tree, and cherish it for the rest of your life."

"That's the worst philosophy I've ever heard," Big Country stated, with a chuckle. "And don't even think about becoming a life coach."

Anthony displayed a hurt expression. "Why not?"

"Because you suck," Big Country answered, causing them both to laugh.

"Anthony Hudson," the P.A. system sounded beyond the cell's door. "You have an attorney visit. Anthony Hudson you have an attorney visit."

"Lucky bastard?' blurted Big Country. "Do you know how long I've been waiting to hear those words?"

"Not long enough, my friend," Anthony replied as he sat up, placed the book beside him, and began putting on his sneakers. "Besides, your lawyer has to come all the way from Savannah, which is not a short drive. You should know because you took that same drive just to check into the Fulton County Hotel. I mean, the jails in Chatham County can't be any worse than ours."

"You're a better comedian than you are a criminal," Big Country remarked. "And, I've never heard of a public defender visiting anybody on the weekend."

That statement caught Anthony off guard. He now studied his cellmate with a serious look. "You know what, Big Country? I haven't thought of that. Why would this piece of shit choose today to piss me off?"

"This could be good news, Anthony."

"On a Saturday?"

Big Country only shrugged.

Anthony stood. "Whatever it is, I'm sure as hell about to find out."

Upon leaving the cell, Anthony's mind wrestled with a multitude of reasons for this extemporaneous visit from his court appointed attorney. Surely, it couldn't' be the notification of the demise of a family member because that imperative rests upon the jail's custodian, not the public defender's office. And, hearing about the death of one of his victims wouldn't do him an ounce of good. Being that there were several others, and the testimony of just one of them could send him to death row. So, as Big Country had predicted, maybe it was good news after all.

Pulling the door open to the attorney's booth, which was void of the electronic surveillance equipment as the others to ensure the attorney, client privacy afforded by the United States Constitution, Anthony stopped in his tracks. The person seated on the other side of the Plexiglass was not his attorney but was indeed unexpected. The eyes that stared back at him were full of familiarity, along with the expression that seemed highly impossible to penetrate.

"Trust me," the visitor spoke through the multiple holes in the glass. "I am not an apparition."

"You came." Was all Anthony cold muster as he entered taking a seat on the steel stool.

"I was in the neighborhood," Ebony explained. "And decided to stop by. Well, actually, I had just left your mother's house. She's a strong woman."

Anthony nodded. "Yes, she is. Though I've put her through a lot growing up, she still remains unbreakable. I have yet to see her lose her composure."

Ebony didn't respond.

Anthony decided to test the water. "I assume you've heard from the DNA analyst. What were the results?"

"Everything's still unclear right now," she answered, leaning forward, and interlocking her fingers on the protruding slab of concrete.

"You should be more worried about getting out of this hot mess you're in. Any idea on how you're going to do that?"

178

Anthony was shaking his head from side to side. "Not one. I was hoping you knew the right string to pull.."

"Is that the reason why you contacted me?"

"At first," he admitted. "My mom told me about Tyrone when I was old enough to understand. She made me watch his broadcasted trials on TV until he was murdered. I knew nothing about you until I saw you on TV, after losing the Brown's case. Initially, yes I was looking for a way out. But that gave way to my wanting to know more about the father I've never known."

"And, you figured I would be the one to fill you in," Ebony stated. "But, what if he didn't father you? In fact, I have a better question. Is finding out about a total stranger more important to you than getting out of here?"

Anthony was shocked by Ebony's line of questioning. Of course, he wanted to know more about the man he'd grown to believe was his father, but escaping the death penalty was irrefutably the most important thing to him at this moment. But, why did it seem as if she was giving him an ultimatum? Was she? Clearly, she would pretty much guess which of these he would choose, but why was she making him choose?

Whatever her motives were, had Anthony suspicious. And, he knew the only way to find out what they were, he had to play along with whatever game she was playing.

"I guess not," he finally answered with a shrug of his shoulders, "It's not like I knew him. My son is my number one priority right now."

Ebony nodded. "Smart man."

"So, how do you plan on getting me out of here?"

"I've never said that I was," she replied, checking her watch. "And, even if that was my intention, it would not be an easy task."

"What if we could convince the judge to grant me a change of venue?" Anthony asked, a hint of hope in his voice.

"It wouldn't do you any good."

"Why not?"

"Linkton County won't even wink at a case of this magnitude," she informed. "But, if I'm able to get you out of this, what are your plans."

Anthony remained silent for he'd never spoken his plans out loud to anyone.

"I see retribution in your eyes," Ebony acknowledged.

Anthony just stared back at her, though he wanted to divert his gaze.

She continued. "Whatever petty beefs you have, you might as well throw them on the backburner because, once your feet hit that pavement, I'll be the one to dictate your every move. You'll be in debt to me so, whenever you take a shit, you won't be able to wipe your ass without my permission. Do you agree to this verbal contract?"

"Maybe we need to—"

"Deal, or no deal?" she cut him off.

The look in her eyes seemed to convey a threat that sent chills up Anthony's spine. This was the same exact look he's periodically seen in Tyrone Davis's eyes while watching him on TV when he was younger. This same look is what had given him the impression that the late Assistant District Attorney Tyrone Davis was a dangerous human being. So, what of his daughter? Did the apple not fall too far from the tree? Did Ebony Davis really have it in her to carry out whatever implicit threat that was hidden deep behind the dark hue of her irises?

He finally opened his mouth to speak. "I um…"
****

Although the sun had descended over an hour ago, Ebony could still feel warmth in the light wind that assailed her upon exiting the Fulton County Jail. Entering the parking lot, enroute to her car, Ebony gazed up at the crescent shaped moon that hung in the dark sky as she mulled over the plan she'd fabricated while riding down on the elevator. She knew that it was a dangerous stunt to attempt. Not only was she putting her career on the line, but she was also putting her life in danger. Which would incontestably affect Samantha's. And, for what? To help Antony escape the death penalty, which is something he probably deserved. He's a total stranger to her. She could easily walk away from this, and never look back.

But, why did it seem like such a hard task?

Disarming her alarm, and starting her car by remote, Ebony slumped down into the driver's seat, and began her slow breathing technique, while mentally rehearsing her plan. Once coercing herself into accepting the consequence, she retrieved her cellular from the cup holder, and dialed Samantha's number.

"Hi, darling!" Samantha's voice boomed through the earpiece.

"Hi, babe!" Ebony responded, voice lacking emotion. "Are you busy?"

Samantha exhaled. "Not really, I was flipping through this lingerie catalog, but my mind was on Albert's party. Are you still indecisive about going?"

"That's what I was calling you about," Ebony told her. "I may need your help on picking out something to wear."

Chapter 20

Saturday

July 15, 2023

"You ever thought about transferring to Atlanta?"

Samantha's question pulled Ebony from her abstract musing. During the drive to Atlanta, she'd been envisioning herself carrying out the plan she'd concocted a week ago. There were two parts to it. She knew that if she could execute the first part similar to how she'd done in her mind over a hundred times, the second part would come with ease. She also knows that even if she's successful, it was still dangerous. Though she had wrestled with this assessment all week, Ebony still hasn't come up with a logical reason as to why she was taking such a risk.

"I've always thought about it," Ebony now answered for the passenger's seat of Samantha's BMW.

Glancing over at her friend. Ebony still couldn't get over how stunning Samantha was tonight, opposed to her everyday look. She was clad in a white dress that came down to her calves and accentuated her curve. Her matching three-inch heeled sandals showed off her flawless feet, and red painted toenails that seemed to bring out the color in her curly hair, in which she had pulled into a loose ponytail. She couldn't help it, but Ebony felt a twinge of jealousy, being that she knew that sole reason for Samantha's embellishment.

Samantha raised her eyebrows. "But?"

Ebony sighed. "I don't know. Maybe it was just a thought. A fantasy perhaps."

"Maybe it has something to do what your father," Samantha offered, keeping her eyes on the road.

"How so?"

"He became a legend in Linkton County," she answered. "Maybe you wouldn't feel right going anywhere else, when you could carry on his legacy in the same domain."

"That could be true," Ebony acknowledged. "But right now, I'm making him look bad."

Samantha chuckled. "Girl, if you think your father came in the door winning all of his cases, then you are highly delusive. He went through the same thing every other prosecutor went through as a rookie. Somewhere along the way, I guess he stumbled upon the most luckiest rabbit's foot on Earth."

Ebony couldn't help but laugh at Samantha's epigram.

"Hell," Samantha resumed. "That's how the storytellers make it seem. Hearing a story about your father is tantamount to hearing about the tooth fairy, and Saddam Hussein."

Ebony regarded her, "Saddam Hussein was a real person."

"Have you ever seen him?" Samantha asked, casting a glance over at her friend.

"Of course, not."

"My point, exactly," replied Samantha. "The things we've heard about Saddam's deportment, sounds like something out of a storybook. It's the same when people hear of the notorious Tyrone Davis. You get what I'm saying.

Ebony nodded. "I get it."

She directed her attention to the governor's mansion, where Samantha had pulled her car into the extended driveway, and joined the line of vehicles that were slowly moving along in search of a place to park. To Ebony, the ten-bedroom home wasn't all too alluring at this time of the hour, being that it was still daytime. She found it more so at nighttime, when it's multiple array of lights made it look like something off a postcard. Though the place was always a beautiful sight, at this moment it appeared an ominous structure in Ebony's eyes.

"Ready?" Samantha asked, after parking and shutting off the engine.

"As ready as I'll ever be," Ebony put on an energetic front. "You just remember not to drink too much. I'm not playing designated driver again."

"Yes, Mommy," Samantha replied, in a child's voice, conveying a broad smile.

"I'm serious." Ebony dismounted, stuffing her cellular into her dark blue Kimberly Mac clutch bag that matched her ankle length Kimberly Mac evening gown. In lieu of resuming with the caliginous color, she adorned her feet with gold spaghetti strap sandals that displayed her pink-polished toenails. After smoothing her dress down with the palms of her hands, Ebony circled around to the rear of the car, joining Samantha, who was replacing her compact into her own clutch bag.

"How do I look?" Samantha asked cupping her surgically done breast that threaten to spew from the top of her dress.

"Like a porn star from the nineties," Ebony answered, jokingly.

Samantha smiled. "Good! That's definitely the look I was going for. Maybe Albert won't need his pills tonight."

"That's entirely too much information," Ebony replied, a disgusted look on her face.

They both moved toward the entrance and joined the line of well-dressed socialites. As they waited, Samantha chatted away with an actor and his wife, while Ebony went over her plan inside her head once more, That's when she realized that she'd forgotten one thing. Time. While spending the whole week colluding, not once did she reflect on timing, which is most essential to her execution. Now, she was wondering if she should chicken out, and try something else. But, what else could she possibly try that would produce such an affect as this one?

"Good evening, ladies!"

"Good evening, Sanchez!" Samantha returned the greeting of one of the governor's bodyguards, when they'd reached the entrance. "How's the newborn?"

"Very good," he answered, with the smile of a proud father. "Right now, she's teething."

"Aww!" Samantha placed a hand on his arm. "I bet she's the most prettiest thing in the world."

"She's a doll," Sanchez concurred, his cheeks turning crimson.

Once their names were checked off on the roster, and they'd cleared the security process, Ebony and Samantha were led down the marble floored corridor, and into the ballroom, where a live jazz band was performing an old song by Amine Chance. The crowd of people already in attendance moved about the vast room conversing, and enjoying appetizers, and alcoholic beverages that were brought around on serving trays by the governor's hired servants.

"Thank you, sir!" Samantha received two glasses of champagne from a passing servant, passing one to Ebony. "Try not to get drunk off this one glass, dear. I will not play seeing eye dog on our way back to the car."

"Very funny," Ebony mumbled as they continued walking purposefully in the direction of the governor, who was standing with his wife, and another couple.

"Hello, ladies!" he greeted, once they'd gotten closer.

"Hello, Mr. Spires," Samantha took the initiative.

"This is an informal event," he told her. "Jennifer and I would like to be referred to by our first names. "

Samantha nodded.

"I remember your face," Albert asserted, as if he wasn't highly acquainted with Samantha. "You're a news reporter, right?"

"Assistant district attorney," she played along. "I'm Samantha Gordon, and this is Assistant District Attorney, Ebony Davis."

"She sure is," the governor's wife seemed to come alive with animation as she stepped forward, extending a hand to Ebony.

"How do you do?"

"I'm fine, thank you!" Ebony replied, shaking the older woman's wrinkled hand that was manicured, and decorated with a wedding ring that looked as if it was in the same price range as the mansion.

"I knew you looked familiar," Jennifer went on. "My stylist and I had watched the Brown's trial from the beginning to the end. And, despite the outcome, you did a splendid job."

Ebony smiled genuinely. "Why, thank you!"

"I think she's your number one fan," Albert said of his wife, sparking laughter from the small group.

"Good Evening, my fabulous looking people."

Lance Stephens was the last person Ebony wanted to encounter tonight. While everyone else greeted the comedian, she rolled her eyes, and looked in the opposite direction, wishing that she was invisible to him at this moment. It's not that she didn't like him. In fact, she thought he was very handsome, with his medium-brown complexion, and dark, low cut, wavy hair. It was just that, after meeting at the governor's party three years ago, he would always bird dog her at subsequent parties, being that the governor has been hiring him to perform his comedy acts. Lance was good at making Ebony laugh, which was something she admired bout him but, tonight, she was not in the mood to laugh, nor be smothered. Now, she has to find a way to *"stiff-arm"* him without hurting his feelings.

"I hope you have new material for us tonight, Mr. Lance." Ebony heard the zaftig governor say.

"Of course," he replied. "That's the good thing about hanging out at the comedy clubs on amateur nights—you get to steal material from the wannabes and make a fortune off of it before they could.

"Doesn't that make you a criminal?" asked Jennifer.

"I don't know," Lance answered, as if he was pondering. "Would something like that make me a criminal, Ms. Ebony Davis?"

Damn! Ebony thought, but turned, and regarded him with a plausible smile. "I don't know, Mr. Lance Stephens. I don't make the rules. I only prosecute the ones that break them," he replied, then addressed the others. "Do you mind if I borrow Ms. Davis for a moment?"

"Spoken like a true prosecutor," he replied.

"Not at all," Samantha prompted, beaming at Ebony. "She doesn't have a curfew, so she can stay as long as she wants."

Ebony glowered at Samantha as she allowed Lance to lead her away with her arm looped around his. After getting them fresh glasses of champagne, he led her through the large, floor to ceiling glass door and onto the patio that overlooked the vast yard that seemed to stretch until infinity. Releasing his arm, Ebony took a gander at the other people gathered along the extensive patio, before perching upon the stone balcony, taking locus to where she could keep an eye on the happening on the inside.

"So, how's that situation of yours going?" Lance asked as he took a seat beside her, his cologne commingling with the aroma of her drink.

"My relationship is just fine, Lance," she lied, taking a sip from her glass.

Lance studied the side of her face. "The last time we talked, you said..."

"That was almost a year ago, "she cut him off. "At that time, Jason and I were going through some things, like any other couple. Yes, I said that I was going to leave him, but I didn't. We've settled our differences, and things have been going pretty well. Thanks for asking, how's your marriage?"

"It's finally over," Lance answered, taking a sip of his drink. "We chose to separate, instead of going through the divorce process which would be one big one headache. The kids remain with Shonte', and I still see them whenever I want. When I'm not on the road."

As Lance carried on about the episode that he referred to as his life. Ebony kept her eyes on Governor Albert Spires, who gracefully sauntered his 5 foot 9, 260 pounds frame around the large room, greeting, and making small conversations with his guests. His frail-looking wife trailed along. Though they appeared the ideal couple to the public, Ebony knew better. She knew of dark secrets that surrounded the whole Spires family. Secrets that Albert had sworn Samantha to secrecy about.

Thinking of Samantha, Ebony scanned the vast room for her friend. It had taken a while to do so, being that there were at least, ten other red-headed white women in the vicinity. But, the bright-haired woman she was looking for, was at one of the tables, helping herself to appetizers, and engaged in conversation with another female. As Ebony watched Samantha, she felt a pang of regret for what she was anticipating. She would never deliberately harm Samantha, nor jeopardize what compact she has with the governor, but her collusion made these things inextricable.

".... in South Carolina," Lance was saying. "If I decide to pursue acting, I'll end up selling it, or renting it to my brother and his wife."

Ebony finally regarded him, "What time do you go on?" I can't wait to hear the newly stolen material."

Lance smiled, causing the dimple in his chin to deepen. "Maybe I should have kept that part to myself."

Ebony giggled.

"I'll go once the band takes a break," he answered her query. "Hell, with the kind of money Albert's paying them, they'll play all damn night!"

"What about you?" she inquired. "I'm quite sure he pays you a nice piece of change also,"

"Of course," replied Lance. "Hell, I'll rearrange my whole schedule to be here. I'll even skip my own funeral. You ever seen somebody do that?"

Ebony was laughing. "No, I can't say I have."

"It happens," Lance insisted. "My mean ass grandfather tried it. My brothers and I were happy when he finally kicked the bucket, but that stubborn bastard would not stay dead. He was the first dead person I'd ever seen sit up in a casket at a funeral. We were like, hell, no! Lay your ass back down! We wrestled him down, and nailed the coffin shut. That had become a ritual. When it's over, it's over. Don't be trying to come back. We'll see your ugly ass on the other side."

This had Ebony laughing hysterically. Through her mirth, she checked her watch, and realized that they'd been out on the patio for over an hour. It had gotten dark, which was something that seemed to magnify her anxiety, being that she was insensible of what time she would make her move. She knew that she only had one shot at this. If her timing was off, it would torpedo her whole plan.

"Lance," she finally spoke, "Would you excuse me? This MiraLAX is still working on my system."

"You took a laxative on the day of the dinner?"

Ebony stood, placing her clutch bag over her stomach. "Actually, I took it yesterday. I'm still feeling the effects of it."

"Just don't forget to wash your hands," Lance quipped, forming a disgusted look on his face.

"I'll try not to forget."

Ebony relinquished her empty champagne glass to Lance, then re-entered the palatial ballroom, intent on dodging Samantha and Albert as she subtly moved through the throng of attendees. She was doing a good job of avoiding them, but she was periodically stopped, and greeted by people she'd held conversations with at prior gatherings at the mansion. The encounters seemed to take forever, but Ebony had finally managed to make it to the entrance, and into the corridor, where she was sure to run into another member of Albert's security detail. But, the guy who was stationed outside the ballroom, earlier, was further down the hall towards the front entrance. To Ebony, it appeared that other members of the detail were having an issue with one of the guests, and he had gone to assist.

Not waiting around to see what it was all about, Ebony ventured off in the opposite direction, which was the same direction of the two bathrooms that were reserved for the current guests. Making it to the one that had the sign that signified female on its mahogany door, she rapped on it with her knuckles. getting no reply. She turned the gold plated knob and pushed the door open. Immediately upon entering, she extinguished the light to prevent the rays from spewing out into the hall. Leaving the door open, she extracted her compact makeup kit from her clutch bag and used its mirror to see in the direction in which she'd come.

Seeing that the security members were still busy with the guest, Ebony wasted no time. She exited, and continued in the opposite direction, moving at a casual pace as she replaced her make-up kit, and tried her best not to look back.

Making it to the top of the carpeted stairwell that curved like a half-moon, Ebony, thankful for Samantha's detailed delineation, made a right, and proceeded to the last door at the end of the hall. Stopping, she finally allowed herself a look back to see if she could hear any movement beyond it. Though she was being cautious, she felt a bit asinine, remembering what Samantha had said about Albert not allowing anyone inside this particular room.

She just hoped it wasn't locked.

After taking another gander down the hall, Ebony turned the knob, and cautiously eased the door open. Entering, she closed the door behind her, and stood there taking in the sight of the bedroom that was analogous to a suite at a five-star hotel. It conveyed a mini bar, snack bar, jacuzzi, an extremely large flat-screen television, and built in wall fish tank with some exotic-looking fish that Ebony know nothing about. The rose petals sprinkled all over the floor and bed, brought erotic thoughts to her mind. The thought of Albert Spires grinding his bulky frame on top of Samantha, projected an image that churned her stomach.

Forcing the objectionable thought from her mind, Ebony crossed the room to the bathroom, where the door was wide open. And just as she'd expected, the place looked as if it had been incessantly sterilized with no subsequent use. She didn't want to precede Albert and Samantha by introducing her very own microorganisms, but she didn't know when she'd get another chance to drain her bladder. Therefore, she took advantage of the opportunity.

After using the toilet, and rinsing her hands with plain water, Ebony used one of her Santi-wipes to dry the sink back off. Exiting, she made her way to the closet, and slid the double doors laterally in opposite directions. She sighed aloud to see that the commodious closet was empty, though for some odd reason she expected to see whips, chains, and paddles of all shapes, sizes, and color, hanging up. It being carpeted was also a plus, because she had mentally prepared herself to sit on the concrete for an indefinite amount of time, which was her way of expecting the worst.

Not knowing how much time she had before anyone shows up, Ebony entered the closet, and pulled the doors shut, but left a gap big enough for her to see the bed. She had to pull the hem of her dress up to her buttocks in order to sit Indian style on the floor. After removing her shoes for a little more comfort, she extracted her cellular from her bag.

"Skyfone," she spoke into it. "Activate Airplane mode."

"Airplane Mode activated," the device responded.

Turning the brightness down on her phone, Ebony placed it in her lap and thought about the meeting she'd had with Rick and Bull last Tuesday, at the house on Wilkins. In the beginning, Bull did apprise her that he was in charge of her father's drug operation but, when he'd approached her about having contacted a connection who would supply her with Marijuana and Crush, she had insisted that Rick handle all transactions. And, just as she'd expected, Bull threw a tantrum, saying that Rick wasn't prepared to deal with these types of people. He argued that since he's the one who's contacted the supplier, he should handle everything on that end, but Ebony remained steadfast. Now, ruminating on the menacing look he'd given her, she couldn't let it go. After he fulfills his end of their consensus, he would definitely be stamped with an expiration date.

The sound of the bedroom door being closed, brought her back to the future. Ebony leaned to the side to secure a view of whomever had entered. She didn't know where Samantha had gone, nor what she was doing until, seconds later, she heard the faint sound of urine splashing onto the water in the toilet. Then, there came the flushing of the toilet, ensued by water running from the sink's faucet. Moments after the water was shut off, Samantha came back into view, dropping her handbag onto the small table beside the bed, and stepping out of her shoes. As if her dress didn't cost close to two hundred dollars, she pulled it over her head and tossed it to the floor, revealing that she had on nothing underneath it, in which Ebony had already inferred.

As if working on her seductiveness, Samantha slowly crawled onto the bed and rolled around in the rose petals, before lying on her back, and rubbing them all over her body. Ebony was so turned on, she didn't know that her hand was slowly making it's way to her vagina. That was until her wrist brushed against some hard object resting in her lap. That's when she remembered her cell phone, and her purpose for being there. She picked it up and, as she fumbled with the features on the dim screen, she heard the bedroom door open and close, followed by its lock being secured.

"Sorry to keep you waiting, beautiful," Albert said, as he came into view, unbuttoning his shirt while looking down at Samantha. "I hope you didn't start without me."

"I wouldn't do that," Big Daddy," Samantha purred, now rubbing her clitoris, and licking the nipple of one of her breasts.

The broad smile on the governor's face could have belonged to a child on Christmas day. The video recorder in Ebony's' phone was already in motion when he tossed his shirt to the floor, kicked off his shoes, and began taking off his pants. Ebony did all she could to suppress her laughter, while regarding Albert's stomach that seemed to overlap his belt buckle by eight inches but, when he'd finally doffed his underwear, she had to parry the bile that rose up to her throat. For, Ebony was highly grossed out by Albert's form. Not only did his penis look as if it belonged on a five-year-old, but the discoloration of it gave the impression of some kind of cutaneous disease. She couldn't see how Samantha could bring herself to touch it, let alone put it in her mouth.

Ebony cringed at the thought of the bizarre scene she was about to witness, hoping she had the stomach to endure it.

***

Getting home, Ebony pulled into their garage, and sat there listening to the engine hum as the garage door closed behind her. During her drive, she was tempted to view the footage of Samantha's and Albert's coition on her cell phone. A part of her wanted to just to make sure the images came out clear but another part of her was reluctant to relive the quaint episode she'd had to endure for, at least, ten minutes. However, knowing that having an accurate and sharp picture quality was a plus when conducting the second half of her plan, Ebony decided to go ahead and view it .

Shutting off the engine, she disconnected her cell phone from it's chargers, and powered it. Before she could re-enhance the brightness of it, she heard the sound of the side door slam into the wall. Ebony looked up to see Jason entering the garage in a mincing stride. His facial features were contorted, and the look in his eyes was frightening. Ebony automatically knew that he was under the influence of drugs and alcohol, and that there was no way she would be able to circumvent an imminent confrontation.

"Get your ass out of the car!" Jason demanded, now yanking on the handle of her driver's door that wouldn't budge, being that all doors were still locked.

Drawing a breath, Ebony calmly placed her phone into her clutch bag, unfastened her seat then retrieved her keys from the cup holder. Usually, her hands would be trembling from fear. Right now, her mind was at ease, and her body seemed to have developed a steely feel that defied the definition of fear. With her keys and bag in tow, Ebony pressed the lock release, and grabbed the door handle. Jason stepped back to avoid being struck by the door but, once Ebony had dismounted, he immediately pounced on her, pinning her back to the frame of the car and wrapping his hands around her neck in a death grip.

"You went out on a date, huh?" he accused, his face just inches away from hers, breath smelling of alcohol, and hint of vomit.

"Get your hands off me, Jason," she spoke through clenched teeth, locking her eyes onto his.

Jason tightened his grip around her neck. "Answer the damn question! You got yourself a new boyfriend? What? You can't talk? If I break your frail ass neck, you won't' be able to—"

What happened next was fueled by pure adrenaline. Letting her keys and bag fall to the ground, Ebony formed her hands into claws, and assailed Jasons, sinking all ten of her polished fingernails into whichever parts of his face she could reach. Jason yelled out in pain as he released his grip on her neck and regressed in an endeavor to escape the assault. But Ebony was relentless. With her hands now balled into fist, she stepped forward with a cannonade of wild punches, knocking him into the garage's wall. Blood drained from Jason's nose and mouth, but Ebony was incapable of pity at his moment. As soon as his back made contact with the ground, she hitched up the bottom of her dress, raised her right leg, then brought the heel of her sandal down into his groin with all her might sending him into another fit of anguish.

With Jasons cries echoing in her ears, Ebony turned gathered her keys and bag off the ground, slammed the drivers' door of her car, then marched into the house with a new mission in mind. She knew that what she was about to do would change her whole life completely, but she was already committed. There was no turning back. At this time, she should've been thinking more rational. She should have been thinking about her career, her grandmother, her dreams of having children of her own. But, all she could think about was the demise of Jason Bryant.

Entering the bedroom, Ebony kicked off her sandals, tossed her bag and keys on the bed, and made for the closet, where she had to stand on the tip of her toes in order to rummage around in the shoe boxes on the shelf. Finding the intended box, she dug inside, allowing her hand to rest momentarily on the cold steel of her handgun. With her mind still on her mission, she attained a firm grip on the weapon, slowing pulling it from the box. Feeling a sense that someone was behind her, Ebony panned around, and gasped at the sight of the blood all over Jason's face that was inches away from her own. On instinct, she attempted to raise the gun, but Jason's hand was quicker. Everything seemed to move in slow motion as his fist seemed to increase in size as it got closer to her face. On impact, Ebony could have sworn she'd heard the gun go off, but wasn't so sure because everything had suddenly gotten dark. The last thing she felt was her numb body crashing onto the floor.

Chapter 21

Wednesday

"You're back!"

This was Ebony's first day back to work since the previous Friday. After sustaining injuries from the altercation she'd had with Jason, on Saturday, she knew that she would need a few days to nurse her wounds. Calling, and complaining of a stomach virus, District Attorney Barbara Hutchins only bided her two days off, and insisted that she return with a written doctor's excuses. That was when Ebony thought she'd put her foot in her mouth, until Dr. McAdams suddenly crossed her mind. And, to her surprise, he was more than willing to falsify the required document for her, plus bring it out to the house.

Ebony was thankful for his generosity, but precarious of his insistence on driving out of her home, being that Jason was already accusing her of finding someone else. Therefore, she chose for the parking lot of a grocery store. She had expected McAdams to question her swollen face, and pierced bottom lip, but he didn't. Though he had an inquisitive look on his face, he handed her the document, wished her a good day, and went on about his business. Again she was thankful.

Now, as she approached the courthouse carrying her briefcase, keys, and cellphone, she encountered Samantha, who was standing out front, confabulating with one of the stenographers. Ebony knew that she was going to run into Samantha sometime today, but she didn't expect it to be this early, being that she would usually be able to make it to her office without being bothered. Well, today wasn't one of those days. And it was incontestable that Samantha was going to bombard her with a million and one questions.

"I'll catch up with you later, Brenda," Samantha told her company.

"Okay," the court reporter responded then headed inside.

Samantha now regarded Ebony with narrowed eyes. "Stomach virus, huh?"

Ebony looked away.

"The sunglasses are always a dead giveaway, Ebony," she resumed. "At first, the stomach virus was cogent, considering how you claimed to be feeling after the dinner party. Then, when you didn't return any of my calls or texts, I started to rule that out. I don't' have to say what my next thought was, do I ?"

Ebony now faced her. "Can we not discuss this right now, Sam?"

'Why do you continue to put up with his shit, Ebony?"

"Why can't we discuss this later?" asked Ebony. "I have a lot of catching up to do. Plus, I have to drop this doctor's excuse off to Ms. Hutchins."

Samantha shot her a questionable look.

"We'll talk about it later," Ebony promised.

They both entered the building and rode the elevator up to their floor in silence. Ebony knew that Samantha wasn't going to let the situation with her and Jason go, which was why she'd already prepped herself for the conversation they would have over lunch. For it was imperative that she made a full attempt to manipulate Samantha's thoughts of Saturday's event and assuage some of the resentment she felt towards Jason.

Parting ways, Samantha made for her office. As Ebony made for Barbara Hutchins'. As always, the head district attorney's door was standing wide open and she was seated behind her desk, sifting through the contents of a manila folder. Being that Barbara has always encouraged her subordinates to enter whenever her door is open, Ebony did just that. She approached the desk with the document from Dr. McAdams. Looking up from her folder, Barbara studied the piece of paper for a brief moment before evaluating Ebony.

"Is the sun out already?" she asked, receiving the document, as placing it on her desk as if she would look at it later.

"Migraine," Ebony answered. Over the years, she has grown accustomed to Barbara's sarcasm but, right now, she was not in the mood.

Barbara squinted as if she was trying to summon the ability to see through the dark lenses of Ebony's sunglasses.

"You're a good prosecutor, Ms. Davis. I would hate to lose you over some personal issues that you can't seem to get under control."

"I don't."

"We all have personal issues," Barbara cut her off. I'm not God. Therefore, I am in no position to judge you, or anyone else. But, whatever your issues are, you need to get them under control, or they'll destroy you."

Ebony didn't respond.

"And," Barbara resumed. "Don't worry about being behind on your caseload. Thanks to Gordon, Briggs, and myself, you can continue on as if you'd never been out."

"Briggs?" Ebony asked, not sure if she'd heard correctly.

Barbara smiled. "Well, of course. Monday was his first day back. I didn't ask him what he was going through because, whatever it was, he didn't let it get him down." Now, there was a pensive look on the older woman's face. "In fact, I've never seen him so energetic. Perhaps, you should ask him what his secrets Who knows? Maybe it could work for you also."

"I'll keep that in mind, Ms. Hutchins," Ebony vowed. "Is the anything else before I began my day?"

Barbara made a face. "I'm afraid not. We're still waiting the case from Bibb County."

"The rape case?"

Barbara nodded.

"Why is it taking so long for the District Attorney's office to release it? Ebony asked.

'I have no idea," answered Barbara. "I don't have the authority to rush them, but I do think I'll place a call to them today and see if I could speed up the process. And, speaking of which, Briggs asked if he could take the case."

Ebony narrowed her eyes behind the dark lenses. "And you told him that it was already taken, right?"

Barbara looked away.

"So, you sold me out?"

"That's such a harsh term," Barbara insisted, now regarding Ebony.

"Well, what term do you prefer? Ebony was heated now. She couldn't believe what Barbara Hutchins was doing. She was basically handing Corey Briggs the D.A.'s position on a silver platter.

"You make it sound as if I've sold out into slavery," the district attorney replied, with a hurt expression on her face.

"I'm actually giving you a break, considering that I' not fully sensible of what you're going through. I don't need you having a nervous breakdown."

"Like Corey Briggs, right? Ebony knew that she was skating on thin ice, but no longer cared. "If I remember correctly, I don't' recall you giving *HIM* a break.

"That's because I didn't see it coming," Barbara purported. "Hell, I don't think any of us saw it coming. Whatever Briggs was going through, he did a good job at hiding it, unlike yourself. For the past few weeks, you've being showing telltale signs of a disaster waiting to happen. Those sunglasses are always a dead giveaway. If it's an addiction, and you're willing to take steps to overcome it, I can contact—"

"I think you're reading too much into this," Ebony intervened. "I attended a dinner party at Governor Spire's mansion on Saturday. Yes, I consumed a variety of alcoholic beverages, and pretty much ate something that didn't agree with my stomach, which prompted the stomach virus, and hangover that spawned the migraine. And as for an addiction, or personal issue, there aren't any."

Barbara raised her hands in mock surrender. "Okay, Okay! I can only take your word for it. I know I promised you the case, but promises are meant to be broken. However, it's not the end of the world. If you could find it in your heart to forgive me, I'll do everything in my powers to make it up to you."

Ebony marched out of Barbara Hutchins' office, disgruntled. She didn't expect for Briggs to return to work after the ordeal he and his family had gone through, and she definitely didn't expect for him to become a cardinal threat to the position that was knowingly promised to her. In the beginning, all Ebony ever wanted to do was to master the art of prosecuting criminal cases like she'd seen her father do several times on TV when she was younger. But now thanks to Rick and Bull, who'd opened her eyes to a power she never thought she could possess, she felt that the District Attorney's position shouldn't go to anyone other than herself.

All threats should be eliminated!

"Good morning, Ms. Davis!" Deputy Taylor, who was conversating with Judge Jackson, greeted Ebony when she entered the courtroom.

Though Taylor's greeting was accompanied by an exceptionally warm smile, Ebony only nodded as she approached the State's table, where she pulled documents she'd retrieved from her office out of her briefcase, before taking a seat. She was cognizant of the stares, that she was getting from Taylor, Jackson and the typist, but made a show of sifting through her case files in an attempt to ignore them.

"Are You still coming down from the flu?" the judge inquired.

"It was a stomach virus, Mr. Jackson," Ebony replied regarding him in his individual capacity, being that he had not yet donned his robe. "Right now," she continued, still feigning interest in her documents, "I'm trying to come down off the migraine."

"You have more migraines than migraines." Jackson pointed out. "Perhaps, you should have that looked into."

"He's right, Ms. Davis," Taylor chimed in. "My cousin went through the same thing. She thought they were migraines, until she made an appointment to see a doctor, and was told that she was suffering from a tumor that required immediate attention."

Ebony regarded them through the dark lenses of her sunglasses. "I will keep what you both said in mind," she promised. "Right now I need to know-"

"Good morning, everyone!"

Ebony's words were cut off by the exuberant greeting of Corey Brigg's, who'd gracefully marched into the courtroom as if he was about to announce that he'd won the lottery. Then, as if his happy go lucky demeanor wasn't annoying, Ebony found the abnormally wide smile plastered on his face, sickening. She watched as she vigorously shook the hands of Deputy Taylor and Judge Jackson, and winked at the typist, who visibly turned red with a blush. Not once did he look in Ebony's direction

"What's the word for today, Briggs?" Taylor asked.

"Golf," he replied, pretending to tee up before swinging an invisible golf club. "That's if you gentleman have any kind of skills."

"You don't find too many black people playing golf these days, Briggs," Judge Jackson asserted.

"Nonsense!" the assistant D.A. contended. "I was just at the Country Club this past Saturday, and there were black people, male and female, all over the golf course."

"Caddies don't count," Taylor said with a smile.

"They were golfers," Briggs replied, returning the smile. "I mean, if you guys can't take being beaten by little old me, I can understand that."

"And, how long have you been playing?" Inquired Jackson.

Briggs answered. "Since Saturday. I'm still going through training, and I was hoping you guys would join me this Saturday. It's a big stress reliever."

Jackson exchanged glances with Taylor, before shrugging and saying, "I guess you can count me in."

"Great!" Briggs looked to Taylor. "And, you?"

"I don't own any golf clubs."

"Neither do I," Briggs told him. "That's why they have rental. I have a membership card, so I'll take care of that."

"Well," Taylor responded, "Since you put it that way, you can count me in also."

"Great!" He shook their hands. "I'll see you men on Saturday."

With another wink at the typist, Briggs made for the exit with only a slight nod in Ebony's direction, which she didn't care to respond to. But she immediately noticed that the radiant smile he'd entered with, had been replaced with a villainous sneer. Ebony didn't want to read too much into it but, before his daughter's abduction, Briggs had never given her such a look. Surely, he couldn't know who was behind that. She thought.

Or could he?

***

"I'm listening," Samantha said, after she and Ebony had chosen a table, and sat down with their lunch.

It was 12:45pm when Judge Jackson called a recess. Being that Samantha was out of court chores for today, she could pretty much break at her leisure. Therefore, Ebony made sure to find her before heading for the cafeteria. Time was of the essence, so she knew that it was imperative that she have this talk with Samantha today.

"I know how you feel whenever Jason and I have our skirmishes," Ebony spoke at a length, dancing the fork around in her salad. "But he's not to blame for this one."

"So, you beat yourself up?"

Ebony scowled at her friend. "I thought you were listening."

"Sorry!" Samantha offered, before biting into her turkey sandwich.

"Anyway," Ebony resumed. "When I returned home that Saturday night, Jason was doctoring on some cuts that were not on his face before I left that morning. His bottom lip was bleeding, and the right side of his face was swollen when I asked him about it, he told me to leave him alone. But I was relentless. I followed him around the house, until he finally told me that he'd gotten into an altercation with some guys he owes money to for drugs. That pissed me off, because he told me that he was done with drugs. He wouldn't tell me what his debt, only that the interest had went up. That's when I exploded. I attacked him with all my might, while thinking about how he'd let these hoodlums know where we lay our heads."

"They came to the house?" Samantha had a frightened expression on her face.

"That's what he said," Ebony answered, taking a sip of her tea.

"Anyway, he got tired of me beating up on him, and defended himself. Had I never hit him, he would have never hit me."

Samantha shot her an incredulous look.

"That was his promise," Ebony expounded, knowing she sounded like a naïve schoolgirl. "I brought this on myself, Sam."

Samantha waved a dismissive hand. "Okay. And, where'd you get that beautiful ring from?"

"It's an engagement ring." Ebony smiled and held out for Samantha to get a better look at the diamond studded ring on her finger, but had her eyes on Attorney Ellen Martinez, who was passing behind Samantha, carrying a tray with the food she'd ordered.

"Jason proposed to you?" Samantha asked, regaining Ebony's attention.

'Right after the fight," she replied, cutting her eyes at Martinez, who's sat at the next available table beside theirs.

"I don't know how long he's had it, but he claimed that he was waiting or the right time."

"Well, he sure as hell picked the darndest time." Samantha offered with a simper. "Are you really gonna marry him?"

Ebony sighed out loud. "Honestly," she began, "Despite what we've been through, I can't see myself walking down the aisle with any other man. And, of course, you can help me plan the wedding."

While they conversed, and finished their meal, Ebony, thankful for the dark lenses of her sunglasses, periodically cast a glance over at Martinez, who'd been doing the same. As always, the attorney seemed timid, but Ebony didn't see any reason for Martinez to be this way around her. Yes, she was sure that Ellen Martinez and Tyrone Davis may have had something going on between each other, but that was beyond her. It was still no reason for the attorney to act the way she did whenever she was in Ebony's presence. Unless, there was another reason why Martinez was reluctant to maintain steady eye contact with Ebony.

Chapter 22

Pulling into her garage, Ebony parked beside Jason's car, and waited for the garage door to close, before shutting off the engine At this time, for some odd reason, she was half expecting Jason to emerge from the house like a bat out of hell in a drug induced rage. But as she stared at the undisturbed door for what seemed like an eon, she realized that he had better things to do besides beating up on her for no apparent reason.

Now, as she toyed with the faux engagement ring on her finger, she thought about the conversation she'd had with Samantha over lunch today. Ebony had never lied to Samantha, but it had to be done. For things were about to get very complicated in Ebony's life, which would entail more prevarications, split decision making, and occasional betrayals. Ebony has genuine feelings for Samantha, but she as highly aware that Samantha could become a casualty of something she has no knowledge of especially if Governor Albert Spires isn't too fond of being *caught with his pants down* in the privacy of his own home.

Leaving her briefcase on the passengers' seat, she dismounted, entered the house, and made for her bedroom, hoping not to run into Jason. Silently celebrating a successful journey, Ebony entered her bedroom, placed her pocketbook, cell phone and keys atop the dresser. Then, began undressing. Getting down to her panties and bra, she pulled a pair of leggings and sports bra from the dresser and donned them. While she was sitting on the edge of the bed, putting on her running shoes, she heard a loud thud come from another part of the house, which made her stop still and listen. But the house was as silent as it was when she'd first entered. This made her want to get Jason's location from the Sen-Tech monitor but, instead, she quickly tied her shoes, placed her cordless earbuds in her ear, grabbed her cell phone and hurried out of the bedroom, hoping to make it to the front door unscathed.

Ebony didn't count her journey as successful, until she'd stepped out on the porch, and closed the door behind her. This is when she realized that she'd forgotten her sweat band but made no effort to go back inside for it. Therefore, she powered up her cellular, selected her workout playlist, then lunged into her pre jog stretch routine, which took no more than two minutes. Done, she sprang from the porch and, as usual, trekked up the sidewalk at her normal pace.

***

He'd been parked across the street from the house since 5:42p.m., so he was there when her Cadillac pulled into the garage at 6:29pm, indicating that he didn't have long before it was time to carry out his mission. This brought on a bit of relief because the fumes from the colorless substance that barely filled half of the 24 oz glass bottle sitting in the cupholder, had him dizzy, and to the point of swooning, which is why he had the four widows of the stolen sedan slightly cracked, though it did him no justice. He'd forgotten the name of the substance but remembered being repeatedly cautioned on how to handle it, which from what he'd heard about it, had him fearing the proximity of the liquid. He wished he could just use his gun as always, but this was at his boss' behest.

While contemptuously staring at the bottle with the potion of a damp cloth dangling from the top of it, he saw movement out the corners of his eyes. Switching his gaze, he saw that she had stepped out on the porch and eased the door shut behind her as if to not alert her boyfriend. She was also now clad in a sports bra and leggings that accentuated her curvaceous figure. That turned him on being that he'd never seen her in such tantalizing gear, but he quickly

208

refocused his mind on what he'd come to do, while watching her stretch, which only took about two minutes.

When she jogged by on the other side of the street, he watched her in the rearview mirror until she was out of sight, before grabbing the bottle with one of his gloved hands and exiting the car. It's been a long time since he'd done a job in the daytime, so he hoped the disguise was foolproof against the prying eyes of anyone who didn't have anything better to do than to stare out their window all day, and watch the goings-on of the neighborhood. Then, of course he'd seen the *Neighborhood Watch* signs posted through the area.

Making it to the front door, he turned the knob, and entered, closing the door behind him. Pulling his handgun from the waistband of his pants with his free hand, he stood listening for any sounds of movement, while taking in the décor of the living room. The house was quiet, save for the ticking of the grandfather clock that he felt would look good in his very living room, amongst the items he'd spotted. But being that he wasn't here on a burglary run, he exited the living room, and approached the monitor in the foyer. After a second, it beeped, then "Sen-Tech" appeared on the screen.

"Sen-Tech," he spoke in almost a whisper. "Locate Jason."

"Locating Jason," came the computerized voice Then, an animated blueprint of the house appeared on the screen with a red indicator blinking at the lower part of it. "Jason located."

"He smiled, thinking how habitual creatures were always easy targets. In the dining room, where he tucked his gun, and grabbed one of the metal, cushioned chairs from the dining table. The door to the basement was just down the hall. Reaching it, he sat the chair down, and slowly pulled the door open, hoping that Jason wasn't on his way up. Thanks to a red glow emitting from below, he was able to see that the stairs were clear. Pulling a cigarette lighter from his pocket, he realized that his hands had started to tremble a bit, which could only be ascribed to his knowledge of the unknown substance he was about to ignite. But, being that he'd murdered more people than he could count on his fingers and toes, he let his killer instinct kick in, and flicked the lighter.

There was a loud whoosh sound as the cloth caught fire and was immediately consumed. Remembering what he was told about having zero to no time to disencumber the homemade weapon, he quickly tossed it down into the basement. The sound he heard while closing the door was something akin to a muffled explosion that vibrated the floor beneath him. Then, came the agonizing cry of Jason though another voice could be heard in the midst, which sounded like a non instrumental threnody.

With the back of the chair wedged under the knob of the basement's door, he made for the front door, thinking that he would have to get his hands on some of the highly combustible substance. Whatever it was called.

Chapter 23

Tuesday

It's been over two weeks since Anthony has heard anything from Ebony. He wasn't really worried, being that he didn't know what kind of outcome to expect from his situation. Sure, Ebony had given him post release instructions but, not once, did she assure him that his release was guaranteed. But, she was just a mere prosecutor from a small town of hillbillies, right? There's no way she would have an ounce of influence on any of the blood thirsty sharks at the district attorney's office in Fulton County. Maybe, Anthony was just hoping that one of her fellow alumni was fortunate enough to land in the huge shark tank and would be willing to do a favor for an old friend. Or maybe he was just desperately grasping at straws. Yes, that was it. So, what if Ebony can't pull this off? What if she's not even trying?

These thoughts were beginning to drive Anthony up a wall. It was already noon, and all he'd done all day was lie in bed, thinking about the unfinished business he had with Marvin and Janell. For he already knew what he wanted to do to Marvin but was still indecisive about his son's mother. Already sick with these thoughts, he forced himself out of bed, and began brushing his teeth, thankful that his cellmate, Big Country was out of the cell. At this time, he knew that this cellmate was out in the day room, watching the news with the other inmates. After washing his face, Anthony exited the cell, deciding that he would join the news watchers to see which one of Georgia dumbest criminals would be joining him on death row.

"Hell, her ass should've been in the house, too!" one of the inmates voiced as Anthony joined the crowd in front of the television.

Anthony directed his gaze to the tube, and thought he'd felt his heart drop to his stomach. He couldn't believe that he was looking at the face of Ebony Davis. And the defiant look he'd seen in her eyes, over two weeks ago, was replaced by a look of distress, as tears cascaded down her face that was illuminated by the bright light of the camera and flashing red and blue lights of the emergency vehicles.

"It was just crazy." Ebony was saying in a calm tone that didn't match her appearance, slowly shaking her head from side to side. "I went out for my routine jog and when I returned home, I saw…"

Ebony let out a sob, and more tears fell down her face as she looked in the direction of the flashing lights. Then, the camera panned, and zoomed in on a house that looked as if it had been strafed. Firefighters and what appeared to be a group of local residents seemed to having a hard time containing the fire that had consumed a large portion of ebony's red brick abode. It produced abnormally dark clouds from it's gold and blue flames that lashed out at the sky like a multitude of whips. When the camera refocused, Ebony was shown from her head to the thighs, in a sports bra and leggings, standing alongside a white, female reporter and more local residents in the background.

"Is it possible that you may have left the stove on?" the reporter asked, before titling her microphone in Ebony's direction.

Still looking off in the distance, Ebony slowly shook her head. "No, that's not possible. I don't cook until *after* my run. My fiancé' doesn't use the stove."

"And your fiancé was inside the house when you left?"

Ebony regarded the reporter with a look of realization. "He was asleep," she answered at a length, voice barely above a whisper. "I left him in there alone."

As she broke into another sob, an older, white woman, from the crowd behind them, moved into console her.

Momentarily, that image had become the image on the wall-screen behind the anchors at Atlanta's Fox 5 News station. The male and female anchors exchanged glances, before the anchorwoman proceeded to read from the teleprompter.

"Linkton Country officials say that the fire had broken out at the prosecutor's home around seven p.m. on yesterday," she promulgated. "As of now, it is still unclear as to how the fire started, and if there were any casualties, though the prosecutor claims that her fiancé was asleep inside the house when she'd went out for her routine run. We'll keep you updated on this story as it…"

"Her ass should've been in the house, too!" reiterated the inmate that was standing beside Anthony.

Anthony turned to the guy, who was of the same height, but slightly larger than his own 6'1, 172-pound frame. "Why would you say something like that?" he asked in the calmest tone he could muster.

The man regarded him with a look of bewilderment. "Why would I say something like that! Are you serious! She's a shit eating prosecutor like the rest of them! She sends people like us to prison. So yeah, her ass should've b.."

Before Anthony knew what he was doing, his left arm shot out like an attacking cobra, and his fist made contact with the guy's chin, knocking him out instantly. The other inmates were whooping with excitement, before the man's body made complete contact with the floor, but Anthony repudiated them as he made for the telephones. Seeing Ebony on the news had caused his hope for freedom to dwindle, well what little hope he had. Now, he was wondering if he should take the state's offer of life without parole or take his chances at a trial, he knew he couldn't win and come out with the death penalty instead.

"Hello?" Anthony's mother voice came through the phone, after accepting the collect call.

"Momma, you won't' believe this," he spoke, trying to contain his anger.

"I already know about it," she admitted. "That poor baby. Not only did she lose her home, she lost her fiancé as well. I know God already has plans for our lives, but I don't think any human being should suffer the way she's suffering right now."

"I need you to call her."

"No, Anthony! This is not an appropriate time to bother her. Besides, I only have the number at her job, and I don't think she'll be going to work any time soon, after what just happened. Give her some time."

Time? Anthony thought. This was something he didn't have much of. His heart went out to Ebony and her losses, but his sympathy wasn't going to help neither of them. If she hadn't already pulled the strings that she was going to pull to get him out, that's to say if there were strings to be pulled, then the State's offer and recommendation were the only optional outcomes Anthony had to depend on. And there was no way he could spend the rest of his life behind bars. For if this were to occur, then Marvin and Janelle would forever be reprieved for what they'd done to him.

He could not let this happen! There had to be another way!

Chapter 24

Saturday

"Ashes to ashes; dust to dust. From the dirt we're created; to the dirt we shall return. May God greet this young man with open arms when he..."

As the pastor drew near the conclusion of the eulogy, Ebony diverted her gaze from the urn upon the stand, to make a show of dabbing at her tearless eyes that were hidden behind the black veil attached to her hat that matched the dress she'd bought on Friday for this occasion. Already conversant with the cremation process and knowing that Jason's body would have to undergo this, once pulled from the remnants of the fire damaged house, Ebony immediately made an appointment with the Linkton County's crematorium, and funeral parlor in lieu of waiting to hear from the medical examiners. Plus, she had never met, nor knew how to get in touch with his parents who, supposedly, resides in Oregon, which pretty much made her Jason's next of kin.

Now, Ebony looked over at her grandmother who'd been holding her hand through the entire funeral session. Her eyes were red from grieving her granddaughter's loss, unlike her husband, who'd remained visibly clinical, though he held his wife's hand, just as she held Ebony's. To the right of Ebony was Samantha. After hearing about the fire, she'd begged Ebony to move in with her, until she gets her life back in order, but Ebony declined. Claiming that she needed to be alone, and would be staying at a hotel, pro tempore. But of course, she wasn't staying at anyone's hotel, being that she was now the owner of her father's old house on Wilkins, which is where she'd been holed up since the fire. Barbara Hutchins had granted her a two week's leave, and left her with the option to return earlier if she was up to it. The leave was much needed, being that Ebony had a lot of strategizing to do, but she was sure that she didn't need a whole two weeks to get the ball rolling.

"Ms. Davis?"

Pulled from her abstract musing, Ebony looked up to see that the pastor was holding the urn out to her. With the aid of Samantha and her grandmother, Ebony was on her feet, slowly moving toward the altar.

"May God's grace be upon you, my child," The paster asserted, tendering the urn to her. "And always remember that your dearly beloved is always smiling down on you form the high heavens."

Ebony was pretty sure that Jason didn't make it anywhere near heaven's gates, but accepted the urn, and the pastor's blessings with a nod, turned, and led her friend and grandparent toward the exit of the small church that was empty, save for the four of them. Outside, they were met by the bright sun and ninety-degree weather that made Ebony feel as if she was going to melt in her thick, fabric black dress They were also met by a white male of average height, clad in dark brown dress pants, black boots, and a dark blue blazer. He was leaning against one of the thin, steel handrails of the steps when they exited. Now, he was blocking their path, standing directly in front of Ebony.

"Ms. Davis," he spoke flashing what appeared to be a wallet containing a badge and photo identification. "I'm Investigator John Pruden, from the Linkton County's Department of Investigations, and I've been trying to reach you to get a statement from you in regards to the fire that was set to your home on Wednesday."

"Can't you see that this is not the right time, Inspector?" Samantha spoke up for her friend. "She's still grieving the loss of her fiancé. Have you any decency?"

He shifted his green eyes to Samantha, without a hint of interest. "You're Samantha Gordon. I have a few questions for you, also."

"I think not!" she snapped. "And, how dare you accost us at a funeral! How would you like it if—"

"Do you have a card, Mr. Pruden?" Ebony finally spoke, nudging Samantha with her elbow to shut her up.

"Sure." He produced two cards, handing one to Ebony, and holding one out to Samantha, who just stared at it.

"Take the card, Sam!" Ebony prompted.

Samantha began to protest. "But, I don't' see any reason why—"

"It's only routine." Ebony already knew what the investigator's intention were. And he didn't know that, by questioning Samantha, he would be playing himself right into her hands. This will be a piece of cake she thought to herself.

After Samantha had dropped Ebony off at the Steinberg Hotel in Macon, Georgia, where she claimed to be staying, Ebony climbed into her rental car and drove out to her new home on Wilkins Street, still wondering what she was going to do with Jason's ashes. For she definitely didn't want to cling to them like some age old widow, which, she thought would be incongruous for a woman for her age. Besides, she didn't love Jason that much.

Entering her home that she'd had refurbished over two weeks ago, Ebony deposited her urn on the coffee table in the living room, and made for her bedroom to change clothes. After finding a white sundress, and matching sandals, she rummaged through her overnight bag to make sure everything was there. While doing so, there was a knock at the front door. Already knowing who her visitors were, she retrieved a small, black pouch off the bed, and re-entered the living room, where she pulled the door open without inquiring on who was on the other side.

"That's exactly how people get abducted from their own homes," Rick asserted, in all seriousness as he entered, followed by Bull.

"I already knew it was you," Ebony replied, closing the door back.

"But what if it wasn't?" Rick's inflection exuded venom. Ebony knew that he meant well by his avuncular, like attitude toward her but, little did he know, it turned her on. Where most women would feel like scolded children, Ebony felt like a high school girl, who had a crush on her teacher. The age difference just made it all the more intriguing. But, she knew that he wouldn't cross the line with her, considering the loyalty he claimed to have had for her father. Or maybe he would.

"I'm sorry, Rick," Ebony said in a tone that she'd used on her father several times.

"Don't be sorry," he told her. "Be careful!"

She nodded, "I'll remember that. So, what's the word on the product?"

"He still wants thirty," Rick informed. "The stuff comes in on Tuesday night."

"Do you trust him?"

"Does a fish need a raincoat?" he tossed back at her. "We have three of your men riding out with us. They'll be hidden out of sight, only to reveal themselves if something goes wrong."

Ebony was confused. "My men? What men?"

"You have four, so far," Bull finally spoke.

"Do I get to meet them?"

"That wouldn't be wise," Answered Rick. "Being seen would only give them someone to point the finger at if things get hot."

"I see." She handed the pouch to Rick. "That's the thirty. Will this stuff need to cooked?"

218

"Not unless you plan on reducing the potency of it," he told her. Then, after a brief pause, he said, "Look, let Bull and I handle this end. You just worry about making it back in one piece. Did you pack your gun?"

"Yes, I did," she lied, now remembering that she'd forgotten to put the weapon into her bag.

"And, how long do you plan on staying?"

"I should be back by Monday night."

"Are you sure you don't want us to go with you?" Bull finally asked.

"I'll be fine," she answered, checking her watch. "In fact, I need to get going. Somebody from Sen-Tech Securities will be here on Monday, to install my security system. Rick, I'll need you to meet them here to let them in. Will you be available?"

"I should be."

"Oh!" she had almost forgotten. "Some, investigator was waiting outside the church for me earlier." She paused to see if she would get some kind of reaction from them. When she didn't get any, she continued. "I assume it's routine, but he claims that he needs to get a statement from me in regard to the fire."

"He actually approached you at the funeral?" Bull asked without a hint of surprise in his voice.

Ebony nodded.

"Was he Fed?" Rick wanted to know.

"No," she answered. "He was a local from the DOI."

"He came to the funeral," Rick pointed out. "Locals don't operate like that, unless they suspect foul play."

Now, Ebony was a bit worried "So, what do I do?"

"Play your part," he told her. "Make an appointment to make a statement. Do it in a public place, and only give a written statement. No recordings. This'll be the time for you to play mind games with him to see if you could get him to reveal his suspicions. But if he chooses to play his cards close to his chest, you'll have to trust your instincts."

"And, what if my instincts are telling me that he suspects me of Jason's murder?"

A smirk slowly creased Rick's visage. "Then, we'll have to pay him a visit."

Chapter 25

"Hello?" Ebony answered the phone in a groggy voice.

"This is your ten o'clock wake up call you've requested, ma'am," a female voice apprised.

"Okay, thank you."

Ebony slammed the receiver into its cradle and rolled onto her back to collect her bearings. For she could still feel the effects of the alcohol she'd consumed at the Downtown Bar & Grill last night. This caused her to reflect on one guy she was conversating with, who must've called her *shorty*, pronouncing it as *shawty*, over a hundred times, in less than three minutes, which was a major turn off. After brushing him off for his lack of vocabulary, she chose not to engage any other man in conversation, lest she be called shorty a hundred more times. But, she did acquire the young man's phone number.

Finally forcing herself out of the huge bed, Ebony padded bare feet across the plush carpet of the hotel room, to the bathroom, where he drained her bladder, showered and brush her teeth. Knowing she would need some caffeine to shake the rest of last night's spirits off, she now clad in a large bathrobe, compliments of the Marriott Hotel, flopped down on the bed, and phoned room service. She ordered one of their breakfast specials also, being that she would probably not have time to stop by a restaurant enroute to her appointment. Concluding that call, she grabbed her cell phone and dialed Rick's number after seeing the missed call from Samantha.

"Talk to me!" Rick answered momentarily.

"Did I wake you?" she asked.

He cleared his throat. "Not really. Is something wrong?"

"No." She smiled at his concern for her wellbeing. "I was thinking about Bull. He knows that the money is in the house. With there being no alarm, he—"

"That's already taken care of." He cut in. "I told him that I'll be staying there until you get back."

"But what if he decided to drive by and doesn't see your car?"

"My truck is parked in your driveway," he told her. "And I don't have to worry about him visiting me. We're not that cool."

Again, Ebony was astounded by Rick's quick thinking ability. It was clear that he knew Bull couldn't be trusted. He too knew that Bull would try to break into the house and steal the money that was hidden beneath the kitchen's floor. And he definitely knew Bull better than she did. For some odd reason, this made her wonder what he would be like as a husband and father.

"Rick?" she finally spoke.

"I'm still here."

"Do you have any children?"

"That's an unprofessional question," he answered, just as someone knocked on the hotel room's door.

"You're right," she said, pulling her handgun from under the pillow, and slipping it into one of the large pockets of the robe. "I'll see you when I get back."

"Be careful," he said, then rung off.

Tossing her cellular onto the bed, Ebony approached the door with her right hand jammed down inside her pocket and wrapped around the gun. "Who is it?" she asked, remembering what Rick had said about people getting abducted for opening their doors without identifying the visitor.

"Room service, "A female voice spoke back.

"Hi!" she greeted the brunette that stood out in the hallway with a pushcart containing her order "Come on in."

222

After paying the brunette a twenty dollar tip, Ebony sat down to eat her breakfast. She wanted to return Samantha's call, but figured she would do so while driving, being that the only things she could have time to do after her meal was get dressed, and brush her hair. Thinking of the impending call, made her think about the possible consequences of her mission, which sent chills down her spine. What will become of Samantha? What will become of herself? For she was dealing with a highly influential person, who has friends in high places, including the White House. As far as she knew, he could be one of the biggest crime bosses of the underworld. Where she only had Rick and Bull, he probably had dozens of indentured henchmen ensconced in different parts of the globe. So, again, why was she putting her life on the line for someone she knew nothing about?

"How are you feeling, baby?" Samantha asked upon answering her phone.

"I'll make it," Ebony replied, purposefully sounding dejected, while driving the Dodge Forum along the semi-busy expressway.

"Why won't you tell me what room you're in?" questioned Samantha. "It's bad enough that you checked in under a false name."

Ebony smiled. "I assumed you'd called the hotel."

"You know I did." She sounded a bit exasperated now. "I understand that you'd rather be alone at a time like this, but loneliness isn't always the answer. I'm worried about you, Ebony. I wish that you would, at least, allow me to come by and check on you from time to time?"

"I won't be here long," Ebony told her. "I plan on returning to civilization this week."

"Are you sure?"

"Of course," Ebony cleared her throat." Despite what I'm going through, I still have a life to live and a career to maintain."

"Where will you be staying?"

"I'll look for a place tomorrow."

Samantha seemed to linger before asking her next question. "Aren't you afraid that those guys may come after you next?"

"What guys?" Ebony asked, genuinely confused.

"The ones who killed Jason?" Samantha whispered, confidently.

Shit! Ebony thought she'd completely forgotten about *those guys.*

After taking a deep breath, she continued in her initial tone. "I don't think so. If they wanted me, they would have waited until we were both asleep. Apparently, they had been waiting at the house, because they waited until I had gone out on my evening jog to do what they did. Not like I know what they look like."

Samantha drew a breath. "I guess you're right," she concluded.

"And, what about the investigator? Why would he want to question me on something I know nothing about? And then, he calls out my full name as if we'd went to school together or something."

"He's just doing what investigators do," Ebony offered, delighted that Samantha had brought up the subject. "They try to interview as many people as they can before turning their findings over to their chiefs with their recommendations."

"So, I should give him a call?"

"Sure." She had just pulled into the lengthy driveway of the governor's mansion. "In the meantime, I need some rest. Thanks for checking on me, sweetheart."

224

"That's what I'm here for, baby," Samantha replied cheerfully.

'Call me if you need me."

"I will."

Parking, Ebony looked out at the huge mansion, thinking of how inspiring it appeared, sans the multitude of opulent vehicles parked outside of it. Figuring the Spires' precious toys were tucked inside the multi-car garage, the only vehicles present were two landscape utility trucks. It's workers were scattered about the place, trimming hedges, running leaf blowers, weed eaters, push mowers, and scags. Neither of them paid her any attention as she dismounted, clad in dark blue, pinstriped dress pants, matching vest, a white blouse, and white sandals. As she'd done as a child, Ebony relished the soothing aroma of fresh cut grass as she made for the large front doors of the house. Before she could reach the steps, one of the double doors opened and Sanchez, one of the governor's bodyguards, stepped out onto the porch to greet her, carrying a handheld scanner.

"I have to run this over you," he informed, looking as if she was sure she would decline.

"Okay," she agreed, climbing the steps, and raising her arms to allow him to run the device over her body. She was only carrying her cellular being that she'd left her keys in the car.

"You're clear," Sanchez told her, shutting off the scanner. "You may enter."

Ebony stepped inside, stopping just beyond the entrance. Once Sanchez had secured the door, he gestured for her to follow him. Despite the cool air coming from the unseen air conditioner, Ebony's palm had begun to perspire around the plastic casing of her phone, as she moved along the hallway, studying the array of portraits on each side containing predecessors of Albert Spires. Taking the stairs she'd used on the night of the dinner party, they encountered a fairly young, redheaded maid, who was descending the stairs, carrying an empty clothing basket. Looking into the girl's green eyes as they passed one another, Ebony couldn't help but reflect on how much she resembled Samantha, though her youthful face made her look as if she was fresh out of high school. And Ebony would wager everything she owned that Albert Spires was clandestinely *robbing the cradle.*"

Reaching the top of the stairs, they made a left, which was in the opposite direction of the special bedroom Samantha shared with the governor, who Ebony now realized, may also share it with the young help. But while trailing behind the guard, she gave in to her urge to look back, and saw that the hall was empty, which made her wonder where Jennifer, the governors' wife, could be at this time. Ebony didn't know that they'd reached Albert's office, until she bumped into Sanchez, who didn't seem fazed by it. Repudiating her apology, he rapped twice on the solid oak door.

"It's open, Sanchez," the governor's voice came back at them.

Sanchez pushed the door open, then stepped aside to allow Ebony to enter, in which she did, closing the door behind her. The office boasted of a large, mahogany bookcase saturated with various tones, a glass trophy case that displayed trophies of different sports, a gun case conveying hunting rifles, and a deer's head hanging about the only window that sat behind the mahogany desk occupied by Albert Spires. As she near, he stood extending his hand.

"Ms. Davis," he spoke.

She shook his hand. "Thanks for seeing me."

"Anything for a friend." He gestured to the cushioned chair in front of his desk. "Please, have a seat. Can I get you anything?"

226

"I'm fine," she responded, taking a seat. Out the window, she could see members of the landscaping detail, tending to the huge backyard.

"Have they made any discoveries in your situation?" Albert asked, once he'd retaken his seat, and was leaning back with his hands rested on his protruding belly.

"Not that I know of she answered. "As of now, I haven't spoken to anyone.

"I see." he was slowly nodding his head up and down with a pensive look on his face. There was a pregnant pause before he asked. "So, what can I do for you?"

"My half-brother is incarcerated," Ebony spoke, not missing a beat. "I don't' know the true nature of the case, but he's facing the death penalty. And as I understand the Fulton County District Attorney office has already filed a notice of aggravating circumstances."

Albert leaned forward, resting his forearms on the desk. "And where do I come into this?"

"I need you to get him out."

"I can't do that, Ms. Davis," he said, shaking his head from side to side. "I can only grant pardons to certain prisoners that meet the qualifications. But they have to be prisoners, not detainees."

"So, there's nothing you could do?"

"I wish there were," he said with a shrug. "The U.S. Constitution only allows me a certain amount of power. I'm sorry."

Ebony narrowed her eyes. "I think you're lying."

Alberts's head snapped back as if he'd been physically struck. "Excuse me!"

"I think you're lying, Albert." She iterated, pulling the video of he and Samantha up on her phone. Pressing play, she slid the phone across the desk to him. "Are you sure you want to stick to your guns on this one?"

She watched him as he picked the phone up and studied the screen with an inscrutable expression. The volume had been purposefully turned up so Albert's and Samantha's voices seemed to vibrate throughout the small office, which had Ebony wondering if Sanchez could hear it out in the hall. Then, came the moans that subsequently led up to them calling out each other's names, and Samantha instructing him on how to please her. Ebony watched the wrinkles in his forehead deepen. The sweat beads that formed at his temple, didn't hesitate to roll down the side of his face. That's when he finally looked up with pure hatred registering in his eyes.

"I can't believe her," he spoke through clenched teeth.

"She has nothing to do with this," Ebony attempted to assure him.

Albert maintained his stare but said nothing.

"Oh! The room, right?" Ebony crossed one leg over the other. "Well, you know girls talk and, just because she told me where it is, that doesn't make her guilty of anything. You may think I'm betraying you two, but I'm not. Samantha doesn't know about my half-brother, or the video."

Albert silenced the phone. "You're sitting here trying to blackmail me, and you don't' think this is betrayal? How dare you bring this nonsense into my home!"

"Nonsense?" Ebony was done with being nice. "Is that how Jennifer would look at it? What about the media? What about the House of Representatives? How many of those guys would be willing to uphold our opinion?"

Placing the phone down in front of him, Albert locked eyes with her. "I think you are bluffing."

"Oh?"

"Suppose I don't' let you make it out of here with this?" he posed.

"Suppose I already have?" Ebony shot back, mentally reprimanding herself for not making a copy of the video. "And I would appreciate it if you'd save your frivolous threats."

"I'm a very powerful man, Ms. Davis."

"Which is why I came to you." She stood and picked her phone up off the desk. "You have thirty days to grant my wish. And, if anything happens to Samantha ... Well, let's just say that I'm a very powerful woman."

Chapter 26

Monday

7:28 p.m.

"How'd it go?"

Ebony wasn't at all startled to see Rick sitting on her living room sofa, when she stepped through the front door, being that she'd called, and asked him to meet her there on her way back from Atlanta. Plus, his SUV was parked at the curb, in lieu of the driveway, where it had been over the weekend. She could have driven back to Linkton County after leaving the governor's mansion but made the decision to drop in on Carol for a quick chat. And it was a good thing she'd done that, because the visit had been very informative. She'd learned that Janelle, Anthony's son's mother, had went into hiding, taking their only child with her. On top of that, Antony had confided in his mother about some guy named Marvin, who was the third accomplice in the bank robbery. According to Carol, Marvin was the reason why Anthony had gotten caught. She didn't get the full story but, what little she did get confirmed the vindictive look she's seen in Anthony's eyes when she'd visited him. This also gave her something to look forward to investigating.

"I don't know yet," Ebony now answered Rick's question. She closed the front door and studied the Sen-Tech monitor on the wall, which had been installed while she was away.

"You'll have to call in for the voice activation," he told her, obviously seeing how she was regarding the screen. "And why don't you know yet? "Didn't you visit with him?"

"Of course." She approached, dropping her overnight bag on the floor beside the coffee table that now stood between them. "I told him what I needed for him to do. He claimed that he couldn't do it. I showed him the video; he said that I was bluffing, and made furtive threats. That's when I bided him thirty days to make it happen, made my own furtive threat, then got my ass up out of there."

"So, what if he doesn't make it happen within thirty days?"

Ebony shrugged. "I don't know."

"You don't know?" he regarded her with a look of uncertainty. "Aren't you going to expose him?"

Ebony didn't answer. She looked away to avoid his penetrating gaze. At this moment, all she could think about was Samantha. Ebony had never betrayed anyone and releasing the video would be the ultimate betrayal. Samantha, whose been nothing but a friend to her since the first day she'd started as a prosecutor for the Linkton County District Attorney's Office, would never forgive her for such an enormity. But what if Albert decides to call her bluff? What if he...

"This is a prepaid phone," Rick said, pulling her from her reverie. He was now standing holding a cellular out to her. "Just in case that investigator has your phone tapped, you should call us on this. And, speaking of which, you need to make an appointment with him, ASAP. We need to know what he knows, so we'll know how to move. In the meantime, get some rest."

With that, Rick was out the door. He'd easily relinquished his quest for the answer to his question, but Ebony pretty much had an idea of what he was thinking. Despite his equilibrium, Rick was a ruthless human being. Plus, he'd worked up under her father, who was as Ebony had come to know as ruthless as they come. It was indomitable that, when Rick looks at her, he sees her father. He actually expects for her to carry on her father's legacy in the same exact manner as he had, especially since he's now working under her. This meant that she had to lead by example. She had to become abominable. She had to cross boundaries that no person in their right mind would cross. She had to... become Tyrone Davis.

Chapter 27

For various reasons, Ebony was divested of a good night's rest. For one, her mind was fully preoccupied with Albert Spires and the burdensome ultimatum she'd imposed on him. Then, whenever she was able to lure herself into a sleep, she was haunted by disturbing images of Jason, crying out for his life, while being consumed by a hell-like fire inside of a huge incinerator, which would cause her to awake in a cold sweat, each time. After the third nightmare, she tried to conjure more, *friendlier* images in her mind, while staring up at the celling, only ended up thinking about the investigator, and how she would comport herself in interview with him, until interrupted by her alarm clock.

Now, stepping off the elevator on the district attorney's floor, Ebony made for Barbara Hutchins office, knowing for sure that she wouldn't be approached by any of her coworkers, being that she'd deliberately left her house thirty minutes earlier than her usual departure time. Everybody knew that Barbara Hutchins was always the first to arrive, so Ebony was relieved to see that the district attorney's car was already parked in the parking garage when she pulled in. And, as always, Barbara's office door was standing wide open. When Ebony made it to its threshold, she saw that the head prosecutor was preoccupied with a newspaper that was spread out on her desk.

"Um, Ms. Hutchins?" Ebony spoke, after several seconds of going unnoticed.

"Oh!" Barbara started, placing a hand on her chest "You're early."

Ebony shrugged. "I didn't sleep so well last night."

"Are you sure you're read to come back?" The district attorney asked with a concerned expression on her face. "I mean, it's obvious that you're still…"

"I'm fine," Ebony cut her off sternly.

233

"Are you sure?"

"Ms. Hutchins," Ebony started slowly. "If I don't' work, I'll go crazy. This is therapy for me. Just trust me on this."

"Well..." Her concerned look seemed to abate as she evaluated Ebony over the top of her eyeglasses. "If you say you're fine, I guess I'll just have to take your word for it. Should I have someone to assist you for today, just in case?"

"I'll manage," Ebony told her. "Thanks, anyway!"

Without giving the district attorney a chance to say anything else, Ebony pivoted and made for her office, thinking about her briefcase she'd left in her car on the night of the fire. After learning about zodine in the Brown's case, Ebony had conducted research, and found that the substance was as dangerous as the fire inspector had insisted, which was why she'd orchestrated Jason's demise by the substance, with hopes of the fire department getting the flames under control before it reached the garage. As she had expected, the firemen were able to save both cars, which were still in the custody of the homicide division's forensic unit.

Entering her office, Ebony closed the door behind her, and took a seat behind her desk, placing her cell phone and keys on top of it. Checking her watch, she realized that she had a little over an hour before she had to report to the courtroom. While her computer was loading, Ebony crossed the room to the file cabinet to retrieve the files of cases she would be handling for the day. But before she could pull one of the drawers open, out of the blue, the name Marvin popped into her mind. Before she could try and retain where she'd heard the name, Anthony popped into her mind, which made her spin around, and rush back to her desk where her computer was ready for use. Taking a seat, she entered her password, then accessed Georgia Criminal Files.

Being that Carol wasn't able to purvey her with a last name, Ebony typed in M-A-R-V-I-N, to see what kind of results she would get. A list of names conveying the appellation, whether first, middle, or last, filled her screen, alongside pictures, and miscellaneous information. She immediately deleted the ones that had Marvin as last names. There were only two with it as middle names. Those were subsequently deleted. She strolled the last seven back and forth, until she remembered that the man she was searching for was Caucasian. This left her with two culprits, but she couldn't make out which one was responsible for Anthony getting caught just by studying their photos. Therefore, she clicked onto View Record for the first one who only had been arrested for failure to appear for child support, and a slew of traffic violations. He definitely didn't seem like someone who'd take on a bank. Closing his file, Ebony logged into the last one, and felt as if she'd hit the lottery. This guy has an extensive line of infractions ranging from aggravated assault, domestic violence, burglary, shoplifting, possession of firearm, and terroristic threats.

He was definitely her man!

Before Ebony could get to the end of the list of charges, her door swung open, startling her for a second. She looked up as Samantha barged in, briefcase in one hand, slamming the door shut with the other. As she approached, her body language bespoke anger, but there was a huge smile on her face. Depositing her briefcase in the visitors' chair, Samantha rounded the desk, cupped her hands under Ebony's chin, and brought her mouth down on hers, smothering her in the longest, passionate kiss they'd ever engaged in. Ebony had always loved this particular kiss. She could tell that Samantha was very happy to see her, and extremely horny. And, just the thought of Samantha's fiery desire for her was enough to send Ebony's hormones into overdrive. Now, she was feeling exactly like Samantha, in dire need of sexual relief.

Ebony wanted to throw Samantha onto the desk, and sex her until the cows come home, but knew that she couldn't. Samantha didn't' show any signs of relenting, so Ebony took the initiative to break the kiss. Standing erect, Samantha was now looking down on Ebony with the same randy eyes that Ebony was regarding her with. The only thing that could be heard throughout the office was the sound of their heavy breathing.

"I've missed you so much," Samantha said, between breaths. "Plus, I was worried about you."

"I'm fine, baby," Ebony assured.

"Can I see you tonight?" Samantha got straight to the point.

Ebony couldn't help but smile at her friend's ambition. "Of course, sweetheart."

As if relieved by the answer, Samantha sat on the edge of the desk. "I had spoken with that investigator last night." She appraised.

"How'd it go?" Ebony asked, just as her computer screen went onto sleep mode.

"It was uncomfortable," Samantha replied, making a face. "He was asking too many personal questions."

"Like what?"

"He asked about your relationship with Jason," she answered.

"He wanted to know if Jason was abusive, or if you've ever mentioned anything about Jason having enemies of any sort."

Ebony leaned back in her chair, waiting on Samantha to resume.

Being that it was none of his business," she continued, "I told him that you and Jason had the kind of relationship that most people would envy." She paused to draw a breath.

236

"I also told him what you told me about Jason being assaulted by some guys he owed money to. Maybe I was wrong for telling him that, but I figured it would help him get some kind of lead on whoever murdered Jason."

"You weren't wrong for telling him that," Ebony assured. After hearing what she was expecting to hear, she decided to change the subject. "So, how's Briggs been holding up?"

"That pig-headed narcissist!" Samantha expressed, making mean face that Ebony found, both cute and funny. "I don't' know what kind of guru he's seeing, or what kind of drugs he'd gotten a hold to but, lately, he's been walking around here acting all high and mighty. You would think he's taken Barbara Hutchins' place."

Ebony smiled. "So, he's no longer following you around like a love sick puppy anymore, huh?"

'Whatever!" she was also smiling. "Are you staying at your grandparents' house or what?"

'Of course, not!" Ebony didn't mean to frown up the way she did. It was a natural reflex. "I bought a house. "

"Where?"

"You'll find out in due time, my pet," Ebony answered, squeezing one of Samantha's knees. "Right now, I have plenty of work to catch up on."

"So do I." Samantha planted a kiss on her lips. "See you later."

"Okay, babe."

Ebony's eyes were glued to Samantha's buttocks that bounced gracefully around in the tan slacks, as she rounded the desk, retrieved her briefcase, and swaggered towards the door. With a look back, and a slight wave of her the hand, Samantha made her exit.

Ebony took a few seconds to force the voluptuous thought from her mind, before tapping a key on her keyboard to awake her computer. When the screen came into focus, she found herself staring into the blue eyes of the man she assumed was the chief object of Anthony's revenge.

"Well, hello Marvin Harris!" Ebony said to the screen. "I think there's a storm coming your way. Well, that's only if you're dumb enough to be staying at the same address."

Chapter 28

Once the judge had called a recess, Ebony made for her office to place the call she'd been anticipating all morning. Investigator John Pruden claimed to be extremely busy at the moment but would be delighted if she'd come by his office after work. Remembering what Rick had told her, Ebony was able to persuade him into meeting her at a diner on the outskirts of Linkton County instead. After the call, Ebony journeyed down to the cafeteria, where she dined lone, being that Samantha was still in court. She was also still in court when Judge Jackson had adjourned for the day. Instead of waiting, Ebony sent a text to Samantha's phone, explaining where she was going, and avowing that she'd see her later.

Now, Ebony pulled her rental car into the parking lot of the not-so-crowded diner, and parked. Thankful for the dark clouds that obscured the sun, and brought on a cooler climate, she crossed the lot, and entered the establishment, looking around. Not seeing the investigator anywhere, Ebony ordered an iced tea, then took a seat at the back of the diner. Before she could take a sip of her drink, she spotted an older model Buick pulling into the lot. She couldn't make out the full feature of the occupant, but she had a feeling that it was John Pruden, though that wasn't the car he was driving on the day she'd met him outside the church.

And, just as she'd figured, the investigator emerged from the car, clad in an inexpensive suit, and carrying a burgundy briefcase. As he neared, he raked his fingers through his hair, which was something she found funny, being that most white men were accustomed to doing such. He automatically knew where she was seated.

"Sorry, I'm late," he apologized, when he approached, gently placing his briefcase at top the table, then taking a seat across from her. "Are you waiting on an order.

"I already have it," she replied, finally taking a sip of her beverage.

"Great!" He opened his briefcase, and pulled out a small notepad, and an electronic recording device, placing them on the table.

"I don't wish to be recorded," she told him.

He regarded her with a look of disbelief. "I think it'd be best if—"

"I don't' wish to be recorded," she reiterated, cutting him off. "And I'd appreciate it if we could speed this up. I have another engagement."

"Yes, ma'am," he replied, flipping through his notepad, and producing a pen. "On the nineteenth of July, what time did you get home from work?"

"Somewhere around six-thirty," she answered.

"According to a source," he begun, regarding his notes, "You like to go jogging in the evening. Did you go jogging on the date in question?"

"I did."

"At what time?"

"I wasn't in the house for no more than ten minutes," Ebony expounded, directing her gaze out at the parking lot. "Once I'd changed into my running gear, I was back out the door. It's routine."

After scribbling something on this notepad, he said, "By the way, Homicide has released your cars. I guess you could go and collect them wherever time permits."

Ebony only nodded.

"Now," he continued, raking his fingers through his hair. "You say that you arrived home around six thirty, and had left for your evening run around six-forty. Fire investigators estimated that the fire had started between six thirty and six forty-five, which would be a theory based on the time that your fire alarm had triggered the alarms at Sen-Tech security. As of now, I have yet to receive the printout from Sen-Tech. However, investigators were able to determine that the fire was ignited by a combustible substance known as zodine. Have your heard of it?"

"I have," Ebony answered, feeling as if he was about to blatantly accuse her of colluding Jason's murder, followed by FBI agents jumping out of the ceiling to arrest her.

Raking his fingers through his hair again, he looked her directly in the eyes. "Do you know of anybody who would want to do such a thing? Any enemies that you know of?"

Ebony shook her head from side to side. "Not that I know of."

"What about Jason? Did he have any enemies that you know of?"

Again, Ebony diverted her attention out the window. For she had already anticipated and prepared herself for this question. Despite his cool demeanor, Ebony knew better than to think of him as anything other than an experienced, and highly trained *crime dog*. He'd probably exposed hundreds of murderers who'd tried their best to maintain their innocent facades. But, luckily for Ebony, she was ten steps ahead of Investigator John Pruden. Now, all she had to do is follow up with what Samantha had told him.

"On the fifteenth of this month," she finally spoke, still looking out the window. "I attended a dinner party at the Governor's mansion in Atlanta, along with Samantha Gordon. When I returned home that night, I realized that Jason was in a foul mood. I also realized that his face was bruised, and it was swollen. I questioned him about it but at the moment, he was too upset to talk. Being that he'd already been drinking, I relented, took a shower, and went to bed, only to be awakened by him asking me to marry him."

"He woke you up to propose to you?" John seemed to find that amusing.

"Yes." Ebony lifted her left hand, showing him the ring. "He claimed to have had the ring for a while and was waiting for the right time." She paused to wipe the tear that cascaded down her left cheek. Then, still looking out at the parking lot, she continued. "I took that time to question him about the condition of his face again. He was reluctant, but gave in, and told me that he'd owed a large amount of money to someone."

"Did he say a name?" The investigator was still scribbling on his notepad.

"No," answered Ebony.

"Did he say how much he'd owed?"

"No," she sniffed for effect. "Whoever he owed, had come by the house, and roughed him up. I figured that when they do stuff like that, the debt is usually considered paid. I guess it wasn't."

Burying her face in her hands, Ebony pretended to weep, making sure that she was loud enough to be heard by anybody seated within the next three tables from theirs. She'd been actuating this award-winning performance ever since she was child. And has always gained the desired effects. Whether this faux emotional display worked on the investigator, or not, Ebony still had the ups on him.

"Are you okay?" he finally asked as Ebony retrieved Kleenex from her pocketbook to dab at the tears she'd summoned.

Ebony only nodded as she made a show of collecting herself. John ran his fingers through his hair. "As of now, I have no other questions. However, if I make any kind of developments in this case, I'll be sure to contact you."

Upon leaving the diner, and enroute to Samantha's place, Ebony could not stop thinking about the interview with John Pruden. She knew that she'd done a great job of misleading him in which she was very proud of. But she could tell that he wasn't the type that one could easily fool.

And, for some odd reason, she felt that he'd been holding something back from her but what?

Pulling into the entrance of Ocean Park, Ebony drove until she'd reached Samantha's trailer, where Samantha's car sat under a build it yourself carport. And Samantha must've heard her pull up because before Ebony could dismount, Samantha was standing akimbo beyond the screened door, clad in a satin nightgown that bared her cleavage, and seemed to show off every inch of her thighs. Samantha's visage was similar to that of a child's on Christmas day, when she let Ebony in and locked the door back.

"I almost started without you," Samantha quipped, plating a kiss on Ebony's jaw.

Ebony smiled. "How many times have I heard that?"

"Not enough," Samantha replied, grabbing her by the hand. "Come on!"

Samantha pulled Ebony toward the bedroom that smelled of scented candles and bodywash. Relieving Ebony of her pocketbook, Samantha gently pushed her down onto the bed, and began taking off her shoes, while Ebony undid her own belt. As soon as Ebony had unfastened the buttons on her pants, Samantha seemed to rip them off in one motion, tossing them onto the floor. While Ebony wrestled with the button on her blouse, Samantha relieved her of her panties and just as she'd expected, held them up to her nose, and inhaled deeply with her eyes closed.

"You smell so good!" Samantha whispered seductively.

"Don't' make me file a restraining order on your obsessive ass!" Ebony jested, just as the all too-familiar ringtone of her cell phone reached her ears from the depth of her pocketbook.

Samantha's eyes snapped open as if by the sound of a gunshot. At any other time, Ebony would be angered by the interruption, and ignore the call. But not this one. She never had and would never ignore this caller, which is why she'd set up this particular ringtone, and always left he phone activated.

"I have to answer that, babe," she asserted, sitting up, and kissing Samantha's stomach thought the fabric of her nightgown.

"I know," she replied. Samantha, who was conversant with the ringtone, sat on the edge of the bed, beside Ebony, still holding on to the panties.

Ebony retrieved her cell phone from the pocketbook atop the nightstand and answered it. "Hello?"

"It's your grandmother," her grandfather's voice sounded through the earpiece. "She's had a heart attack."

***

It had only taken thirty-seven minutes for Ebony to reach the hospital where her grandmother had been rushed to for heart complications. Samantha had insisted on accompanying her, but Ebony declined, being that she wasn't sure of what the outcome maybe and didn't want to drag anyone into her family's business. As far as Ebony knew, this made the third time that Regina Davis has been hospitalized for a heart attack. The lady was almost seventy years old. How much more could she endure?

Ebony didn't bother with inserting coins, nor her credit card, into the parking meter as she dismounted, and hurried inside of the hospital that was crawling with people. By the time she'd reached the desk of the receptionists, she was covered in sweat that caused her clothes to stick to her body. And, it didn't make it any better that she'd rushed out without putting her panties back on, which made her assume that Samantha was having a field day with them.

"How may I help you?" the receptionist asked, once she was done with the person that was ahead of Ebony.

"I'm trying to find a Regina Davis," Ebony apprised, and the receptionist began typing on her keypad. "I was told that she was rushed in for heart complications."

"According to my display, "the receptionist started, "She's still in O.R. That would be on the fifth floor; east wing."

Ebony shot off toward the elevators without taking a second to thank the woman. Well, of course, it's hard to think straight when you're on the brink of losing a loved one. And, Ebony was definitely to this point, commingled with the notion that the smallest thing could exasperate her. It just so happened to start with the elevator taking forever to arrive. On top of that, it seemed as if a thousand people had tried to cram into one shaft. Then, the elevator stopped on every floor before reaching the fifth. By the time Ebony had stepped off, she'd almost convinced herself that she hated all human beings, reprehending them for being inconsiderate to what she's going though. She knew that this was irrational thinking, which was why she'd forced it from her mental, before entering the large, not-so-crowded, waiting room looking around for her grandfather, who was seated in a section by himself with his head down, fidgeting with his fingers. He must've checked his watch five times, before Ebony approached, standing in front of him.

"What's her condition?" Ebony asked unceremoniously.

Terrance Davis slowly lifted his head to meet her gaze. "She's in and out," he answered, in almost a whisper.

"And, what the hell is that supposed to mean!" she hissed, hoping that he wasn't implying what she was already thinking. He dropped his gaze to the floor before saying, "They're doing their best to keep her alive."

It felt as if Ebony's heart had dropped to her stomach. Her grandmother's last visits were for mild complications of the heart, whereas Ebony wasn't notified until after she was stabilized. This time her grandfather had called her, using her grandmother's cell phone, insisting that she drive out to the hospital. That, plus the tone of his voice, should've been enough to let her know how critical this visit was.

Now, as she paced back and forth in front of the nurses' station, Ebony thought back to how devastated she was when she'd lost her mother and father on the same day.

She was only eleven at the time and felt that it was that experience which made her compassionate towards other children who'd endured the same ordeals. This had also started her ambitions of wanting to be a mother and wife, promising herself that she would ever leave her children to grow up without her. Well, she was only eleven so, of course, this was foolish thinking, being that no one actually knows the date and time that they will cease to exist.

"Mr. Davis?"

The unfamiliar male's voice caused her to stop in her tracks, and turn in the direction from whence it came. Her grandfather was now regarding the man that approached him, clad in a long, white coat with a stethoscope about his neck. They were only a few yards away from her, so she could clearly hear their exchange.

Terrance cleared his throat, before answering. "Yes?"

"I'm sorry!" the doctor apologized, sounding sincere. "We've done all that we could."

Tears instantly clouded Ebony's vision, before cascading down her face. She wanted to run until she was on the other side of the hospital's wall, but felt that, if she tried to move, she would only crash onto the thin-carpeted floor, being that her legs were feeling fragile all of a sudden. For she'd just lost the last person she'd loved more than anything in the world, and all she could think about was that somebody would have to pay dearly for bringing this pain upon her.

Chapter 29

Saturday

July 29, 2023

Ebony watched with tearless eyes as her grandmother's casket was being lowered into the earth beside her father's plot that was contiguous to her mother's but her mind was elsewhere. Though she'd lost the last person she'd cared dearly for, she knew that she had to go on with her life. The deaths of her parents had prepared her for this, being that the first cut is always the deepest. She'd always promised herself that she would somehow avenge their murders. Now, she had to add the death of her grandmother to her list. Yes, Dr. Taft or whatever his name was, had explained that Regina Davis had died from cessation of heartbeat but, for some strange reason, Ebony was leery of his synopsis. For this would definitely need further investigation.

"Are you ready?"

Snapping out of her thoughts, Ebony regarded Rick, who was standing to the left of her, looking as if he was dressed for a photoshoot, instead of a funeral, in his black tailormade suit, and ever present sunglasses. He'd been by her side ever since she'd informed him of her grandmother's passing. He'd volunteered to stay at her house with her, making the living room his temporary lodge, being that it, and the master bedroom were the only rooms furnished in the three-bedroom house. Ebony was grateful for his benevolence, though she didn't expect for him to cook, and clean up after her the way he did, which seemed to boost her sense of security around him.

Now, not trusting her voice at the moment, she nodded in response to Rick's question then tossed the bouquet of lilies she was holding onto her grandmother's casket. With a mere glance at her grandfather, who was standing at a respectable distance to the right of her, Ebony turned on her heels and allowed Rick to lead her back to the white 2023 Cadillac Safari she'd purchased after trading in hers and Jason's cars. Bull, who'd refused to wear a suit, was leaning against the car with his arms folded over his chest. Once he'd opened the rear door for her to climb in, he and Rick climbed in up front, and they made for the exit of the cemetery in silence. The only sounds that could be heard were the car's engine, and air conditioner unit.

"Is this an appropriate time to discuss business?" Bull asked after a while.

"Is there a problem with the business?" Ebony inquired, knowing that he was referring to the drug game, in which she'd found herself an anonymous player in.

"Not at all," he answered. "I was just wondering—"

"Now's not the time," she cut him off, directing her attention outside window. "If neither of you have any question about tonight's mission. I would like to be left to my thoughts."

There were no questions.

It was almost thirty minutes later, when Bull had pulled the Cadillac into the driveway of Ebony's house, where Rick's truck was still parked at the curb. Before Bull could kill the engine, Ebony dismounted, and made for the front door, rummaging through her pocketbook for her keys. Just as she was about to slide the key into the first lock, the euphony of children laughing and playing about caused her to cease movement. Pivoting slowly on her heels, Ebony took a moment to survey her neighborhood, which was something she hadn't done since she'd moved in. Despite the fact that she was still grieving the loss of her grandmother, the smiling faces of the children capering about carelessly seemed to put a smile on her own face. For she vividly remembered when she was just a child and didn't think it possible to lose the people that were responsible for her very existence.

Now, turning back to the door, she saw that it was standing wide open. Then, not seeing Rick, nor Bull, she deduced that they'd gone inside. Rick used his spare key and left her to her thoughts as she'd requested earlier. Maybe, they thought she'd fell into a state of delusion while watching the children play and didn't believe it was sagacious to bother her. Ebony almost laughed aloud at the thought as she entered the house, where Rick and Bull were standing around in the living room, clearly awaiting further instructions.

"I haven't lost my marbles yet," she asserted, not liking the looks they were giving her.

Rick and Bull only exchanged glances.

Ebony resumed. "Whatever affairs that you two need to tend to right away. Now's the time to do so. My expectation hasn't changed. In the event that they do, I'll make contact."

With that, Ebony made for her bedroom, where she placed her pocketbook and keys on the dresser and began undressing. While doing so, she heard the front door close, indicating that Rick and Bull had left. Being that Rick had driven out to pick Bull up, he was responsible for making sure that Bull made it back to his residence. According to the clock on the nightstand, it was 1:44 p.m., in which, Ebony deemed was the perfect time to take a cat nap.

Now, down to her panties and bra, Ebony climbed into bed, pulled the covers up to her chest, and didn't realize that she'd fallen asleep until she was awakened by the alarm clock that she set last night just in case she'd needed a reminder. Seconds later, the alarm on her cell phone sounded from inside of her pocketbook. She had also set that one, just in case she was out of the house, doing God knows what.

Being that it was already dark outside, Ebony activated the small lamp on the nightstand, before deactivating both alarms. After a trip to the bathroom to drain her bladder, she donned the pants and shirt she'd picked out earlier, then slipped into her tennis shoes. Only retrieving her keys from her pocketbook, Ebony exited the house without resetting the alarm. The neighborhood was quiet and deserted, save for the young hoodlums on the porch of the house at the end of the cul-de sac, who'd began whistling, and yelling out obscenities which was something they'd been doing since she'd moved in, unless Rick was with her. But, as always, she ignored them, and climbed into her car.

It had only taken her forty-two minutes to reach her grandparents' house, where it seemed as if there were no lights on inside, save for the constant flicker of lights from the television in the living room. Ebony made sure to extinguish her headlights before turning into the drive and parking behind her grandfather's truck. Only taking a minute to reflect on what was about to take place, she killed the engine, got out, and walked the stone walkway up to the front door, where she used her key to get inside. She was about to disarm the alarm but saw that it wasn't activated.

As she moved about the semi-dark house, Ebony couldn't help but inhale the familiar fragrance of her grandmother, which had lingered about the house ever since she could remember. Making it to the kitchen, she disengaged the locks on the backdoor, then made a B line to the living room, where her grandfather was seated in his favorite recliner, staring blankly at the muted television As she neared, she noticed the pint of gin sitting on the edge of the coffee table, nearest him whereas the contents of the bottle was well below the halfway mark.

'I knew you were coming," he avowed, not taking his eyes off the set.

Saying nothing, Ebony took a seat on the middle cushion of the sofa, which was to the left of him.

"I've must've dreamed of this day over a hundred times." He continued, voice slurring from the indefinite amount of alcohol he'd consumed. "You're too much like your father, who was too much like me. It's in our nature to hold grudges."

Terrance finally looked up from the tube, when Rick and Bull entered, both clad in dark clothing, and wearing gloves. Never taking her eyes off her grandfather, Ebony was surprised that the old fart showed no sign of fear. In fact, he impassively watched as Rick handed her a pair of gloves, and placed a small, black case on the table in front of her. After donning the gloves, she popped the two latches on the case, and lifted the lid, revealing a brand-new chrome .38 caliber pistol that gleamed in the glow of the television. Checking to see that the gun was loaded, she placed it in her lap, then looked over at her grandfather, who diverted his attention back to the TV, as if everything was normal.

"It's in our nature to hold grudges," he repeated, just as Rick placed a white, letter size envelope on the table. "We find it hard to forgive the people who wrong us. That's how I knew you were coming."

"Why wasn't I informed about the money that was left by my father?" Ebony now asked." The money that arrived in the briefcase?"

"So, you knew about that," he stated as if talking to himself.

"I used to hear you and momma argue late at night," she pointed out. "She would get on you about smelling like other women. The money came up quite often. Something about you spent money on the other women that you were cheating on her with. I've even heard her cry during these arguments. Then, I think she hid the money from you. That's when you stopped staying out late. You had once again become a regular at the dinner table. I guess, without the extra money you could no longer live out your sexual fantasies. That's when your perverted ass mind conjured a new fantasy that included your very own granddaughter."

Ebony paused to let her words linger in the air. She didn't even look in the direction of Rick and Bull who were standing in their same positions. Up until this moment, she and Terrance were the only two that knew of this violation of her childhood, and she had planned to keep it that way until Terrance's demise. It would have made her sole holder of the secret that she was going to take to her own grave. So much for that, she thought. Now, Terrance drew a breath before replying.

"Yeah, I guess I did you both wrong. I could easily blame the alcohol, but that's the coward's way out. I know that I would end up paying for what I did to both of you. As I've said I must've dreamed about it over a hundred times, and I accept my punishment like a man. Also, if it means anything to you, I'm sorry.

Though he'd been watching the TV the whole time, Ebony could see the tears forming in his eyes, which prompted her to mentally alter her plans a bit. For this was the first time she'd ever seen Terrance Tyrone Davis display such emotions. And, she knew that she would be foolish to not take full advantage of this moment. She looked up at Rick.

"Retreat!" she ordered.

Rick narrowed his eyes, shot a glance at Terrance, then back her. Ebony clearly knew what he was thinking.

'I got it," she assured him.

"Are you sure?" he finally asked.

"Take the case with you," she said, repudiating his question.

"I'll make contact tomorrow."

Rick seemed to linger for an eon, before retrieving the gun case from the table, and exiting the living room, followed by Bull. All the while, her grandfather's eyes remained transfixed on the tube. A tear had already made a trail down his face. But, Ebony remained clinical as she ejected the cylinder of the .38 caliber and dumped all six bullets into her gloved hand. Slipping one back into the chamber, and the other five into her pocket. Ebony got up and stood in front of Terrance, who'd finally looked up making eye contact with her.

"If you're really sorry for what you've done," she said, placing the gun in his lap, "Prove it."

He glanced over at the table, then back up at her before asking. "Can I, at least, finish my drink first?"

"By all means."

With that, she exited the living room, and made for the kitchen, where she locked the back door. Heading for the front door, she stopped at the Sen-tech monitor and instead of voice activating, manually called up the touchpad to activate the house's security system. Done, she exited, using her keys to lock the house up. Then, she headed for her car, thankful that her grandfather had requested to finish his drink. For this would give her enough time to be as far away as possible when the gun goes off, and neighbors peer out their windows in hopes of seeing something that they could report to the authorities.

Now, as she drove, she thought about what her grandfather had said about it being in their nature to hold grudges. Did he really know that she was coming? Had he really dreamed of her coming back for him? Well, of course. He'd acknowledged that she was too much like her father, who was too much like himself. Terrance was cognizant of what he would have done, had he been in Ebony's shoes. Here fore, he knew that she was now on the road for revenge, and that it will be hell to pay for whomever that may have caused her pain in the past.

Chapter 30

Wednesday

August 9, 2023

"I think the blue crabs are the best ones." Big Country avowed. It was well after lockdown. He and Anthony were lying on their bunks, engaged in their usual conversation about anything under the sun. Though Anthony kept up with the conversation, he could not stop thinking of Ebony. If the death of her boyfriend wasn't enough, her grandmother dies of a heart attack the following week. Then, on the night of her grandmother's burial, her grandfather commits suicide by shooting himself in the head. It was said that authorities found a suicide note he'd typed upon, responding to the emergency call. After hearing of all this, Anthony relinquished his thoughts of Ebony coming to his rescue. All he could hope for now is a miracle. Perhaps, some deadly disease would break out and kill all the victims in his case. For that would definitely be a start.

"You don't' know which ones are the best," Anthony now responded to his cellmate. "Your fat ass'll eat anything."

"That's a lie," Big Country contradicted. "Before I started working at Wood's Seafood in Savannah, I wouldn't dare eat crabs, or lobsters. Matt, one of the white dudes that goes out on the boat to catch them, turned me onto the seafood thing. Now, I'm a seafood fanatic."

"Big Country," Anthony stared, "You're a fan of all foods, I bet your big ass—"

Anthony stopped mid-sentence when their steel door slowly rolled back on its mechanical hinges. Not knowing what to make of this, Anthony sat up and slipped his feet into his tennis shoes. The jail was locked down for the night, but inmates were known to bribe officer into opening their doors, and the doors of an enemy ,for a surprise attack. But Anthony couldn't think of anyone he would peg as an enemy in the dorm. Just as he was about to get up, a male officer appeared in the threshold.

"Anthony Hudson," he said with authority. "Pack you things! You're being released."

"I don't' know which one of these suckers paid you to participate in this prank," Anthony bristled. "But I'm not the one! You might wanna—"

"You have five minutes to pack that shit!" The officer cut him off, then walked away.

Anthony was still leery of the cabalistic request. For if this was a prank, funded by one of the inmates, then that inmate should give the officer a bonus for the award winning performance he'd just put on. Anthony regarded Big Country, who had a half-smile, half smirk on his face.

"This has to be a prank, huh?"

"It may be a prank," his cellmate offered. "But at the same time, it may not be a prank. Hell, it could be a computer error. I've seen that several times."

"So have I," Anthony replied, rubbing his chin.

"Now's not the time to be a good Samaritan," Big Country sermonized. "It's also not the time to waste time. Once that computer error is corrected, and you're not beyond that front door, you'll never get beyond it. Take advantage."

It had only taken a split second for Anthony to take heed of Big Country's advice. Prank, or no prank, he packed his belongings. Which were only a bundle of letters and pictures within two minutes, said goodbye to Big Country and made for the dorms' exit, where two officers were waiting to escort him down to intake. He knew that he would have to fill out paperwork, get fingerprinted and sit around for hours before being able to walk out the front door, which had him hoping the computer maintained its *stupidity* until after he was long gone. But upon entering intake all they had him to do was change into his stained clothes that he was arrested in and escorted him to the front door. No paperwork, no fingerprinting and no hours of sitting. Something wasn't right about this but, as Big Country had pointed out, now's not the time to be a good Samaritan.

Upon exiting the building, carrying a brown paper bag containing his mail, Anthony moved along the parking lot looking around as if he was expecting agents from some kind of foreign agency to pop up out of nowhere and rearrest him on charges that didn't' even exist. But the night was still, and nothing seemed to stir in the parking lot that was lit by multiple lamp posts.

However, Anthony didn't feel safe, until he had cleared the jail's parking lot, and was marching up Rice Street, enroute to the train station. He was thankful that there were no vehicles roaming the streets at this time of night, being that he was on high alert, and didn't know what to expect or what to trust. Up to the moment he'd thought this, a Fulton County Sheriff's car rounded the curve, moving in his direction at a casual pace. It was safe to say that he was scared at this moment. But the deputy drove by with just a mere glance in his direction.

Realizing that he was holding his breath, Anthony exhaled, and intentionally picked up his pace. For he could take no more of these close encounters. But just as he'd gotten over his anxiety of the squad car, another car rounded the bend at a casual pace. Anthony was not that good with make and models of certain cars, but he could tell that this one was a newer model Cadillac. He could also tell that it was occupied by three people. He figured the car would ride by, just as the last car, but it didn't. The driver slowly brought the car to a halt beside him. Anthony's eyes immediately locked on the two, hard looking, older men seated up front, being that all the windows were rolled down. Plus, the handguns in their laps were visibly displayed. At this time, he realized that he'd stopped walking.

"Are you trying to skip out on our agreement?"

At the sound of her voice, Anthony averted his gaze to see Ebony seated in the backseat as if she'd won the presidential election. The scene was very uncanny to him being that she didn't seem like the type that would be in the company of such men as the ones seated up front. But, hell, she was the daughter of Tyrone Davis. There was no telling what other things he was bound to find out about her.

"I was on my way to see my mother," he now avowed.

"Some other time." Ebony told him. "As of now, you make no moves unless I give my permission. Now, get in!"

Ebony slid over to make room for him, but Anthony lingered for a few seconds. The men up front were looking as if they were waiting for him to flout, so that they could put their guns to some use. Ruminating this, Antony climbed in beside Ebony, and the driver moved on. He waited for Ebony to explain how she was able to get him out or hit him with a litany of dos and don'ts but they rode in silence as she appeared to be interested in the world outside the window.

"So," Anthony decided to break the ice, "You kept your word."

"I'd never given you my word," she replied, still looking out the window. "But I do intend to uphold our agreement. However, if you don't' think you'll be able to uphold your end, now's the best time to say so."

"I don't' have a problem with upholding my end," he replied.

"But could you at least tell me what I'll be doing?"

She finally turned, and locked eyes with him. "Whatever I tell you to do."

258

The Saga Continues in: Crime Boss 3: Road to Revenge

Lock Down Publications and Ca$h Presents
Assisted Publishing Packages

BASIC PACKAGE	UPGRADED PACKAGE
$499	$800
Editing	Typing
Cover Design	Editing
Formatting	Cover Design
	Formatting
ADVANCE PACKAGE	**LDP SUPREME PACKAGE**
$1,200	$1,500
Typing	Typing
Editing	Editing
Cover Design	Cover Design
Formatting	Formatting
Copyright registration	Copyright registration
Proofreading	Proofreading
Upload book to Amazon	Set up Amazon account
	Upload book to Amazon
	Advertise on LDP, Amazon and Facebook Page

***Other services available upon request.
Additional charges may apply
Lock Down Publications
P.O. Box 944
Stockbridge, GA 30281-9998
Phone: 470 303-9761

Submission Guideline

Submit the first three chapters of your completed manuscript to ldpsubmissions@gmail.com, subject line: Your book's title. The manuscript must be in a .doc file and sent as an attachment. Documents should be in Times New Roman, double spaced and in size 12 font. Also, provide your synopsis and full contact information. If sending multiple submissions, they must each be in a separate email.

Have a story but no way to send it electronically? You can still submit to LDP/Ca$h Presents. Send in the first three chapters, written or typed, of your completed manuscript to:

LDP: Submissions Dept
Po Box 944
Stockbridge, Ga 30281

DO NOT send original manuscript. Must be a duplicate.

Provide your synopsis and a cover letter containing your full contact information.

Thanks for considering LDP and Ca$h Presents.

NEW RELEASES

SOSA GANG 2 by ROMELL TUKES
KINGZ OF THE GAME 7 by PLAYA RAY
SKI MASK MONEY 2 by RENTA
BORN IN THE GRAVE 3 by SELF MADE TAY
LOYALTY IS EVERYTHING 3 by MOLOTTI

Coming Soon from Lock Down Publications/Ca$h Presents

BLOOD OF A BOSS **VI**
SHADOWS OF THE GAME II
TRAP BASTARD II
By Askari
LOYAL TO THE GAME **IV**
By T.J. & Jelissa
TRUE SAVAGE **VIII**
MIDNIGHT CARTEL IV
DOPE BOY MAGIC IV
CITY OF KINGZ III
NIGHTMARE ON SILENT AVE II
THE PLUG OF LIL MEXICO II
CLASSIC CITY II
By Chris Green
BLAST FOR ME **III**
A SAVAGE DOPEBOY III
CUTTHROAT MAFIA III
DUFFLE BAG CARTEL VII
HEARTLESS GOON VI
By Ghost
A HUSTLER'S DECEIT III
KILL ZONE II
BAE BELONGS TO ME III
TIL DEATH II
By Aryanna
KING OF THE TRAP III
By T.J. Edwards

GORILLAZ IN THE BAY V
3X KRAZY III
STRAIGHT BEAST MODE III
De'Kari
KINGPIN KILLAZ IV
STREET KINGS III
PAID IN BLOOD III
CARTEL KILLAZ IV
DOPE GODS III
Hood Rich
SINS OF A HUSTLA II
ASAD
YAYO V
Bred In The Game 2
S. Allen
THE STREETS WILL TALK II
By Yolanda Moore
SON OF A DOPE FIEND III
HEAVEN GOT A GHETTO III
SKI MASK MONEY III
By Renta
LOYALTY AIN'T PROMISED III
By Keith Williams
I'M NOTHING WITHOUT HIS LOVE II
SINS OF A THUG II
TO THE THUG I LOVED BEFORE II
IN A HUSTLER I TRUST II
By Monet Dragun
QUIET MONEY IV
EXTENDED CLIP III
THUG LIFE IV
By Trai'Quan
THE STREETS MADE ME IV
By Larry D. Wright
IF YOU CROSS ME ONCE III

ANGEL V
By Anthony Fields
THE STREETS WILL NEVER CLOSE IV
By K'ajji
HARD AND RUTHLESS III
KILLA KOUNTY IV
By Khufu
MONEY GAME III
By Smoove Dolla
JACK BOYS VS DOPE BOYS IV
A GANGSTA'S QUR'AN V
COKE GIRLZ II
COKE BOYS II
LIFE OF A SAVAGE V
CHI'RAQ GANGSTAS V
SOSA GANG III
BRONX SAVAGES II
BODYMORE KINGPINS II
By Romell Tukes
MURDA WAS THE CASE III
Elijah R. Freeman
AN UNFORESEEN LOVE IV
BABY, I'M WINTERTIME COLD III
By Meesha

QUEEN OF THE ZOO III
By Black Migo
CONFESSIONS OF A JACKBOY III
By Nicholas Lock
KING KILLA II
By Vincent "Vitto" Holloway
BETRAYAL OF A THUG III
By Fre$h
THE MURDER QUEENS III
By Michael Gallon

Playa Ray

THE BIRTH OF A GANGSTER III
By Delmont Player
TREAL LOVE II
By Le'Monica Jackson
FOR THE LOVE OF BLOOD III
By Jamel Mitchell
RAN OFF ON DA PLUG II
By Paper Boi Rari
HOOD CONSIGLIERE III
By Keese
PRETTY GIRLS DO NASTY THINGS II
By Nicole Goosby
PROTÉGÉ OF A LEGEND III
LOVE IN THE TRENCHES II
By Corey Robinson
IT'S JUST ME AND YOU II
By Ah'Million
FOREVER GANGSTA III
By Adrian Dulan
GORILLAZ IN THE TRENCHES II
By SayNoMore
THE COCAINE PRINCESS VIII
By King Rio
CRIME BOSS II
Playa Ray
LOYALTY IS EVERYTHING III
Molotti
HERE TODAY GONE TOMORROW II
By Fly Rock
REAL G'S MOVE IN SILENCE II
By Von Diesel
GRIMEY WAYS IV
By Ray Vinci

Available Now

RESTRAINING ORDER **I & II**
By CA$H & Coffee
LOVE KNOWS NO BOUNDARIES **I II & III**
By Coffee
RAISED AS A GOON I, II, III & IV
BRED BY THE SLUMS I, II, III
BLAST FOR ME I & II
ROTTEN TO THE CORE I II III
A BRONX TALE I, II, III
DUFFLE BAG CARTEL I II III IV V VI
HEARTLESS GOON I II III IV V
A SAVAGE DOPEBOY I II
DRUG LORDS I II III
CUTTHROAT MAFIA I II
KING OF THE TRENCHES
By Ghost
LAY IT DOWN **I & II**
LAST OF A DYING BREED I II
BLOOD STAINS OF A SHOTTA I & II III
By Jamaica
LOYAL TO THE GAME I II III
LIFE OF SIN I, II III
By TJ & Jelissa
BLOODY COMMAS I & II
SKI MASK CARTEL I II & III
KING OF NEW YORK I II,III IV V
RISE TO POWER I II III
COKE KINGS I II III IV V
BORN HEARTLESS I II III IV
KING OF THE TRAP I II
By T.J. Edwards

Playa Ray

IF LOVING HIM IS WRONG…I & II
LOVE ME EVEN WHEN IT HURTS I II III
By Jelissa
WHEN THE STREETS CLAP BACK I & II III
THE HEART OF A SAVAGE I II III IV
MONEY MAFIA I II
LOYAL TO THE SOIL I II III
By Jibril Williams
A DISTINGUISHED THUG STOLE MY HEART I II & III
LOVE SHOULDN'T HURT I II III IV
RENEGADE BOYS I II III IV
PAID IN KARMA I II III
SAVAGE STORMS I II III
AN UNFORESEEN LOVE I II III
BABY, I'M WINTERTIME COLD I II
By Meesha
A GANGSTER'S CODE I &, II III
A GANGSTER'S SYN I II III
THE SAVAGE LIFE I II III
CHAINED TO THE STREETS I II III
BLOOD ON THE MONEY I II III
A GANGSTA'S PAIN I II III
By J-Blunt
PUSH IT TO THE LIMIT
By Bre' Hayes
BLOOD OF A BOSS I, II, III, IV, V
SHADOWS OF THE GAME
TRAP BASTARD
By Askari
THE STREETS BLEED MURDER **I, II & III**
THE HEART OF A GANGSTA I II& III
By Jerry Jackson
CUM FOR ME I II III IV V VI VII VIII
An LDP Erotica Collaboration

268

Crime Boss 2

BRIDE OF A HUSTLA **I II & II**
THE FETTI GIRLS **I, II& III**
CORRUPTED BY A GANGSTA I, II III, IV
BLINDED BY HIS LOVE
THE PRICE YOU PAY FOR LOVE I, II ,III
DOPE GIRL MAGIC I II III
By Destiny Skai
WHEN A GOOD GIRL GOES BAD
By Adrienne
THE COST OF LOYALTY I II III
By Kweli
A GANGSTER'S REVENGE **I II III & IV**
THE BOSS MAN'S DAUGHTERS I II III IV V
A SAVAGE LOVE **I & II**
BAE BELONGS TO ME I II
A HUSTLER'S DECEIT I, II, III
WHAT BAD BITCHES DO I, II, III
SOUL OF A MONSTER I II III
KILL ZONE
A DOPE BOY'S QUEEN I II III
TIL DEATH
By Aryanna
A KINGPIN'S AMBITON
A KINGPIN'S AMBITION **II**
I MURDER FOR THE DOUGH
By Ambitious
TRUE SAVAGE I II III IV V VI VII
DOPE BOY MAGIC I, II, III
MIDNIGHT CARTEL I II III
CITY OF KINGZ I II
NIGHTMARE ON SILENT AVE
THE PLUG OF LIL MEXICO II
CLASSIC CITY
By Chris Green
A DOPEBOY'S PRAYER

Playa Ray

By Eddie "Wolf" Lee
THE KING CARTEL **I, II & III**
By Frank Gresham
THESE NIGGAS AIN'T LOYAL **I, II & III**
By Nikki Tee
GANGSTA SHYT **I II &III**
By CATO
THE ULTIMATE BETRAYAL
By Phoenix
Boss'n Up i , ii & IIi
By Royal Nicole
I LOVE YOU TO DEATH
By Destiny J
I RIDE FOR MY HITTA
I STILL RIDE FOR MY HITTA
By Misty Holt
LOVE & CHASIN' PAPER
By Qay Crockett
TO DIE IN VAIN
SINS OF A HUSTLA
By ASAD
BROOKLYN HUSTLAZ
By Boogsy Morina
BROOKLYN ON LOCK I & II
By Sonovia
GANGSTA CITY
By Teddy Duke
A DRUG KING AND HIS DIAMOND I & II III
A DOPEMAN'S RICHES
HER MAN, MINE'S TOO I, II
CASH MONEY HO'S
THE WIFEY I USED TO BE I II
PRETTY GIRLS DO NASTY THINGS
By Nicole Goosby
TRAPHOUSE KING **I II & III**

Crime Boss 2

KINGPIN KILLAZ I II III
STREET KINGS I II
PAID IN BLOOD **I II**
CARTEL KILLAZ I II III
DOPE GODS I II
By Hood Rich
LIPSTICK KILLAH **I, II, III**
CRIME OF PASSION I II & III
FRIEND OR FOE I II III
By Mimi
STEADY MOBBN' **I, II, III**
THE STREETS STAINED MY SOUL I II III
By Marcellus Allen
WHO SHOT YA **I, II, III**
SON OF A DOPE FIEND I II
HEAVEN GOT A GHETTO I II
SKI MASK MONEY I II
Renta
GORILLAZ IN THE BAY **I II III IV**
TEARS OF A GANGSTA I II
3X KRAZY I II
STRAIGHT BEAST MODE I II
DE'KARI
TRIGGADALE I II III
MURDAROBER WAS THE CASE I II
Elijah R. Freeman
GOD BLESS THE TRAPPERS I, II, III
THESE SCANDALOUS STREETS I, II, III
FEAR MY GANGSTA I, II, III IV, V
THESE STREETS DON'T LOVE NOBODY I, II
BURY ME A G I, II, III, IV, V
A GANGSTA'S EMPIRE I, II, III, IV
THE DOPEMAN'S BODYGAURD I II
THE REALEST KILLAZ I II III
THE LAST OF THE OGS I II III

Playa Ray

Tranay Adams
THE STREETS ARE CALLING
Duquie Wilson
MARRIED TO A BOSS I II III
By Destiny Skai & Chris Green
KINGZ OF THE GAME I II III IV V VI VII
CRIME BOSS
Playa Ray
SLAUGHTER GANG I II III
RUTHLESS HEART I II III
By Willie Slaughter
FUK SHYT
By Blakk Diamond
DON'T F#CK WITH MY HEART I II
By Linnea
ADDICTED TO THE DRAMA I II III
IN THE ARM OF HIS BOSS II
By Jamila
YAYO I II III IV
A SHOOTER'S AMBITION I II
BRED IN THE GAME
By S. Allen
TRAP GOD I II III
RICH $AVAGE I II III
MONEY IN THE GRAVE I II III
By Martell Troublesome Bolden
FOREVER GANGSTA I II
 GLOCKS ON SATIN SHEETS I II
By Adrian Dulan
TOE TAGZ I II III IV
LEVELS TO THIS SHYT I II
IT'S JUST ME AND YOU
By Ah'Million
KINGPIN DREAMS I II III
RAN OFF ON DA PLUG

Crime Boss 2

By Paper Boi Rari
CONFESSIONS OF A GANGSTA I II III IV
CONFESSIONS OF A JACKBOY I II
By Nicholas Lock
I'M NOTHING WITHOUT HIS LOVE
SINS OF A THUG
TO THE THUG I LOVED BEFORE
A GANGSTA SAVED XMAS
IN A HUSTLER I TRUST
By Monet Dragun
CAUGHT UP IN THE LIFE I II III
THE STREETS NEVER LET GO I II III
By Robert Baptiste
NEW TO THE GAME I II III
MONEY, MURDER & MEMORIES I II III
By Malik D. Rice
LIFE OF A SAVAGE I II III IV
A GANGSTA'S QUR'AN I II III IV
MURDA SEASON I II III
GANGLAND CARTEL I II III
CHI'RAQ GANGSTAS I II III IV
KILLERS ON ELM STREET I II III
JACK BOYZ N DA BRONX I II III
A DOPEBOY'S DREAM I II III
JACK BOYS VS DOPE BOYS I II III
COKE GIRLZ
COKE BOYS
SOSA GANG I II
BRONX SAVAGES
BODYMORE KINGPINS
By Romell Tukes
LOYALTY AIN'T PROMISED I II
By Keith Williams
QUIET MONEY I II III
THUG LIFE I II III

Playa Ray

EXTENDED CLIP I II
A GANGSTA'S PARADISE
By Trai'Quan
THE STREETS MADE ME I II III
By Larry D. Wright
THE ULTIMATE SACRIFICE I, II, III, IV, V, VI
KHADIFI
IF YOU CROSS ME ONCE I II
ANGEL I II III IV
IN THE BLINK OF AN EYE
By Anthony Fields
THE LIFE OF A HOOD STAR
By Ca$h & Rashia Wilson
THE STREETS WILL NEVER CLOSE I II III
By K'ajji
CREAM I II III
THE STREETS WILL TALK
By Yolanda Moore
NIGHTMARES OF A HUSTLA I II III
By King Dream
CONCRETE KILLA I II III
VICIOUS LOYALTY I II III
By Kingpen
HARD AND RUTHLESS I II
MOB TOWN 251
THE BILLIONAIRE BENTLEYS I II III
REAL G'S MOVE IN SILENCE
By Von Diesel
GHOST MOB
Stilloan Robinson
MOB TIES I II III IV V VI
SOUL OF A HUSTLER, HEART OF A KILLER I II
GORILLAZ IN THE TRENCHES
By SayNoMore
BODYMORE MURDERLAND I II III

THE BIRTH OF A GANGSTER I II
By Delmont Player
FOR THE LOVE OF A BOSS
By C. D. Blue
MOBBED UP I II III IV
THE BRICK MAN I II III IV V
THE COCAINE PRINCESS I II III IV V VI VII
By King Rio
KILLA KOUNTY I II III IV
By Khufu
MONEY GAME I II
By Smoove Dolla
A GANGSTA'S KARMA I II III
By FLAME
KING OF THE TRENCHES I II III
 by GHOST & TRANAY ADAMS
QUEEN OF THE ZOO I II
By Black Migo
GRIMEY WAYS I II III
By Ray Vinci
XMAS WITH AN ATL SHOOTER
By Ca$h & Destiny Skai
KING KILLA
By Vincent "Vitto" Holloway
BETRAYAL OF A THUG I II
By Fre$h
THE MURDER QUEENS I II
By Michael Gallon
TREAL LOVE
By Le'Monica Jackson
FOR THE LOVE OF BLOOD I II
By Jamel Mitchell
HOOD CONSIGLIERE I II
By Keese
PROTÉGÉ OF A LEGEND I II

Playa Ray

LOVE IN THE TRENCHES
By Corey Robinson
BORN IN THE GRAVE I II III
By Self Made Tay
MOAN IN MY MOUTH
By XTASY
TORN BETWEEN A GANGSTER AND A
GENTLEMAN
By J-BLUNT & Miss Kim
LOYALTY IS EVERYTHING I II
Molotti
HERE TODAY GONE TOMORROW
By Fly Rock
PILLOW PRINCESS
By S. Hawkins

BOOKS BY LDP'S CEO, CA$H

TRUST IN NO MAN
TRUST IN NO MAN 2
TRUST IN NO MAN 3
BONDED BY BLOOD
SHORTY GOT A THUG
THUGS CRY
THUGS CRY 2
THUGS CRY 3
TRUST NO BITCH
TRUST NO BITCH 2
TRUST NO BITCH 3
TIL MY CASKET DROPS
RESTRAINING ORDER
RESTRAINING ORDER 2
IN LOVE WITH A CONVICT
LIFE OF A HOOD STAR
XMAS WITH AN ATL SHOOTER

Made in United States
Orlando, FL
13 November 2024

53875880R00153